To Each His Own

To Each His Own

a novel by

Valerie Chandler-Smith

This novel is a work of fiction.
Any references to real people, events, establishments, organizations, or locales are intended to give the fiction a sense of reality and authenticity. Other names, characters, and incidents are either the product of the author's imagination or are used fictitiously, as are those fictionalized events and incidents that involve real persons and did not occur or are set in the future.

ISBN 0-9769440-0-6

For

Maceo,

Nico, Daisha & Zion

Thanks for being the best part of my life.

thanks!

Mommy, *I love you so much! Thanks for being both, a mommy and a best friend! Thanks for sharing your wisdom to trust God and teaching me about the power of prayer. It's the best gift you could have given me. God is truly the center of my joy! I thank Him for blessing my life with you!* **Ms. Gwen,** *You are a wonderful big sister but most of all, someone I can count on. I know if anyone is praying for me, it's you. Thanks for being a super Auntie to my children.* **Greg,** *Whew, it was touch and go there for a moment. Your trials have humbled me. I didn't feel right going to God on your behalf when there was stuff I needed to get out of my way. I wanted to help you so much that I gained courage to straighten my walk. Stay strong.* **Pookey,** *Just saying your name makes me laugh. We get the hate because we have too much fun when we're together. I enjoy the laughs but it's the tears that do it for me. Every time we're together you make me laugh so hard I cry. What a great feeling to release tears of joy. Life is short and you make it so pleasant. You are good medicine and I'm your biggest fan.* **Desa,** *Who knew? It's been 23 years and we still giggle and whisper just like we did in 1982. I love it! I won't go into details (wink) but our friendship has never been boring. Thanks for being there for the real exhale. Always remember Regina and Janice. Hello* **Paula,** *It's been a while since we've been clubbing but the memories will never fade. You and* **Derrick** *stand next to Pookey with the laughs and tears. Love you both!!* **Laverne** *aka Bernie Mac, what's up girl? Thanks for the southern fried fish and dirty rice.* **Theresa,** *you are one in a million. Thanks for the education.* **Felicia** *you put the Toe in Ghetto. Thanks for keeping it real!* **Monica,** *you put bartenders to shame. Big shout out to the Dogg Pound.* **Rosezette,** *what a true friend, thanks for believing in me.* **Monica C,** *I'm praying for you! Stay out of Iraq.* **Deb,** *I'm not going to even go there with you.* **Sheryl,** *my unofficial prayer partner—thanks!* **Pat,** *you've been nothing but a blessing- everyone needs a Pat in their life -- thanks!* **Malissa,** *I'm so proud of you. Stay in prayer! Congratulations on MiAsia.* **Charlene,** *we just click like that-- thanks for the new friendship.* **Pearl,** *years ago, you asked me a very important question. Thanks!* **Melissa,** *thanks for the encouraging words to move on this project.* **Craig,** *thanks for creating a fabulous cover.* **Kev,** *thanks for your help in the beginning, your support will never be forgotten.* **Much Love to you all!**

Also by

Valerie Chandler-Smith

Youth Plays

Reversing the Plan
(Teenage drug issue)

&

Trading Place
(Teenage pregnancy dilemma)

TO EACH HIS OWN

PRINTED IN THE UNITED STATES OF AMERICA.

ISBN #0-9769440-0-6

Whatever is

blocking your way ...

Grab it by the throat

Don't take no for an answer

And don't give up

Be passionate about your dreams

And do something everyday

to bring you closer to it.

-- mixture of folks

To Each His Own

A novel by

Valerie Chandler-Smith

Maya

Still in her bed at 11:56 am Maya refuse to get up and face the realization of April 19th. Three years ago, and the memory of being left at the altar still pained her. Reaching for a dry pillow to comfort her soul, Maya buried her face and continue to cry over the most undeserving day in her life.

****

A beautiful spring morning greeted Maya as she got up, opened her blinds and embraced the blessing of the bright morning sun. She closed her damp eyes, smiled and inhaled the sweetness of her wedding the day. Gently kneeling by her bedside, Maya brought her hands together and began to thank God for her life, for all that it was, and all that it wasn't. She praised him and lifted his name for being God all by himself and blessing her with this special day and a loving man to share her life. Kneeling longer than she ever had before, Maya continued to thank God for everyone and everything around her. She was so pleased with where she was in her life she could not thank God enough. When her prayer had ended Maya rose to her feet with the satisfaction and confidence that every word was heard. She hugged herself and repeated the words "thank you" once again. "I'm so happy" she whispered and then she giggled out loud. Today was her day and now that her quiet time with God was done she felt sure about the plans for the day.

Maya blushed at the thought of being pampered all day in preparation for her big walk down the aisle. Arrangements had been made for her hair, nails, facial, and massage all to be taking care of by noon. Maya twirled and twirled around her room until she was in front of her full-length mirror that hung from her closet door. She threw herself a kiss and then she pulled out her stunning wedding gown. She hugged it then danced with it. "This is the happiest day of my life" she told herself, as she squeezed the dress tight enough to make it wrinkle.

With no desire to eat, Maya reached for her kettle and decided to make a cup of her favorite tea. Maya loved the Tazo brand and the exhilarating aromas and flavors they offered. This morning her choice was *Passion*. Passion delivered a mind cleansing awakening that gave her every reason to feel great. And it was just what she needed to take the edge off the excitement she held inside while waiting to call her best friend, Tyrone. Knowing she had at least another half an hour before she could call, Maya kicked her feet up and inhaled the delicious fragrance of hibiscus and other exotic flowers and natural ingredients. She savored each sip, closed her eyes and rehearsed the words "I do."

Beautiful inside and out, Maya had plenty girlfriends yet Tyrone was her best friend and she cherished their unique relationship. Depending on which day of the week it was, some would think they were siblings and on other days, lovers. But they were just good old fashioned friends, the kind that you rarely find today.

"Good morning Princess." Tyrone responded on the first ring looking at his caller ID.

"Ooooh Tyrone, I can't believe it's here! My wedding day is finally here!" Maya gushed.

"Whup de do." Tyrone replied dryly.

"Uhn-uhn," Maya stop him short. "You promised you wouldn't go there. You know how much I love Perry -- so don't start." She warned.

"I'm not starting -- I just hope he loves you as much as you love him."

"Tyrone!" Maya whined.

"Alright, alright, I won't say another word." Tyrone promised, throwing his eyes in the air.

"Good. Now listen it's almost eight what time will you be here?"

"Give me about ten minutes."

"Okay hurry up, I'm so excited!"

"I'm on my way." he quickly responded before saying the wrong thing.

Placing the cordless phone down, Tyrone shook his head with pity. Certainly, he was happy for his girl, but on the other hand, he, being a gay man, didn't trust Maya's fiancé.

****

Tyrone and Maya had been out for drinks when she met Perry. Perry was sitting across from them, at the bar alone. Tyrone spotted him first, thinking what a sexy man. No sooner than Tyrone thought it, Maya whispered the exact sentiment in his ear. Tyrone didn't let on that he found Perry attractive he just smiled and waited to see which one of them Perry would make his move on. After discreetly peeking across the bar several times Tyrone finally got impatient and went into the men's room, hoping that Perry would follow. But instead Perry sent a drink over to Maya, applying for an opportunity to get to know her better. A few short weeks following that night, Maya and Perry were an item.

For several reasons, this situation drew a red flag with Tyrone, so he decided to call Maya out on a few things:

"How did he know that you weren't my women?"

Maya almost choked as she smiled then answered, "He said that you just didn't seem to be paying me as much attention as you were paying the other men in the bar."

"Whaat?!" Tyrone was clearly offended.

"Tyrone, he noticed that you were gay." Maya said without hesitation, knowing it was no secret. She also hoped Tyrone would just let it go.

"Gay? Tell me something." Tyrone sucked his tongue for sound effect and started slowly. "How do you notice someone is gay from across the bar? I wasn't even standing." Then he hesitated and flicked a piece of lint off of his sweater and said. "I guess what they say is true."

And just like clock work, Maya fell right in and asked.

"What do they say?"

"They say," Tyrone cleared his throat for more sound effect. "It takes one to know one. So go run and tell your little bi-friend that his behind is busted. No don't do that he might like that -- tell him . . ."

"Tyrone stop!" Maya interrupted and then tried to hide the fact that he hit a nerve. "You always go there -- everyone is gay in your world. Perry is definitely not gay." She assured him, thinking how sweet Perry had tasted and then she giggled like a school-girl with a secret.

"Keep laughing Honey, but remember . . . just because he showed you a hot time doesn't mean he can't show me one too." Tyrone replied knowing the sting would end the conversation. And he was right, without saying another word Maya grabbed her Coach bag and strutted out the door, leaving it wide opened.

Weeks had passed before Tyrone finally broke down and called her to apologize. Maya was his closest friend and he refused to let a man come between them. Still, he didn't trust Perry, he was almost certain that Perry gave him the eye that same night. He couldn't figure out what the game was about but he knew that there was something foul in the air. Unfortunately, by the time Tyrone had apologized, Maya and Perry's relationship had blossomed into a serious engagement.

"Of course I forgive you. Now, guess what has happened since the last time we spoke?" Maya zoomed right pass his apology and into her news.

Tyrone thought. Please don't be pregnant.

"OK, let me see . . . you're pregnant." The words rushed out of his mouth as he closed his eyes and crossed his fingers.

Maya loved the thought, blushed and said "Nope. Guess again."

Thankful that she wasn't pregnant Tyrone guessed again.

"You broke up with him."

"No!" Maya quickly responded annoyed at the mere thought.

"Perry asked me to be his wife." She announced proudly.

Tyrone was both shocked and disgusted.

"No. Tell me you're lyin'!"

"Nope, I'm staring at my wedding band right now."

"Band?" Tyrone wanted to comment about the band, but other issues were pressing, so he said. "Hold up, you mean to tell me you've accepted his proposal? You've only known him for a few weeks, what's the rush?"

"No rush, Perry said that he wants to take care of me and the only way he knows how" she paused "is to marry me. Plus I could care less about what kind of ring he offered me. I'm only concerned about his love for me."

"C'mon Maya, you sound silly. You barely know him. I know you are not seriously thinking about marriage. Did he put it on you like that?

"No, as a matter of fact, we haven't really done it yet. Perry wants to wait until our wedding night."

"Maya, girl you better snap out of it, there's something wrong with that picture."

"Look, I thought you called to apologize? I guess not. I will talk with you later. I'm not trying to hear none of that. I just told you I was engaged, can't you just be happy for me?"

Not wanting to go back to not speaking for weeks, Tyrone lied and said. "You're right, I don't know why I'm tripping. You go, Girl!"

****

Ten minutes had passed before Tyrone realized he was still sitting by the phone thinking about the whole Perry situation. He quickly yanked off his oily socks, slipped his bony feet into his white mules and ran out the door to pick up the bride to be.

Maya was already outside when he turned the corner -- her face lit up by her smile, her eyes sparkling in the bright sun.

"Look at you, you're glowing." Tyrone said squeezing her tight.

Still in his arms, Maya said "Tyrone, I know that you're not crazy about Perry but, please be happy for me."

"I am, for real, I'm happy for you." he leaned and kissed her making sure she knew he was for real. "I promise that I will do my part as your brother and best friend to welcome Perry into our happy world."

"I know you will." Maya replied easing into the cozy Escalade."

"OK you know the drill, cover your eyes." Tyrone said handing her a silk scarf.

Maya exhaled as the luxury vehicle slipped out of Jersey City through the Holland Tunnel into downtown New York.

"Can I take off my blindfold now?" She questioned knowing full well what his answer would be.

"No. Just hold tight we're almost there."

Maya was fidgety, twisting and turning around in her seat trying to get comfortable, but it was no use. Blindly reaching for the radio she told Tyrone "Put some music on, I need to hear Stevie."

"Too late, we're here." Tyrone announced, anxious to see the expression on her face when she realize where he had taken her.

"Now you can take off the scarf. No wait." He said reaching in the back seat for his digital camera.

"OK, now."

Maya gasped when she realized that he had taken her to *Soft*, the exotic beauty spa she often fantasized about. A staff of six stood outside the elegant establishment, all of them perfectly posing with a white towel draped over their arm. Neatly dressed in soft periwinkle scrubs and white shoes, each of them greeted her with a warm smile.

"I can't believe this." Maya turned and faced Tyrone. "All of this for me?" She literally cried and grabbed him, lifting his thin frame off the ground.

"OK, ok calm down. Let go of me." he said trying to hide how elated he felt seeing her light up like that. "Go ahead, get inside, you only have a few hours here, then we have to eat, get that hair done, meet the make up artist and the photographer all by 2pm."

"Meet them where?"

"Well I was going to save that little surprise for later but, you might as well know, for a wedding gift I got you two a suite at *Adore.*"

"Shut up, no you didn't!" Maya screamed and went to grab him again.

"Yes, I did."

Maya then began to feel guilty for all the times she doubted their relationship and said. "Tyrone, I'm sorry I didn't call you first. I meant nothing by it, I was just so happy to be in love, I got carried away and I'm sorry. I should have known that you are always looking out for my best interest. Please forgive me."

"Girl, if you don't get inside. We'll talk later."

Maya gave Tyrone one last kiss and hug before she floated inside to receive her luxurious pre-wedding spa experience.

The remaining few hours had come and gone too fast. Maya was now pampered, fed, beautiful and ready to take the big step. The wedding staff applauded her as she walked out of the Master bedroom into the living room area where she admired the many gifts, flowers and well wishes that were sent. Whispers of how she looked like a queen trailed amongst the staff. The photographer was delighted at his assignment and snapped countless shots of her adding that with her height and beauty she could have easily been a professional model.

****

As the limousine whisked away in the direction of the church, Maya waved bye at the crowd outside *Adore.*

Sitting next to the "queen for a day", Tyrone was amazed at how stunning Maya looked and frowned at the fact that his hard work would only be seen by a few, since Perry insisted that the ceremony be small, just a few close friends and his parents. Tyrone exploded when he heard this but instead of telling Maya he told his partner, Wes. It took a lot for him to hold his peace on this one but he promised Maya and said nothing against Perry. Several times he wanted to tell her that this was her day too, and she should have more than four friends there. But all he said was, "whatever."

When they arrived at the church, Tyrone quickly escorted Maya out of sight so no one could see her before she came down the aisle. He didn't see Perry, so he motioned for an usher to let Perry and the best man know that the bride was in place and ready. After a few short minutes the usher returned letting Tyrone know that it was time to escort Maya down the aisle.

The atmosphere in the church was chatty as the musician entertained the small audience with his above average keyboard playing skills. But soon he would get the signal that it was time. Maya closed her eyes and lightly swayed from side to side as she connected to the soft and lovely rendition of something by Luther. And then out of nowhere and a little sooner than expected the soft and lovely music stopped and the thunder of the wedding march began to infiltrate every inch of the pristine sanctuary. The sudden pounding of the keys disturbed the sleeping butterflies that rested at the bottom of Maya's belly. Startled, they jumped up and started to fly wildly bumping into each other, falling down and flying back up. Maya grabbed her middle and took a deep breath.

Tyrone grabbed Maya's hand and said in a fatherly tone, "This is no time to faint, Princess. Let's do this." Even though he had planned a superstar's pre-wedding extravaganza, watching it unfold was more spectacular than even he could have imagined. These plans were extraordinary, not just for anyone but for his Maya. And under the circumstances of Maya not having much family, Tyrone wanted this day to be very special.

Maya placed her gloved hand into Tyrone's sweaty palm and the two strolled down the aisle to the rhythm of the now softer and slower solo, Here Comes the Bride.

While strolling down the aisle, neither noticed that Perry wasn't in his place at the altar, and now it was too late to turn back. Tyrone gestured for the best man to bring his ear close and whispered.

"Where the hell is Perry?"

"I don't know." the best man lied.

"What do you mean you don't know?" Tyrone asked with the words choked behind his teeth.

"Like I said, I don't know." The best lied again this time turning his back to Tyrone letting him know that he didn't care and that's when it hit Tyrone. The best man was the same man that was at the bar less than six months ago, arguing with Perry. What also came to Tyrone's mind was the fact that not once could he recall Perry calling the hotel to speak to Maya. Her girlfriends called and even stopped by to give her little old and new things to wear for good luck. Her co-workers and business associates sent flowers and gifts since they were not invited to the ceremony but not a peep from Perry or anyone in his family. Tyrone wanted to question Maya about what appeared to be odd, but he didn't want to rattle her. Everything was going so well, besides, he was a man of his word and he refuse to break his promise to never speak negatively about Perry again. But the more Tyrone thought, the more the pieces came together, he also recalled how Perry suddenly became ill the night of the pre-wedding dinner last Friday when the bride's maid and best man was suppose to meet. The dinner reservations were set for eight, Maya, her girlfriend, Tyrone and his friend, Perry, the best man and Perry's parents. And just like today no one on Perry's end showed up. Perry created this fabulous story about how he and his parents ate some bad seafood the night before and how they all were feeling pretty sick. He never made it to any rehearsals but continuously assured Maya that there was nothing to saying "I do". Why didn't any of this alarmed Maya? Was she that desperate to be married? Tyrone questioned. And what was up with the cheap band? Tyrone never did understand how she let they fly.

Witnessing all the red flags, Tyrone still didn't see this coming. Tyrone even attempted to crash the bachelor party last night but couldn't get in touch with Perry. He figured Perry didn't want him to know anything about it because of the closeness he had with Maya. So he placed it in the back of his mind and focused on making sure everything was in tact for Maya's big day.

"C'mon." Tyrone motioned for her to move with him.

"Stop." Maya whined playfully popping Tyrone on his hand. "Perry is probably just downstairs he'll be up in a minute. Why don't you have one of the guys run downstairs and tell him that the ceremony has started." She continued smiling and waving at her guest with all the confidence in the world. There was no doubt in her mind that Perry wasn't on his way up the stairs to marry her. There was no reason for such a thought. He loved her and she adored him. So why was Tyrone over reacting?

"Princess you don't understand." Tyrone stopped not able to continue.

"Shhh. You're starting to upset me. He'll be here just hold on, he's just a few minutes late. Have the girl sing another song." Maya then noticed that the best man was not in his place. "What happened to the best man?"

Tyrone motioned for the young woman to sing another song and for the ushers to come to the front. He then asked them to go outside and search for Perry and the best man. Fifteen minutes and two songs later, the small crowd started whispering that the groom didn't show. Maya was still holding onto her smile with hopes that Perry may have gotten stuck in traffic or have overslept. She smiled for a couple of pictures and then she began to peek over her shoulder at her attendees. The pew where Perry's parents were supposed to sit was empty. Then she noticed that none of his friends were there. She looked at her side of the church and saw her two co-workers, Mrs. Green who owns the brownstone that she lives in, her three girlfriends and some church members she did know that well. Since the members sat on both the bride and groom side, Maya didn't notice when walking down the aisle that Perry's crew was missing.

"Look Princess, let's just go in the back and relax until Perry gets here." Tyrone suggested, trying to save Maya from as much embarrassment as possible.

"I am not moving out of this spot!" Maya gritted, emphasizing on the word not. "Hand me your phone."

"Maya don't." Tyrone begged. "Don't call him."

But Maya was ready to face her worst fear. Just like Tyrone, she witnessed all the red flags. Each time Perry called with an excuse she felt like there was more to it, but chose to ignore it. She neglected to tell Tyrone that she had never met Perry's parents, not even on the phone. That none of Perry friends were friendly to her and all that Perry would allow her to do to him is perform oral sex. He insisted he wanted to wait until they were married for the real thing, even after she explained to him how she really needed taken care of and begged him for several hours one night. Still he wouldn't budge and repeatedly told her no.

With her hands shaking nervously, Maya carefully dialed Perry's number and was sickened at what she heard on the other end. By the sounds in the background, it appeared that there was some kind of party going on at his place. "Perry?" Maya called his name thinking she may have dialed the wrong number. But the number was right and now the music in the background had stopped and what she heard next was Perry whispering "On the count of three: One, Two, Three" and then in unison the all male crowd in his apartment chanted an old hit from the eighties "Another man is beating your time." And then she heard them breakout into a roaring laughter, and then the line died.

Turned out Perry was gay and his whole proposal to Maya was a sick scheme to win back his ex-lover's heart.

The night Perry met Maya was an hour after he and Gene had broken up. Gene was a married man sleeping with men on the down low and Perry had given him an ultimatum that he had better leave his wife or it would be over between them. Gene told Perry to do what he had to do because he wasn't planning on ever coming out of the closet. He had far too much to lose. So in a confused state Perry decided to get a wife of his own. After news broke out that Perry was seeing this gorgeous woman and they were soon to be married, Gene quickly packed his bags and left his wife with no explanation. The reality of being abandon devastated her but her feelings didn't even rate in comparison to what Gene wanted most. So he moved on and landed back on Perry's doorstep two weeks before the wedding.

Perry was elated that Gene chose to follow his heart and be with him. He wanted to stop the wedding and explain everything to Maya. But Gene didn't trust that idea, he was insecure about his power over Maya's and wanted to make sure she hurt. He wanted Perry to go on pretending that the wedding was still on. He told him to leave her standing at the altar so that there could never be a chance of her ever forgiving him. So to please Gene, Perry went along with pretending that the wedding was still on. Then to commensurate Gene and Perry's new beginning, Gene decided to throw a party on Maya's wedding day.

Tears quickly streamed out of Maya's eyes as her mind played back the roaring laughter. Painfully her eyes met Tyrone's loving and understanding heart. Once again the butterflies had returned, this time bitter and crazed, bouncing up, down and all around the insides of her stomach searching for an exit. She started to feel sick as Tyrone took her by the arm and boldly walked down the center aisle not looking at any of the guests. The butterflies grew agitated and hot forcing their way out of her stomach and up into her throat and finally in her mouth. She then paused from walking and swallowed hard forcing them back down into her belly. When the couple reached the church doors, Tyrone grabbed Maya by her waist and carefully eased her down the church stairs. Still determined, the butterflies were ruthless and decided to get out any way they could. So as Maya took her last step she felt a warm sensation creeping out of her behind and flowing down her backside. The butterflies were now free, leaving her white lacy garter and underwear soiled. The guests pushed their way through the double doors of the church and watched in disbelief as the limousine drove off leaving behind an expensive and beautiful pair of white satin diarrhea filled shoes by the curb side.

****

Finding herself reminiscing about that day yet another year, Maya dried her face with the sheets, got up and blew her nose. She looked in the mirror and was sick at the sight of herself. She began to strip the linen off the bed and thought the only way she could get over her pain was to confront Perry. She thought about paying him a visit a thousand times over but never got up the nerve to actually do it. It wasn't until Tyrone offered to have Perry and Gene slip into an unfortunate accident that she realized that it wasn't them that made her mad. She blamed herself for allowing it to happen. She saw every sign and her first impression of Perry was the same as Tyrone's, yet she ignored everything she knew to be true and proceeded with the wedding.

But why? The question haunted her night and day. Not allowing her to eat, sleep, laugh or concentrate on anything too long. Why would she allow this to happen to her? Three years had pass and she was still in denial about what was going on with her at the time of Perry's charade. But the question would not go away and she would be forced to re-visit her painful childhood that made her feel so needy that she would attempt to marry a man that was clearly gay.

When Maya refuse to get back at Perry, Tyrone suggested that she seek a therapist and move on with her life. Agreeing that she needed to move on and still too embarrassed to face the church Maya contacted Dr. Weaver and shared all that she could remember about the mother she never knew, the cold and hateful aunt who raised her and the twin brother that she was separated from. Along with prayer, the sessions proved to be very helpful, through the tears and pain Maya got through her issues and when April 19th came by for the fourth year, Maya treated it just like any other day - Blessed!

New beginning

Maya smiled as she stared into the face of the man she met last night. Yes, he was still handsome, and no she didn't forget his name. Basil. Basil was tall, with a perfect tanned complexion and a neat mustache. He spoke with a deep, sexy, voice and laughed with a quiet one. The hairs on his chest were thick and soft, his body muscular, his belly missing. Maya's hands went wild exploring every part of him. Kissing him from head to toe, she celebrated his presence. Basil had been Maya's first lover since Perry. Now, with his eyes wide open lying on his back, he lifted her over him and licked the crease between her breasts. She eased down on him, sucked his tongue, and eagerly spread her thighs to receive more of the celebration she desperately longed for. Ignoring the punishment of his strength her needs begged him to take all that he wanted. Taking pleasure in the look of pure ecstasy on her face, Basil's neat mustache smiled at her and then he flipped her over and took control of the heated rhythm their oneness created. Adding more fuel to the fire as his body chased hers, they were in perfect harmony. Maya was in her glory and began shouting finally getting the release that she often times yearned for. She felt alive and wanted to go on like this forever but Basil struggled to conserve his cream. His grip on her ass tightened as he felt the sweet victory of her nails clawing the skin on his back. She begged him to stop and to keep going. But soon her voice died, it was over for her. He locked her body in his giving her the last stroke he had in him, treating her to the cream of life as his heavy body collapsed on top of hers. In unison the two let out a heavy sigh, both breathing hard, then Basil rolled off of her, grabbed her by the hand and softly began to speak. Maya missed what he said and just smiled. She batted her eyes and scooted closer, still his voice was too low so she reached over to shut off the alarm clock and that's when she realized that she had been dreaming, again. She reached down between her thighs to confirm her release and although she wished it wasn't a dream she was pleased that she got something out of the deal without having to go to great lengths to get it.

This was Maya's third wet dream this week and although they felt good and carried her all day long, she was feeling a little uneasy about what they meant and if she was becoming some kind of freak. She was getting annoyed with herself and didn't know what to make of her constant dreams about the perfect man and sex all the time. Maya stripped the bed down and threw the soiled sheets in the hamper. She didn't know what to make of herself, but she knew that she didn't like it. She also knew that it was after eight and she couldn't afford to waste anymore time analyzing her recent behavior, she had to be at work by nine.

Another beautiful day, Maya thought as she walked to the Grove Street PATH Station to catch the 33rd Street Train. Everyone on the train seemed to be reading something so she pulled out her copy of Toni Morrison's Song of Solomon, and pretended to read through her dark shades. Maya couldn't concentrate -- her mind kept switching back and forth between her book and her dream. Maya scolded herself, after realizing that she was enjoying the memories of her dream. When the train doors opened Maya stood still, allowing everyone else to get off the train first. It didn't matter that she was late. She hated being squeezed, pushed, and confronted by the rude crowd. Maya held her breath as she walked through the underground station.

"Can you spare some change?"

A toothless homeless woman greeted Maya. A lot of strange homeless people lived and begged in the train terminal but, this woman was no stranger to Maya. She was the same woman that asked Maya for spare change every morning. For years, she had been living in the 33rd Street Station wearing the same shiny black raincoat with the belt fastened securely around her waist. She wore a pair of what seemed to be purple rain boots and a purple rain scarf holding down her untamed mixed gray hair. Maya never thought much about the homeless. She gave when it was convenient for her but never really went out of her way to give them money. But this woman was different she had something about her that drew Maya closer and closer each day. Maya couldn't quite put her finger on it, but she knew there was something interesting about this woman. Someone she may have known as a child, a school teacher or the lunch lady or maybe a librarian. Maya had attempted to talk with this woman several times, to ask her name and whereabouts. But each time the woman just dropped her head, until Maya walked away. It was pretty clear that she didn't want to be close to anyone and that all she wanted was 'spare change'.

Maya respected that and made sure she always kept singles in her pocket to give the woman each morning. On Fridays or long holiday weekends, Maya would give her extra money to hold her over.

Feeling such a strong connection, Maya often spoke about her to anyone who would listen. But each time she would be warned not to get involved. But Maya couldn't help it she couldn't shake the way she felt. Every time she handed the woman money, their eyes would meet and Maya's heart would swell. It was kind of freakish the way this woman would look at her almost as if she knew something about her.

Getting up close, Maya could smell the rank that rose from her body. She could see the dried saliva that stained her face and hands, the garbage and layers of dirt that coated her skin, the bugs and gnats that circled around her head and the stray cats and rats that shared her home. But none of these things deterred Maya's feelings for the woman. Her feeling grew stronger. Eventually, it got to the point where Maya could not bare to look into the woman's eyes anymore. She weakened every time she saw those big, dark eyes looking back at her. At first they were beautiful and then they were sad. The woman's eyes were mirrors to a forgotten soul.

Maya believed that part of the homeless problem was that they had no love, which propelled low self-esteem to none at all. It wasn't long before Maya's thoughts were confirmed, one day while handing the woman money, their fingers touched and in that moment, when their eyes met, the woman's eyes quickly filled with water expressing gratitude. Again Maya asked her name and she quickly pulled away and dropped her head, removing her boot to hide the money all the while saying. "God bless ya, chile."

Monday

Even though she knew that in an hour or so she would be complaining that she was cold, Maya was relieved when she walked into the air-conditioned Macy's building. Just getting across the street from the 33rd St. Path Station was enough to make her want to turn back and go home. Outside was very humid, and congested, thousands of people going in different directions, everyone pushing, shoving and stepping over each other. Cars, cabs, limousines, buses, pedestrians, police, horses, peddlers, bums, tourists, evangelists, screaming ambulances, phone booths, garbage, garbage cans, baby strollers, hand trucks, you name it, it was there and it was in the way. It took a good 5 minutes just to cross the street. Regardless of how insane everything seemed, it was just an average day in mid-town Manhattan.

"Hey girlfriend." Her co-worker Toy sang from down the hall. Toy was bubbly as usual. "What's wrong with you?" Toy frowned getting a closer look at Maya. "You look like you just woke up out of a bad dream or something!"

Maya sighed, put on a phony smirk and said. "Look again, it wasn't bad and it wasn't a dream."

"I heard that," Toy said loudly, slapping Maya a hi-five. Toy was excited she loved hearing about people getting off. Then she got nosey and said, "Anybody I know?"

Maya looked at Toy from toe to head and said, "Do I look like a whole fool? Like I would really tell you -- c'mon now."

Toy just grinned and said "Pleeese, I don't need details -- just as long as you're getting paid or should I say laid."

The two of them cracked up laughing, hi-five and got on the elevator. Toy was just going on and on about everything and anything while Maya just stood there dazed, still wet from her dream. When the doors opened on the 11th floor the two got off.

Maya liked Toy because she was so full of life, even if she did always seem to talk about sex, parties, parties and sex. Toy was young, well groomed, smart, petite, and happy. She loved to gossip but wasn't a trouble-maker, she was the only girl that Maya knew that was always laughing and smiling. But Maya thought, being married, she had to have some kind of problem although it never showed. The girl never stopped talking, laughing or singing. Co-workers have accused her of using some kind of happy drug, but Maya knew better. Toy was too smart for that, her perspective on life was good. The glass was always half full, she was more than optimistic, she was encouraged.

Despite the fact that she was late today, instead of going to her office, Maya headed straight to the ladies room. She had to check herself out. All that laughing with Toy did not make her forget Toy's first impression of her. She wanted to see why Toy thought she had a bad dream. She looked in the mirror and could tell that her eyes were puffy from crying and her make-up was a little off. So she pulled out her black shiny patent leather cosmetic bag and gave herself a quick touch up. She didn't worry about her outfit, she could tell from the many stares and hellos that her peach Armani single-breasted suit was doing its job. She adjusted the skirt a little, making sure the seams were in the right place and then checked out her heels to make sure the concrete didn't add its signature to her new Cole Haan shoes.

Her beautiful brown skin went well with almost every color but, peaches and reds complimented her complexion the most. Maya was a beauty, her tall, full-figured body, and small waist, carried well with her long shapely legs and size 7 feet. She had clear dark brown eyes and extremely long lashes that fanned every time she blinked. She had full lips, and clean wet teeth, that invited you to hold her in conversation longer than necessary. Today she wore her silky thick wavy hair pulled back and neatly pinned at the nape of her neck. For extra security she added another dab of her sensuous perfume behind her ear and headed for her office.

A buyer for Macy's children department for 6 years, Maya loved the freedom of her job and did it well. Arthur, her immediate director, refused to acknowledge the fact that Maya was the best children's clothes buyer that he's ever seen. Was he insecure because she was female, and smarter than he was? Or was it the obvious?

After all the interviews, Arthur didn't want to hire her. It was a toss up between a college grad with no experience that knew very little about the industry and a sister with a degree and two previous buyer's position under her belt. Arthur wanted the younger college graduate. He said he wanted someone he could 'train'. Besides, he never worked closely with an African-American female before and wasn't sure he wanted to be associated with one in his department. But the final choice was not up to him and so it was announced that Maya Taylor would be the new senior buyer for the Macy's children's department.

Although Maya exceeded expectations on the job, Arthur felt that it was necessary to give her grief. He was not prepared for the educated, energetic, well-groomed, black woman that made shrewd dealings that even he, was not familiar with.

So poor Arthur had no choice, after all he's the boss and he's miserable, so he had to take it out on Maya. Whenever he spoke to her, he barked. His laugh was barely a smile, and his thank-yous were never even considered. He treated Maya as if she was an odor that he couldn't stand smelling.

Maya walked into her office and opened the wooden blinds allowing the sun to share her space. She enjoyed the sun, the heat from the rays made her feel loved. She closed her eyes and let the warmth hit her lids, then began imagining she was somewhere tropical. Not long after getting settled into her workload her phone ranged.

"Yes!" she said annoyed at being disturbed.

"I need to see you in my office right away Ms. Taylor". It was Arthur.

"I'll be right there." Maya answered in a sweet but phony voice.

She grumbled, slipped into her shoes and complained under her breath all the way to his office. When she arrived Arthur was standing at the window pretending to be interested in something happening on the streets, knowing that he was blind as a bat, and could not see anything much from the 11th floor.

"Good morning, Arthur, what can I do for you?" Maya said, getting right to it.

He ignored her for about 45 second, cleared his throat, turned around slowly and began to inform her that there had been some kind of problem with the quantity she had purchased last month and that he wanted it fixed immediately. Maya hated him and his office, and wasn't in the mood for his daily drama. She wanted to go back to her cozy space.

Annoyed, she sucked her teeth louder than she had planned, then took a deep sigh and said, "Arthur, be more specific, exactly what is the problem?"

He looked at her, checked out her outfit from head to toe as if he was planning to wear the same thing later on that evening, and said, "Someone is stealing from the shipments."

"Arthur, what does that have to do with me? I'm pen, paper & calculator. I don't drive trucks, and I don't count stock, I just do the selecting, pricing, ordering and purchasing. How does this involve me?"

He took his time again and answered, "It involves all of us. You need to be exact about your figures, we have an idea of who's doing what but we don't want to be made fools of and we need our end to be accurate."

Maya knew then that this was just another one of Arthur's 'I don't have anyone to talk to' moments and he just wanted her in his office for some color, some show, some big secret he hoped someone on the floor was going to start talking about. He wanted a life, a life that included interesting people.

So she played along with the game and said, "Okay Arthur, I'll be extra careful. Is that all?"

Arthur couldn't think of anything else to say, so he gave her a pitiful look and nodded yes. She couldn't wait to get out of his clammy, dark office. She hurried hoping that her morning boost of hot water and lemon was still warm.

It was now ten thirty and time to pull together some figures for her meeting at twelve with distributors from Sean John, Baby Phat and Polo. Maya enjoyed these meetings because most of the distributors were her friends and after all the haggling was done, they would enjoy a delicious lunch on one of the company's tab.

Maya loved the many perks that came along with her job. Because of her rank she received thirty percent discount storewide and because of her many connections she met a lot of interesting designers and famous people. Unfortunately no one she would consider dating.

When Maya returned to her office, there were two messages on her desk, one from Alycia the other from Roz. These were her girls. Maya gulped down her now lukewarm lemon water and started dialing them back.

"Alycia Moore's line." a clear voice announced.

"Hi, is she there?"

"Yes, may I ask who's calling?"

"Tell her it's Maya."

"Hold on please." Maya didn't mind waiting for Alycia because the hold line was on the radio station WBLS and they were playing Baby Face.

"Hey, Girl what's up!" Alycia shouted, "I've called you four times this week, where were you?"

"I was home. I didn't want to be bothered so I turned off my ringer."

"No wonder I kept getting that weak message. Why don't you change that tired recording. Oleta Adams is my girl and all but "Get Here" sounds so desperate on an answering machine."

"I'm not desperate." Maya informed her.

"Anyway, forget that, here's the scandal, you remember that guy Jeff, the one I met at the Paradise Garage umpteen years ago?

"No." Maya said out of spite because Alycia called her desperate.

"Stop playing, I know you do. He's that gorgeous brother with the caramel skin. You remember, he looked like he was honey dipped."

"Oh yeah Jeff from Brooklyn."

"Right, well I was coming back from lunch through the Financial Center and who did I see?" not waiting for a response Alycia continued. "Yes girl, Jeff! He was eating an ice cream cone, and I said to myself, that guy over there is so handsome I wonder if he wants to share his ice cream. So, you know me."

"Oh no! What'd you do?"

"I purposely bumped right into him and knocked over his cone."

"You didn't."

"You know I did! Girl he was pissed, but when he looked up I could've died. He said, Alycia?! Nothing came out of my mouth I just stood there smiling. He leaned in and kissed me, girl I almost peed on myself. I could not believe it was Jeff, the only brother I still brag about."

"Don't I know it?" Maya responded sarcastically.

"We had the best understanding. There were no pre-arrangements, but whenever we bumped into each other at the club, it was understood that we were together for the rest of the night. Every time I went up the ramp into the Club, I would have my fingers crossed that he would be inside, ready to snag my body on the dance floor. Girl I can't tell you how it felt to be in his company again. And from what he's told me, the feeling is mutual! He wouldn't stop about how sweet, sexy, sophisticated and all that he thought I was. You know me, girl, I was eating it up, smiling and giving him that I-love-every-word-you're-saying-grin."

"So are you going to see him again? Did you get his number?"

"Now what do you think? Of course I did. I'm an opportunist, Honey. If I have my way, I'll be marrying his ass next spring!" Alycia shouted with excitement.

"Oh no, I know that tone, you're serious."

"You know it, anyway, get this, tomorrow is our big night out, were going uptown for an after work drink. He mentioned a Reggae club but I told him that I wasn't feeling that and prefer to do something light like listen to some Jazz. You know me girl, I love a mellow setting. What's the name of that new New Orleans place? Huh? Hello, Maya, are you there?"

"I'm listening."

"What's wrong with you girl, lately you've been so blah?"

"You would be blah too, if you haven't been getting any. I haven't had any in months, and I am tired of sleeping with pillows between my legs. This morning I woke up with wet gook everywhere. I'm over due, and I'm cranky. I'm sure you can understand."

"No. Not really. I keep me some meat." Alycia bragged ignoring Maya's feelings.

"Excuse me! I forgot I was talking to Sizzlin' Susie! So Jeffrey is back on the block? Mmntn, mntn, mntn, I have to admit that's one man I wish I had met before you. Everything about him is beautiful. His personality, skin, eyes, hair, teeth, and oh that body. Besides, the way you use to act all of those next days after, I know he did you right. I know you're looking forward to getting back with him."

Alycia blushed proudly, thinking just that, "If you want, I'll see if he has a friend."

"No thanks, I've been on that ride before and I'm still dizzy from it."

Alycia laughed confirming that Maya was definitely still dizzy. They jumped on another topic then promised to talk later.

Lunch

Eleven thirty: time for Maya to leave and meet with the distributors for lunch. She exhaled, relieved and glad to get out of the office for a few hours and away from Arthur. Plus she was excited about seeing everyone especially Tyrone -- he, too, was having men troubles. And the two of them would spend hours going on and on about how trifling men could behave. Maya appreciated how Tyrone discussed men differently from her girlfriends he had more of an open mind, more fact than assumption. Despite who he slept with he was still male. He would joke, *"Maya, honey if I wasn't gay, I would have to snatch you up, but you know I prefer steak over fish any day of the week. Girl, you haven't had any real problems with men, until you have two or three of them chasing your ass like it was the last one on earth. With everyone wanting to do me, I don't even have time for a . . .* Maya would cover her ears like she didn't want to hear the rest, yet she would hang onto his every word, stretch her eyes and fall out laughing.

She loved Tyrone, he was a class act. He fancied himself by wearing the finest silks, leathers, suede and linens, his only objection were furs. He hates fur and calls it "hair". As a child his mother brought him a rabbit coat for Easter and he complained that "hair" was in his mouth and ever since then he never forgave fur and refuse to put it on, even on the coldest evenings when he was stepping out in style. Despite the absence of furs, his closet was a work of art, everything color coordinated, neatly folded, hung and pressed as if it all had been delivered by the dry cleaner. On a wall of just shoes, every pair appeared new, freshly shined and neatly arranged. Tyrone took a lot of pride in how he looked and what he wore. He would really show off in the winter. Winter white was his favorite color, coats, hats, scarves, gloves and boots all in sync for his big entrance at every upscale event in and around town.

If you didn't know Tyrone, your first impression would be that he was good people, smart, clean, an honest. His aura was inviting.

He always kept his face clean shaven, teeth white, eyes clear, nails well manicured and hair cut close. He was well groomed and always smelled good. Although very gay, Tyrone attracted all kinds of people, beautiful women in particular.

Once the women got to know him better and found out about his sexual preference they were attracted to him even more because now he'd become non-threatening. Plus they loved his flair for what worked and what didn't. They would consult him on colors, cuts and fabrics. They would ask him to go shopping with them and to help them pick out the right outfit to get a man's attention. If they were going to a major party or had a big meeting or any situation where they wanted to make a lasting impression they would speak to him first on the dos and don'ts. Tyrone loved acting as their personal stylist and gave them what they needed to get the results they wanted.

Tyrone's lover, Wesley, was a designer, and most of the people they associated with were up and coming designers on the verge of making it big. As a favor, Tyrone often modeled for them, introducing their new line to buyers at exclusive designer boutiques.

At their last exhale session, Tyrone complained to Maya about Wesley's spending too much time with a hair dresser named Dane. Dane was a messy looking thing and Tyrone could not understand why a sophisticated designer like Wesley would be caught seen with a skank like Dane. His skin was bumpy yellow, his hair was over-permed and dyed a cheesy blond, he had a big nose that didn't appear to belong to him, and was always seen flirting with that long nasty looking tongue that seemed thin enough to have holes in it. He looked disgusting and talked with an irritating baby voice, *"Dad-dy,"* he would call Wesley *"Daney wants to go for a ride. Dad-dy, Daney wants some ice cream."* Tyrone knew just what kind of ride and cream Dane was talking about and he wasn't having it. He knew that Dane wanted Wesley in the worst way and he was not about to sit back and let it happen.

Unfortunately for Tyrone, the situation grew out of hand and he didn't know how to handle it. It wasn't so much that Wesley had a lover, because Tyrone had his occasional fling too. But in his mind that wasn't the issue. The fact that Wesley's lover had a reputation of sleeping with almost everyone in town was the issue. Not to mention that there was no discretion involved. Dane let it be known that Wesley was hopeless and that he wasn't going anywhere anytime soon.

Tyrone was not only afraid of losing Wes to Dane but losing him to AIDS. He was certain that Dane would be the one to bring the virus into their little circle and kill off everybody. Although he had his points of weakness, Tyrone was very particular about whom he'd danced around with and never entertained without a condom, except when he slept with Wesley. But now even their skin to skin relationship was over. Wesley, too, would have to slip on his raincoat.

Maya was too shocked to respond, she just shook her head in disbelief. She knew Wesley well and couldn't believe that he would be taken in by this Dane person. In the design/fashion community, Wesley was the cream of the crop. Educated, talented, kind and gentle, he was an athlete, a teacher, a mentor and a good friend. He always looked as if he just stepped out of a magazine. Outside of being gay, she thought he was the ideal man, tall, very dark and lean with the perfect amount of thickness. Wes was humble and very reserved and falling prey to someone like Dane was totally out of his character. He and Tyrone had been together for more than seven years and as much as Maya would prefer men to be with women, she thought that Tyrone and Wesley was a very fitting couple.

****

Briefly scanning the menu, Maya got impatient. She was 10 minutes late and surprised that she was the first person there. Just to be doing something, she flagged down the waiter.

"Hi. Can I get a club soda with lime?"

Just as the waiter completed her order and walked away, Sheila and Ian walked up to the table. Happy to finally have some company, Maya got up and kissed them both.

"Where's Tyrone?" She asked.

"Oh he called my office just as I was walking out to say that he'll be a half an hour late and for us to go ahead and order -- the tab is on him." Sheila reported and offered Ian and Maya a hi-five. They all laughed and ordered a round of drinks and appetizers.

It was business as usual, Sheila had a new line she wanted to show and Ian had some orders for Maya to sign. At about a quarter to one, Tyrone came strutting in, giving everyone a big Hollywood style hello. Ian and Sheila were just as excited about Tyrone's presence as Maya. Tyrone sat down and jumped right into the mozzarella sticks.

"I'm starving. I hope half of the meeting is over. Fill me in. Where are we?"

Everybody began talking all at once, the meeting was a success and finished right as their entrees were being served. The food was excellent, Maya had the shrimp parmesan without the ziti, Ian had baked sole with potato, Tyrone had a crab-cake sandwich, and Sheila had the vegetable lasagna. Tyrone's company paid the tab as promised.

Ian and Sheila took the subway back to the World Trade Center, Maya and Tyrone shared a cab. Maya release a sound of pleasure as she leaned back into the cab seat. She felt good to be out of the office during office hours, hanging out with her associates.

"So what's up boyfriend?" she asked Tyrone.

"Same shit, Wesley had the nerve to bring Ms. Thing to our place."

Maya's mouth flew opened. "No he didn't!"

"Hmph, yes he did, and It had the nerve to speak to me, '*Hi Ty,*' with that razor blade tongue poking out of Its mouth like It was a snake or something."

"Whaaat! I can't believe Wes, sounds like he's all in -- I wonder what's up? I hope it's not a drug thing."

"I doubt it, we mingle with some pretty powerful people and they always have enough drugs to give away. We usually have it around the place for months, neither one of us really enjoy using -- it just sits there. I keep telling Wesley we better get rid of it before we get busted for having it in the house."

"So if it's not that, what does Ms. Thing have that you don't?"

"No. It's what It doesn't have. And the answer is Respect. Take those big greasy lips and that worn out tongue and you get a nasty tramp."

Maya had to clench her legs; she didn't say anything but the way Tyrone talked about Dane's work made her wish she had a man of her own. The cab driver pulled up in front of Macy's and Maya gave Tyrone a kiss and said "Hang in there, this will all be over soon. Wesley loves you."

It was 3:05, and Maya was ready to leave work and meet with Selina, she had promised her they would go bike riding after work. She placed her ear plugs in her ears and worked steady hoping that 5pm would come soon. She loved listening to music and had all her favorite artists downloaded on her computer. She clicked through her computer files and highlighted Indie Arie's *Strength, Courage and Wisdom*.

At 5:05 Maya was already sporting her fucshia with lime biker suit, her Nike cross-trainers, and biker hat. She didn't forget her ear plugs and was now listening to Patti Austin. Maya loved Oleta Adams, Diane Reeves, Randy Crawford, Carmen Lundy, Sade, Basia, Anita Baker, Phyllis Hyman, Dinah Washington, and Ella just to name a few. She felt a connection with their style and often had them blasting in her car and apartment.

Selina was already outside waiting; her hours at Chase Manhattan are 8:30 to 4:30. Out of all of her friends Maya knew Selina the longest. They grew up together, same neighborhood, same teachers, same everything, they were close as sisters.

"Hey Honey, you ready to free your spirit?"

"Of course and what's up with the helmet?" Maya asked rolling her eyes.

Selina had on a helmet, knee pads, gloves, elbow pads and goggles.

"You look like a messenger."

"That's all right I'd rather look like a messenger than to look like a fool with my head all bandaged up. You should take lessons, but no you gotta be styling. That styling shit is gonna catch up with your ass."

Maya just laughed, and began peddling.

Selina was a faster rider than Maya and she liked leaving her behind. They circled Central park three times before they decided to walk their bikes to get some frozen yogurt.

"Girl, we got to start going out again, I feel it coming on. It's this weather it just makes me feel like grinning in some man's face."

Selina choked and laughed at the same time. "Is that all you want to do, is grin in their face?"

"Shut-up."

"I'll call Roz, you know if we go out Roz got to come. She likes starting things."

"Oh good, ask her if next Thursday work for her, we can skip biking for one week."

"Okay, but let's do something crazy, lets bar hop." Selina suggested with two places in mind.

"Bar hop?! That's dumb. Bar hopping is tacky. How many of those places can your stomach stand in one night? One is usually enough to make me wish I'd stayed home."

"Oh boy here we go with Ms. High and Mighty. You always find reason to kill a good plan. And you wonder why you can't find anyone. You would meet somebody decent if you would just adjust your standards a little bit."

"My standards don't need adjusting, it's these men. And the women, they're really the ones that make my stomach ache. They can't go anywhere without looking like they're on sale."

"True, they are pretty disgusting these days."

"You know what I'm talking about. Remember the changing room at the Garage?"

"Yeah unisex." Selina eyes lit up.

"We used to rush in there, take off our clothes and put on our flats, slip into our body suits and shorty-shorts."

"Chile, there were breasts hangin' and pieces swingin' in that place. It was deep."

"And, you didn't get any funky looks or stares."

"Well," Selina admitted, "I did take a couple of good looks at everything that was swinging and hanging.

Maya fell out laughing, and said "I know you did. But it was cool that nobody bum rushed you because you had a big ass, or plump breast. Everybody just did what they had to do to get on the dance floor."

"Yeah, that was back in the days."

Speaking of back in the day, Alycia called me and told me that she bumped into that guy Jeff."

"Not eat-it-all-Jeff?"

"Yes, eat-eat Jeff."

"Please don't tell me that I'm gonna have to hear that chile brag about that boy again. We just got her to shut up about him last year, why did he have to come back?"

"Oh stop, as long as she's happy I'm happy."

"I guess." Selina said not really caring.

Maya couldn't wait to get on the PATH train to Grove Street. She was tired and wanted to close her eyes and enjoy the seven minute ride home. There weren't that many people on the train now that the rush hour was over and the crowds had died down. She closed her eyes and smiled thinking how nice it was reminiscing with Selina about the good old days at the Paradise Garage.

Girl's night out

Thank God it's Friday, Maya said through her yarn as she stretched. Her Friday outfit already pressed and waiting to be worn. Glad that she didn't have another one of her dreams she thought it must have been the biking and the milk bath that put her right to sleep -- making no room to fantasize about love making with the perfect man.

It was 9:20 when her phone rang.

"Hey girl, heard you were ready to hang out?"

Though, Maya loved Roz, it was just too damn early in the morning to hear her voice.

"Yeah, I was going to call you later and set up something for next week."

"Next week? Girl, I'm calling you about tonight. There is this after work spot called Manilas, it's on 41st and 7th and my girl Latisha told me that it's the place to be."

"Oh please not another 'place to be'; I don't want to be there already."

"Look, hussy, don't get shady with me this is Roz you're talking to. Not one of your other tired girlfriends. If it's not the 'place to be', then we'll just have to make it 'the place to be', okay."

Maya sighed, Roz was so damned bossy.

"Look, I didn't plan to go out tonight; my hair is pinned up and . . ."

"Oh stop with the excuses, your hair is always pinned up."

True, Maya thought. "Okay. Who else is hanging?"

"Me, you, Selina and Alycia. Oh yeah, there is a slight catch, I'm very busy so you'll have to call them." Click.

"Witch." Maya said to the phone, complimenting Roz's sparkling personality.

Maya worked on changing her mood before she called the other girls. She knew that Roz was right and that tonight was as good as any other to go out. She decided to make the calls now while it was fresh in her mind. First she called Alycia.

"You know I'm down. What time?"

Then she called Selina.

"Just tell me when and where."

It was set, "girl's night out" on the town. The details were that they would meet at Chelsea Place for their initial drink and then leave for Manilas.

Arguing over who deserve the crown for sexiest man, Will Smith or Morris Chestnut, the women giggled walking towards the restaurant.

"Ooh good. Men." Alycia whispered as they entered Chelsea Place. The place was packed with wall to wall men, the music was mellow and everyone seemed to be talking. The brothers were definitely in the house but . . . they were either blind or shy, or maybe they just forgot their manners, because no one said hello, no one offered to buy them drinks and no one asked them to dance. They had two drinks each and decided that the men wanted to be the ones spoken to; drinks bought for, and asked to dance. Just because they had on fancy suits and wore expensive cologne, they wanted to be treated like women like to be treated, but these ladies had too much going on for that, so they decided to leave and go somewhere where they would be appreciated.

They giggled out of Chelsea's and attempted to hail a cab. That's when Roz surprised them and pulled out a joint. They hadn't seen a joint since the good ol' days. Roz was an occasional weed-smoker, but the rest of them grew out of it.

"Anybody want a boost?"

Since they were already boosted from the Absolute and cranberry juice, they all said "Yeah" except Maya. Roz and Selina took about 2 pulls apiece as they all jumped into a cab. They were happy and singing and flirting with the cab driver. It took them all of four minutes to finally gather up the $6.25 for the fare. Outside of Manilas you could hear the music pumping.

The men at Manilas were altogether different. They were very friendly, and rushing at them -- offering to buy drinks. They weren't there for 20 minutes before they each were grinning in some man's face. Maya winked at Roz to let her know that this was indeed 'the place to be'.

After what seemed like a night of dancing, they decided to get a table. All of them met someone new. It took about 10 minutes to introduce everyone over the loud music. Maya's friend's name was Gary, Alycia's, Brad, Roz's, Lance and Selina's, Thomas.

Brad ordered a round of drinks for everybody. That's when Alycia kicked Maya from under the table, it was a signal that not only was he good looking . . . he wasn't cheap. After the drinks arrived, Brad held up his glass and made a toast *"to new friends."* Everyone lifted their glass, looked at each other and grinned.

Gary, Maya's friend, didn't waste anytime getting the details on her.

"Maya are you single?" he said in a warm, direct tone.

Maya smiled a quick smile she wasn't prepared for such a personal question. She was feeling too nice and didn't want to have to think. So she said, "No." and then she thought, *what am I doing?* And said, "Yeah, sort of." She knew that this was not a smart move, but decided to worry about it later.

He smiled, thinking that her being confused was a positive sign. Then he pulled her chair close to his and whispered in a low voice. "What do you mean sort of? Will I be able to see you after tonight?"

Maya was uncomfortable by his forwardness and avoided his eyes, when he spoke. It's been so long since she allowed herself to get close to a man that she didn't know how to act. So she batted her eyes, licked her lips and said, "Depends on how you act tonight."

Even though he loved her reply, it shocked him. Sexy and sassy, he thought. Maya found herself shocked too, what made her say that? Finally she excused herself and got Selina's attention to go with her to the ladies room.

"Pinch me." She said.

"For what?"

"I want to make sure I'm not dreaming. Did you see him?"

"Who?"

Maya plucked Selina on the side of her head and said "stop playing girl. I'm talking about my husband to be, my babies daddy."

"No more drinks, for you – you don't even have kids."

"I know I don't have kids, Silly, I'm talking about my future."

"Maya, you're drunk and things just seem like this for now, call me in the morning and tell me if you still feel the same way."

" Oh, you don't think I can get him? Bet I will, mark my words, Gary's the one. I will be Mrs. Gary whatever his last name is."

"Through her laugh Selina said yeah, Mrs. Gary X." They laughed, got themselves together and went back to the table.

Before they reached the table Gary stood up and pulled out Maya's chair.

"How did you do that?" he asked

"Do what?"

"How did you make yourself more beautiful than you were a minute ago? You are absolutely stunning." Maya blushed, and thought; *good he's still singing my tune.*

"Can I get you another drink?"

"Well, uh no."

"You seem a little unsure."

"I had my limit."

"Limit? It's Friday night and its only 9:30. You appear to be a big girl; don't tell me you have a curfew?"

"No, I don't have a curfew. I just tend to pace myself when I drink. I do have to catch a train to Jersey."

"Jersey? What part?"

"Jersey City."

Maya blushed thinking about her adorable Hamilton Park brownstone apartment.

"Jersey City, get outta here! I work in Hoboken. My car is parked there now." Then he pulled her chair closer to his again and said, "You don't have to worry about getting home I'd be glad to escort you to your door."

He did it again, Maya thought, he's moving too fast. Then she remembered that none of her girlfriends were going to Jersey so it would be nice to have a strong, handsome brother escorting her to her door. Then she thought is he trying to be slick, escorting me to my door? Was he a dog in disguise? Or was he just being a nice brother, making sure that I made it home safe?

Before Maya accepted his offer she asked him, "Where do you live?"

"Queens, Jamaica Queens."

"Oh, how long have you lived there?"

"Three years. I'm originally from Georgia."

That's it. Maya thought, I knew there was something different about this guy. He wasn't raised in the City. He had too many manners, and he seemed so sure about himself. This was a plus for him. Maya became more relaxed and said, "Oh well, if it's not going to be too much trouble, I would appreciate the company going home."

That's when he took her hand and kissed it softly. Maya just purred.

The deejay was in rare form and Roz, Alycia and Selina were out on the dance floor with their new friends -- feeling no pain. Finally, Gary and Maya decided to join them. Maya pretended to be in a dancing mood, but she really just wanted to be alone with her new friend, and get to know him better. Fortunately for her, after two songs the music had stopped. It was show time and Maya was glad.

They took their seats and Gary ordered a round of drinks. Thomas was excited about show time because his sister was part of the show. He had guaranteed them that, "this is one show they'll never forget." That's when Maya received another kick from under the table. This time it was Selina, she was happy because he was happy, and Maya was tired of being kicked, but figured she'd tell them off tomorrow and enjoy herself tonight. For people who just met, Roz and Lance seemed very tight. At the first half of the show the women decided to go to the ladies room.

"Roz, what's up with this lubby-dubby act? You act like you've known Lance all your life."

"Girl, can I help it if that's the way he makes me feel? Like a sponge, I'm just soaking it up. And Maya, I know you're not talking, the way what's-his-face is all up in your face."

"Is he? I haven't noticed." Maya replied with her nose up in the air and her eyes closed. "But check it out, I'm going to let him escort me home tonight."

"Girl, are you crazy?" Alycia cautioned.

"That's right Maya, you better think again, you don't even know him." Selina jumped in and said.

Roz stepped between them and said. "Oh chill, Maya's a big girl she knows what time it is. The boy is harmless. Y'all just trippin' cause we're scoring." Then she threw her hand up to catch Maya's hi-five.

"Don't even act like its all about you two. Didn't Maya tell you that I was seeing Jeff again? Hello." Alycia was being facetious, holding her hand to her ear. "I just came out to come out. Give me a couple more weeks and you'll be hearing me singing 'Do It To Me One More Time, Once Is Never Enough With A Man Like You.'"

They fell out laughing.

"Sure Alycia, so why aren't you out with Mr. Do It To Me tonight, if he's all that? Is he with the wife?"

"No, he doesn't have a wife, besides Jeff's the kind of guy that you don't want to rush. Plus I plan on having a little fun with what's-his-name out there tonight."

"Oh? Just a minute ago, you were trying to tell me not to let Gary escort me home. Which is it?"

"Maya I was just looking out for you. You know you're practically a virgin."

Everybody laughed, even the women in the bathroom that didn't know them.

"Can I help it if I'm not easy?"

The laughter started again. "Oh shut-up, what about Selina?" Alycia said getting the attention off of her.

"Yeah Selina, you've been awfully quiet. What's up with Thomas?"

"What do you want to know, he's a man." Selina said as if being a man was like being a wall.

Nobody touched that. Everyone secretly thought that Selina was bisexual, though no one ever mentioned it to the other or questioned her about it. So they left it at that, he was a man.

"C'mon let's get outta here, Maya said snatching a last look at herself in the mirror."

The men were getting along well. They were giggling like school boys. Gary saw them coming and cleared his throat as he stood up to help Maya to her seat.

"What's so funny?" Roz asked Lance knowing that the joke was on them.

"We're just joking about the guys here, who didn't get to meet you and your girlfriends first." Then his tone changed. "It's clear that you all are the most beautiful women in here."

Roz made an oozing sound of appreciation and kicked Maya then made a face that said, *'how long do you think this will last.'* Selina motioned for more drinks.

"This round is on me," Thomas announced, peeling out a crisp fifty dollar bill.

"No more for me." Maya said in her sweetest voice. Then she whispered something in Gary's ear.

"It's been a pleasure meeting you ladies." Gary stood up and smiled at each one of them. "Lance, Thomas, Brad." He said as if he was reciting roll call, "Make sure these precious women get home safely." They all stood up to shake his hand and Lance mumbled a few words that made Gary blush.

Wait until you hear . . .

It was 7 a.m. when Maya's phone rang. Her head was hurting and she didn't want to be bothered. She heard her voice say, "You got the right number, at the wrong time, please leave a message." Then she heard Roz shouting.

"He just left, he just left, pick up the phone!"

"Why me?" Maya grumbled reaching for the phone. "I could strangle you. This better be good."

"Girl, Lance put it on me."

"Y'all sure didn't waste any time." Maya said removing dry crumbs out of her eyes.

"That's right, we didn't waste any time and why should we? He wanted me and I wanted him. And to top it off, it was excellent."

"Excellent? I've never heard sex referred to as excellent."

"Well now you have."

"Now Roz, you know how brothers are, you can't be giving them the impression that you're easy."

"Maybe you didn't hear me. I said I wanted it and he did too. It's not about being easy. I'm grown! If you look at the whole picture, you will see that he was just as easy as I was. I wouldn't have just screwed anyone. Lance turned me on. He was a total gentleman the whole night. It was me, who invited him in and got things started. It was my game, he had the right piece and we both won. I don't care if I ever hear from him again, he satisfied me and I know I satisfied him, the proof is in the sheets. So now what?"

Maya knew she hit a nerve, she was supposed to relish in the exciting news. She didn't know how to respond, nor had the head for it. But she knew she had to say something that would bring the excitement back and remove the bitterness.

"Girl, you know I'm just hating."

"Mmm girl, I can still feel him. Maya, the boy did me like I was his favorite flavor. Oh the chills are coming back." Roz said hugging herself.

"Do I have to hear this?" Maya groaned.

"Yes, you do!"

"So did you return the favor?"

"I tried, but he wouldn't let me. He said he gets his pleasure by giving pleasure. Can you believe it?"

"No."

"But girl, I have to admit, it was so pretty I wanted to treat him."

"OK, I'm sorry I asked, I don't need to hear anymore about that. What time did he leave?"

"About an hour ago, he woke me up at 5:30 and told me his last name. Walker, Lance Walker. Isn't that a nice name? How do Roslyn Reid- Walker sound to you?"

"Ridiculous." Maya wanted to say but lied and said. "Beautiful."

"And girl, get this, he's never been married, doesn't have any children and lives alone. He's an architect for Mitsubishi Bank. Owns his own home and drives a Volvo 740."

"OK, what's the catch? You know if it sounds too good to be true, it probably is."

"I don't know, but I think it'll be fun finding out. On the way home last night we stopped at one of those Korean deli-fruit stand-florist-cold and hot salad bar-grocery stores so that I could get some gum and when I walked out, Lance surprised me with a lovely bunch of fresh flowers."

"You lucky dog."

"Girl, that's when our tongues met, I knew right then I wanted him in my bed. His mouth was fresh, his teeth clean and his grip was strong. It was one of those kisses that did all the talking."

"Ooh," Maya cooed. "He sounds so nice. I checked him out last night he's fine and followed you all night like a little puppy. Wait a minute Roz, hold on." Maya got up to check out the noise in the hall. "That's Chase scratching the door, I got to let his fat ass out.

Girl, Gary didn't even attempt to come in after he heard Chase barking like he was ready to kill. And when I told him that Chase was a Rottweiler his behind was half way down the stairs."

"So nothing happened?"

"Nothing compared to your great adventure. Gary suggested we take the Ferry to Hoboken instead of the train. We stood on the top deck, while the moon watched over us. He told me that he was Gary Steven Cooper, a pediatrician. He's 41, has two sisters, both older and he, too, lives alone. I know it's ridiculous to get excited about a man you've just met, but everything about Gary seems right.

"Oh boy. How many times have I heard this?"

"I'm not sure, since you haven't heard it from me. Well, not lately anyway. Sure I fell for the wrong guy in the past but that's over I know what signs to watch for now. Anyway we all make mistakes I don't know anyone who hasn't. Do you?

"Mmm hmm, well we'll see, but girl, you should have shut that mutt up and got some filling."

"I'm not like that, and the next time you bring your ass over here I want you to tell Chase he's a mutt."

"Later for Chase, you claimed not to be 'like that', but I know you wanna be. But do it your way, I hope he can wait."

"If he can't, he can't. But I already told you it wasn't like that. We had a couple of soft kisses at my door, then he slobbed me down, gave me a peck on my forehead and said good night. That was enough to soil my panties."

"Boooring" Roz sang. "I'm just kidding girl, he's too cute, let me know if you don't want him."

"Forget it, Roz, you're not his type."

"Oh, excuse me. Don't blame me if you never see him again."

"For your information, I'm seeing him tonight, his place. He invited me over for the best home cooked meal in Queens."

"Now you're talkin'! Finally we're getting somewhere. He wants you to come over to his place, so he can cook? Let me guess what he'll be serving."

"Bye Roz, you're pathetic, plus I gotta go. Chase is starting to panic. I'll talk to you later."

"Okay, but I want details when I talk to your ass later."

Maya took a quick shower and threw on a t-shirt and some sweats, grabbed Chase and headed for Hamilton Park. Chase was Maya's baby. Her brother Gregg, who raised Rottweilers upstate New York, had given him to her for protection. Though Chase was still a pup, he weighed 85 lbs. His coat was rich black with rattan brown sections inside the ears and at the neck. He had a short stubby tail and the compliments never stopped when it came to Chase. The whole neighborhood admired his strong posture and confident stride. The thing Maya liked most about Chase was that he took no mess. No one could just walk up on her if he was around. He would let out a mean growl, bark loudly and pull to get loose. That was just fine with Maya since she didn't appreciate her flaky neighbors coming up to her with their silly conversation.

It was a beautiful clear morning and Maya took pleasure in it as she sat on the bench gazing while waited for Chase to do his thing. She thought about her invitation for the evening. What was she going to wear? What should she bring? Can he cook? Was Roz right about this just being a ploy to do the wild thing? And if so, should she? She smiled, thinking about him, and then his face appeared, a younger version of Karl Malone, that's who he looked like, the Mailman of the Utah Jazz basketball team. She laughed out loud at her thoughts and yanked Chase's leash. "Let's go baby."

The guys

"Man I'm telling you this woman is gorgeous. She's like a fine glass of wine. She has to be the prettiest woman I've ever seen."

"Yeah, sure, I bet she's a real bow wow." Dice nudged Pookey.

"Okay, wait until you see her. You're going to flip. I bet you can't name a star that's prettier."

"Lisa Rae."

"Good call, but Maya's got her beat. Next."

"What about Janet Jackson?" Pookey said slamming his beer down, like there was no one that could possibly be prettier.

"Little Janet? Man I'm talking about a real woman with long shapely legs and beautiful eyes. Janet Jackson is cute and short."

"Okay, okay I got it. What about that pretty woman that used to be the host on BET?"

"Which one?"

"I don't know, but she's real pretty and she use to host a while back."

"How pretty can she be? You can't even remember her name."

"I got it." Dice laughed. "Is she prettier than Wesley Snipes?"

"Ha ha, real funny, you're going to eat those words when you see her."

Selina

Left, two, three, four, and right, two, three, four . . . was the beat that Selina watched herself exercise to in the full wall mirror. From the first day she saw her apartment she envisioned turning it into her personal gym. Her bedroom was the locker room, the bathroom was the steam room and her living room was the main area for the gym equipment. The raw brick walls and the hard wood floors, also added to the look she wanted to achieve. Living on the third floor, Selina could get away with having nothing but a shine on her tall, black-framed windows. The one air conditioner and the two ceiling fans she had, kept her cool from the sun and the heat exercising generated. A fanatic about her weight and health, with the exception of beer, Selina's diet consisted of frozen yogurt, cranberries, leafy vegetables, almonds, sunflower seeds and tofu. She would only eat meat when she visited her parents or when invited to a cookout. But for her lifestyle at home, she would not eat or buy meat.

Exercising was Selina's way to release any unwanted tension, stress and anger that blocked her from being productive. Today she wanted to remove the incident that happened at the club the other night. She was upset with the girls for not mentioning the fact that she wasn't into Thomas, the guy she met at the club. Thomas was a "good catch" a bachelor, a pharmacist at Duane Reade, handsome face and loved the Lord. So why didn't they act surprise when Selina left without exchanging numbers with him? She wanted one of them to say, *'girl, you crazy, I'll give him some'* like they would have said to each other. Selina hated the fact that they knew about her and pretended not to know.

Now sitting and feeling lonely, Selina thought back to the days when life was simple. Living with strict parents, she was not allowed to mingle or go to school with the kids in her neighborhood. Compared to the other families there, Selina's parents appeared wealthy. They owned the home they lived in and had two cars parked in the garage. Attending private school, Selina only got to see the kids in her neighborhood on Saturdays when she walked around the corner to the beauty salon to get her hair pressed. Although she barely came out, she was popular. All the teenage boys would pass her letters as she turned the corner, some even watched through the glass while she got her hair done.

Being one of the only two black girls in her school she didn't have many friends. The kids teased her about her color and wrote horrible things on her locker. When Selina begged her parents to take her out of that school, they told her to just ignore the teasing. Education was far more important, and when she got older, she would understand. Her parents were right, and she did start to understand but what she understood most was the kids at school didn't like her because they didn't know her or anyone like her, except Maya. But Maya didn't count because back then, lighter skin was more acceptable. Selina took her parents advice, made top grades and thought of the kids as being ignorant and narrow minded. Besides, the kids in her neighborhood were being friendly and trying to get to know her better.

Because she never wore braids, went to a private school, dressed real nice and was laced with expensive jewelry, the boys held her out to be the neighborhood princess. At the age of fourteen, and shortly after receiving several intimate letters, Selina got the urge to disobey her parents. At nine o'clock when they dismissed her from the family room, she would kiss them both goodnight and climb out of her side window to meet with her new friends, mostly guys. Selina's new friends were into things that even her parents didn't do. They smoked weed, drank large amounts of beer and liquor and talked about having sex. Selina embraced her new friends and provided them with money to pay for the stuff that made them have fun. After about six months, Selina got tired of climbing out of her window and appealed to her parents to allow her out to be with her new friends. Busy with their own life, they told her that they thought it was nice that she had new friends and for her to go ahead and play along.

Selina enjoyed all the attention she was getting from the kids her age. The girls would ooh and ahh at her fancy perms and stylish clothes. They would ask to borrow some of her nice things with the intention of never returning them. But material things didn't matter much to Selina, she had plenty things that she could give away and was just happy to have new friends.

Not a day would pass, without two or three guys from the neighborhood standing outside of Selina's school. They argued over who was going to carry her books and who was going to hold her hands. Flattered by the attention and kindness, Selina felt that it was time to make a choice about who would be her man. Each guy wanted to be able to say that she belonged to him. They all dreamt about the good time they would have with her and the nice life it would be. Having everything that she wanted, it was hard for her to make a single decision. So she picked them all, they each had a turn with her and some how it worked. No one condemn her or called her out.

Selina squeezed herself as she reminisced about those good ol' days. But out of all of those days, what stayed in her mind more than anything was the night she went out with her last boyfriend, Ben. Ben had invited Selina to a strip poker party. He knew that she was on the loose side and that she wouldn't mind having a little extra fun with some of his friends. He was right Selina accepted the invitation without question.

When they got there Selina was introduced to three girls and three guys. Everyone seemed pleasant and seemed to be enjoying themselves. Beer and weed were the complete refreshments. Not long after the game started, all the girls had stripped down to their bras and panties. Selina remembered that it was the point when the lights went out and the music seemed low. She could still hear Ben's words, *finder's keepers*. She remembered giggling trying to find him, when she felt a hand grab her wrist. She knew it wasn't Ben, but she didn't mind, because she understood the rules of the game and thought all the guys there were kind of cute. But when the person touched her chin and kissed her mouth until she freed her tongue, Selina noticed something very different. The kiss was real, very passionate and tender. Selina felt her body weaken and tripped backwards until the wall broke her fall. The kiss continued and Selina reached out to feel the body, she searched for the legs, hoping to find something extra large between them. When she didn't feel anything she ignored it, thinking that it'll be up soon. So then Selina traveled up top to feel the masculine chest. Instead Selina felt a soft warm breast and jumped, breaking the kiss. The girl grabbed Selina's mouth and said '*sssh*' and then she released Selina's breast from the under wire cup bra and with her tongue, she began circling around the nipple. Selina's brain told her to push the girl off and ask her was she crazy, but it was too late, her nipples were erected and her flesh was weak. Selina heard Ben call out her name. He wanted to know where she was hiding. Then she heard him and another guy saying that they bet the girls were downstairs hiding behind the bar in the basement. So off they hid.

When the guys couldn't find them, they came back upstairs and threatened to turn on the lights, but the other couples complained and reminded them of the rules. Without a kiss goodbye, Selina's girlfriend eased away from her, then Selina heard the other guy say, '*I fount mine*', so she caught on and eased over by Ben.

"You're not suppose to really hide", he complained, but little did he know that Selina had a big surprise for him. She kissed his neck and couldn't feel the passion that she felt with the girl so she unbuttoned his shirt and sucked his chest -- still there was no passion. Selina needed the passion bad; this girl had started something that needed to be finished. So Selina's tongue raced down his stomach until she reached the hairs before his penis. With a slight tug she placed his penis in her mouth and treated him to something he'd never had before.

Selina was satisfied when the lights came back on, then she realized that she didn't know which girl made her feel so good. She studied the three girls carefully, but none out of the three seemed possible. Leaving, they all told her goodbye and gave her a big smile.

On their way home that night Ben got down on his knees and asked Selina to marry him. He said that she made him feel like a real man, and that he wanted to be with her for the rest of his life. But Selina didn't hear him. She didn't care about him. She was introduced to something she liked a lot more and couldn't wait to experience it again. She ignored his question and began questioning him about the females that were there. She told him not to hesitate to let her know the next time he wanted to go there. He agreed hoping that she would treat him special again.

Four days later Ben told Selina that it was going to happen again. For completely different reasons, they both were excited about going. But when they arrived, Selina noticed that there was only one of the girls there, and that girl was Trudy. Trudy was Ben's best friend's girl. She was real pretty and didn't seem like the type that would even consider such creative behavior. The other two girls from the party were friendlier, one even winked at her. The other nudged her as if to say, *'wasn't that fun?'* So this time, when the lights went out, Selina didn't even bother hiding. She knew that one of the guys would get her this time; after all, the object of the game was trying out new partners. She moved slowly letting whoever grab her, grab her. When the grab was made Selina backed into the wall until she fell down on something comfortable. And then she spread her legs allowing the guy to go ahead and get it over with. But instead she was kissed. The kiss registered instantly, now Selina knew that Trudy was her lover. Knowing that they didn't have much time, the two girls took off everything. They wanted to go further than they did the last time, and they would have if Ben wouldn't have shined a flashlight on their faces and their naked locked bodies.

Nervously Selina started laughing, she persuaded Ben to join them -- she was just seventeen and couldn't handle people knowing that she enjoyed being with another girl. Ben being two years older but less mature, was pleased by the invitation. After giving him all he could handle Selina convinced him that it was a ploy to turn him on. She told him that she loved him and would do anything to turn him on. He believed her and vowed not to say a word to anyone.

Tricking boys to meet girls was always Trudy's intention. Her date knew exactly what she was up to and didn't mind just as long as he got what he wanted in return.

Trudy

Coming from a mixed race family, her mother Philippine and her father African, Trudy had an exotic look. A small mouth, full lips, slanted eyes, flat nose, thick wavy hair and a peachy colored skin tone. At a size 9 she had healthy thighs and shapely legs, heavy breasts and thick arms, no belly and a big behind. Men accused her of being too cute to speak when they yelled *'yo momma, yo baby, hey thighs, hey tits'* and all of the other charming phrases that they enjoyed hearing themselves say. Trudy would ignore them and keep walking. That's when they would change their charming phrases to phrases more suitable like, *'f-you -- you stuck-up witch, keep on walking -- you big titty hoe, I don't want to talk to your stank ass anyway.'* Trudy was relieved when they became angry; she smiled at the thought of them changing their mind.

At the age of four, Trudy's parents had split. Trudy's father had chosen to spread his love around the rainbow and fell in love with a Spanish woman. Leaving New York, Trudy's father left her with a mother who stayed depressed and wanted to die. After months of getting in trouble and running away, Trudy fell into the hands of her father's sister. A year later when her father returned with his new love, this time a red-head Irish woman, Trudy cried that she wanted no part of him and wanted him to stay away.

Gradually, it happened, it never occurred to Trudy that she was being seduced or that she was being turned out. She enjoyed living with her aunt and playing with her cousins. She had no clue of what kind of lifestyle she was being led into. Even though she wasn't kept clean, or went to school everyday, she loved her aunt and liked the things that went on in the house.

Unlike Trudy, Selina could not blame her behavior on anyone. Until she met Trudy, she never had any intimate feelings for females. Not realizing the explanation for her promiscuous acts, Selina thought she loved the many sex partners she encountered. Cheating on every boyfriend seeing one in the day and one at night, Selina faked having orgasms every time, but didn't know why she kept trying. It took Trudy to come into her life for Selina to realize what she was searching for.

Living with her aunt, Trudy was allowed to have sex anytime she pleased and made love to many women, but Selina was her first virgin, her baby. Right away she wanted to take Selina in and treat her like she was her property. She could not understand why it was so hard for Selina to accept the fact that it was alright, and that if her friends and family loved her they would understand. Selina disagreed and was not ready to let anyone know what was going on between her and Trudy. After months of failing to make Selina understand, Trudy walked.

With angry tears in her eyes, Selina sat on the corner of her weight bench. She was tired of her secret life, the mystery and the assumptions. She no longer wanted her sex life to be private. It was too painful. She wanted to share her thoughts and feelings with someone. She wanted her friends to know and understand, that yes, she prefers a woman over a man. And yes it's the most beautiful thing she has ever discovered. She wanted to tell them why Thomas wasn't for her because she needed something that he did not have. Getting together with him would have been a waste for the both of them.

Selina picked up her weights and began lifting again, left, two, three, four, and right, two, three, four.

Okras

It was 7:30 pm when Maya stepped out of her brownstone apartment. The air around her was filled with her perfume. She took a deep breath and inhaled the foggy mist. The evening was calm after all the sun showers they'd received earlier. She was relieved that her car was parked in front of the door; she had on heels and didn't trust the cement with them. Her black, Toyota Avalon was looking especially sleek tonight, she had asked the kid next door to '*do the works*' and he did. For twenty bucks he did a great job, and had the insides smelling like fresh fruit. Maya re-adjusted her rear view mirror and threw herself a kiss with her tango-bronze colored lipstick then she selected her La La Hathaway CD, turned it up and pulled off. Maya had no doubt about how she looked tonight, she knew she was flawless and that was part of her plan to make him want her. She knew that her white sleeveless, silk jumpsuit danced sexily around her body with every move she made. She adjusted the volume a little more and sped through the Holland Tunnel feeling like tonight is going to be a wonderful night.

The fellas had just left and Gary was pitiful, his place was a wreck. When they invited themselves to his house to watch the games, Gary explained to them that Maya was coming over and that he had his whole afternoon planned. First he was going downstairs to do his laundry then he was going to make his place shine like new, after that, he was going to his favorite gourmet deli and buy all sorts of treats for his new and very special lady. And that there was not going to be any games watched at his house, not today. But when the last guy walked in with the case of Bass Ale, Gary smiled and said "let the games begin."

Now it was 7:55 and all the help the fellas promised they would do, turned out to be no help at all. It was bad enough the place wasn't cleaned when they arrived, now it was worse. Empty bottles, cigar butts, potato chips, salt from the pretzels, pizza boxes were all over the place. Plus the foul odor of sweaty men drinking and smoking clung to the air and in the carpet. Gary knew that time was not on his side, so during the last quarter of the game he embarrassedly got up and started picking up things, and then he sent Butchie to the grocer to get some fresh bread and vegetables and a bottle of fancy wine. Dice and Junie tried to help by watering his plants with their hot beer and feeding the fish, pretzel crumbs. Gary kicked them all out, when Butchie returned with a can of pork 'n beans, a box of stone crackers and a bottle of Four Roses White Wine.

Looking at the clock Gary realized that Maya would be there any minute. He threw some carpet fresh on the carpet, collected all of his clothes, poured pine down the toilet, and sink, stuffed all of his dirty dishes into the refrigerator, fed the fish, took a shower, threw some deodorant and cologne on and got dressed.

Standing outside of his home, Gary had on a pair of baggie khakis, an oversized orange shirt that allowed you to see that he had hair on his chest, and brown penny loafers with no socks.

Maya was prompt. She parked her car four houses from his, grabbed the flowers she had for him and stepped out of her car. He spotted her but couldn't move. He had forgotten how beautiful she was. He could not believe that this sexy woman was coming to be with him. He was no stranger to pretty women, but none like Maya. She was graceful – a real natural beauty it was in her walk, her smile and her eyes. She was perfect, he thought, as they faced one another again.

"Hello beautiful." He said and then slipped his tongue into her mouth. "You are so beautiful, I had to do that." He said starring at every part of her.

"Thank-you." Maya responded pleased that he felt moved to kiss her. All her life, she was told that she was beautiful, but when Gary said it, she felt beautiful. "These are for you." She said blushing.

"For me? Maya?" He looked into her eyes questioning her actions. The flowers blew his mind. It was his first time he received flowers from a woman before making love to her.

Maya knew she had him so she loosened up and said. "So, are you going to just stand there looking at me or are you going to invite me in for dinner?" Then she motioned to climb the stairs.

"Dinner? Oh-oh dinner . . . Maya, there has been a change in plans." Lost in her presence, Gary had forgotten all about dinner. About the fact that his apartment had not been clean in months and that the smell alone would turn her away. He was disappointed with himself, here she was prompt, beautiful and ready to enjoy the evening with him, not to mention the flowers that she brought to grace the table. He felt stupid, letting the fellas talk him into drinking and fooling around watching games all day instead of getting prepared for a special evening with her. "Would you be too disappointed if we went to a restaurant instead of eating here?"

Maya was relieved. She didn't trust herself to be alone with him, afraid of what she wanted. His body was so tempting. The two kisses that he already took from her were enough to make her surrender to anything he wanted.

"Of course not, did you make reservations?" she said still batting those long eyelashes and being pretty.

"No. But there's this great Soul Food Restaurant a few blocks from here called Okras, if you like soul food, you'll love Okras."

"Ooh, the name alone sounds good."

"Good let's take my car." He said grabbing her hand. "Wow you have soft hands."

Maya just smiled and squeezed his hand a little more. He opened the door to his late model Saab and surprised her with another slip of his tongue. Maya returned the favor with an extension of his kiss.

"You're going to like Okras. They cook better than my momma." He said over the relaxing flow of Joe Sample.

"Where is your mother?" Maya asked, not really interested in the answer but, the sound of his voice and the parting of his lips turned her on and so she wanted to see them move again.

"Oh, she's lives in Georgia. You couldn't pay her to come out here. She says there's too much crime in New York for her."

"She's right. It must be nice to live in Georgia with all that land. Why did you move up here?"

"Oh, I'm not one to live where I was born. I like to explore and meet different people." Maya just smiled not sure of what he said. He pulled up in front of Okras and handed the keys to the valet.

"I hope you're hungry."

Hungry? Maya was starving. She was too nervous to eat all day. Plus she had faith that Gary was an excellent cook, coming from Georgia and all. So she starved, saving herself for his treats. Maya just smiled.

An old black gentleman with very short white hair opened the door, and with his southern drawl he said. "Greaaat Gawd! You two 'bout the prettiest things I've seen dis ebenin', com'on heah and take a seat!" This man had hidden powers, Maya thought. He didn't look strong enough to hold the door, nor did he seem to have a voice as powerful as the one he used. "Someone will be heah to hep you two shortlay."

The atmosphere of the restaurant was pleasant. There were plants and floral arrangements all over and a sophisticated collection of old black and white photos from the 1930s era creatively displayed on the walls. Maya studied each photo and loved the way they were arranged and she would have loved to own a similar collection for her home.

When the waiter approached them they ordered a carafe of wine and traded smiles. Maya's insides were doing a dance. Finally she was with her honey again. All day she dreamt about being with him. The wine was soothing and the jazz was mellow, they both seemed relaxed. Gary had taken off his shoe and slipped his naked foot up Maya's pants leg and massaged her from ankle to knee. He watched her face as he did it and to his surprise her eyes were closed. She was swaying back and fourth with the music and to the rhythm of his touch. Then he lifted her hand and kissed the tips of her fingers. She opened her eyes and said, "This feels so good."

"I want you to feel good." he continued tasting her fingers.

When the waiter returned, he placed in front of Maya, a hot bowl of gumbo, a side of white potato salad and a big square of buttered cornbread. Gary plate contained red beans and rice, cabbage, bar-b-que baby back ribs and a side of macaroni and cheese. The waiter filled their glasses with ice-cold sweetened iced tea and brought over a neat brown bag for Gary to put his rib bones in. Gary joked. "What's this for? I plan to chew these bones."

Maya just blushed thinking how much she liked him.

Gary was right, Okras was definitely special. Everything was seasoned well and delicious. But now the two of them were stuffed. They shared a slice of sweet potato pie and decided to go to the other side of the restaurant for more wine and to enjoy the live jazz band.

"Now, you two, don't be no stranjahs. And de nexx time ya come, ya gotta have some my okra." The gray haired man said, helping Maya out of her chair. "She shoore is a pretty thing, you take care of dis heah gal." He continued, shaking Gary's hand and patting him on the back.

The couple reached for each other's hand and walked over to the other side. They got a cozy table with a small candle in the center and ordered more wine.

Maya was having the time of her life. So far Gary has been the man she had been craving. Allowing the wine to tell her what to do, she reached over and kissed him twice, the second one being the most passionate. Then somehow her shoes were off and now her feet were rising up the side of his hairy leg.

"You know, a girl can get herself in all sorts of trouble doing something like that." He said, pouring her more wine.

Until he mentioned it, Maya didn't realize she was being so forward, so she quickly stopped.

"Hey, why did you stop? It's alright, baby. I know you're feeling good, so am I. You don't have to stop, I like the way that feels. C'mon don't stop." he rubbed his leg against her foot to get them going again.

But, too embarrassed to continue, Maya changed the subject. "What time is it?"

Time to make love to you, Gary wanted to say. "Its 1:30, did you want to get in at a certain time?"

"No, I just wanted to change the subject." She said not looking at him.

"Oh I see, but baby," he said grabbing her hands, making sure she focused on his words. "You don't have to play games with me. Tonight is your night. You're the queen, whatever you want is alright with me." Then he kissed her hands and placed them back on the table.

Maya wanted to die; she did not know how to accept this kind of care. Then she thought, hey, let me try out my new powers.

"Let's dance." she whispered.

That was right down Gary's alley, the wine, the music, the low lights and of course Maya had him only too hot and eager to get close to her body. Besides he was a great dancer. He held out his hand and lifted her out of her seat and strolled onto the floor. He held her face and kissed her forehead before he wrapped his strong arms around her. Maya's eyes were closed as they moved slowly, side to side to the soft sounds of Jazz. Gary's body was firm and strong, while Maya's was tender and vulnerable.

"You smell so good." She said softly.

"You do too." He said with his mouth on her earlobe.

Before the music stopped, Gary whispered. "C'mon baby let's go."

Maya didn't answer she just followed. "You're going to have to hold me tight. I didn't realize how much wine I had."

"My pleasure." He said, lifting her by the fingers and into his arms. Face to face he could smell the fruit from the wine on her breath, and then leaned in for a long taste her tongue.

The flash from the camera interrupted their hot kiss, and as much as they both wanted to ignore their gracious host, Maya and Gary smiled as the white haired man took another picture.

The walk to the car was slow, both of them savoring the perfect feeling. They had already been out for over four hours and it was time to take this pretty lady home, Gary reasoned unwilling to jeopardize making a bad move. But it was Saturday night and the feeling was so right. So what does a man do with a five star lady on a Saturday night? Not say thank-you, dinner was nice, hope to see you again; no he would take her home, have a night cap and listen to some soft music and maybe make love to her. But that was out, he could sense that she was fragile and was probably hurt in the past and the thought of taking her to his place was certainly out.

Maya was in her glory, she felt so secure with her Gary. He was positive, strong and smooth. He didn't fumble on a word or trip over his feet. He took his time eating and she imagined that he would do the same when making love. He clearly had it going on and from the confident way he act, he knew it. If she had her way they would end the night strolling along the sands of Long Island's Beach until dawn. But that too, was out, they were in Jamaica Queens. So she assumed that they would just chill at his place for another hour or so, kissing and getting to know each other better.

"Baby, do you think you'll be alright driving back to Jersey?"

"Oh, I hadn't even thought about that. I'm sure I'll be fine." She said with a worried look on her face. Unconvinced Gary leaned over while waiting for the light to turn to green. He sucked her bottom lip and said, "I think it would be better if I drove you home. I wouldn't want anything to happen to you."

Maya was fascinated everything about him was inviting and exciting. Especially his scent, the cologne that he was wearing mixed with his body temperature was enough to send her to the floor of the car. At one point she didn't even remember leaving Okras, going by his place and switching cars. All of that seem to just poof and happen. It wasn't until they were half way through the Holland Tunnel that Maya partially sobered up and noticed that Gary was driving her car. How is he getting back? Don't tell me he's planning on staying? Who said he can stay? What is he trying to pull? If he wanted to do the wild thing, why didn't we just stay at his place? We were already there, weren't we? Then she studied his face as he took a right turn out of the tunnel and all she saw was the man she wanted to be with in Jersey, in Queens, in a tent, on the moon, wherever. When they got to the red light before her house he leaned over and sucked her neck. It wasn't until a car behind them blew the horn that the two straightened up and continued on their way.

Her neighborhood was quiet as usual. They got out of her car and strolled around Hamilton Park across the street from her brownstone. Since they've only known each other for a day, Maya knew that it wouldn't be smart to invite him in, especially since she was horny and would probably scare him away with what she really wanted to do. She also knew, regardless of what men say, they usually never let you live it down -- that you did it with them on the first date.

With the realization of no sex tonight, Maya let out a deep sigh of frustration as they leaned against a wide oak tree that covered them like an umbrella. Her back to his front, he pulled her close, wrapped his arms around her and lightly placed his chin in the crease of her neck and shoulder, and then the words she's been dying to hear floated in her ear. "Maya, let me make love to you tonight."

Her insides dropped. You would have thought he proposed marriage to her the way she lost her balance. He gently turned her around slowly and went straight to work, letting her feel the manhood that rose to the occasion. Maya was pleased at the presence of his manhood and grew weaker -- she separated her thighs and leaned into him. He squeezed her real tight guiding her hips as his hands explored her backside, she could not believe the stiffness and was ready to receive him. But she didn't, they spent a couple more minutes exploring each other's body against the tree, then Gary whispered, "Let's go."

They took sloppy steps toward her house, stopping to kiss every other second until they reached the top step and into the building. His skilled fingers traveled pass her button and bra and directly to the nipples of her breast, he bent down kissed it and she moaned. Taking that as a sign to please continue, he attempted to acknowledge the other nipple but then she stopped him.

"Not here, c'mon." She said taking his hand and leading him through the hall door. Before they could climb a second stair, he stopped her, unable to wait he eased her against the hall wall and greeted her other breast. Her body quivered and she grabbed his neck and kissed him like he was leaving for Iraq. They stopped and motioned to climb the third step leading to her top floor apartment when his cell phone vibrated then beeped.

"What's that?" Maya questioned, nervous that Ms. Greene may come out of her apartment. Gary had her so hot; she thought it may have been the fire alarm.

"Damn!" he barked, switching into an unknown gear. "It's an emergency, baby I gotta go. I need you to take me to Hoboken, to St. Mary's Hospital, now!" She nearly passed out. Hoboken? Hospital? Now? She didn't want to move, she didn't want him to leave.

"C'mon baby I gotta go now." Gary reiterated as he headed toward the door. Sweet Gary was now Serious Gary and he didn't spare a minute getting out of the building and into her car.

"Oh, of course." She said moving fast behind him.

It took them all of eight minutes to get to the hospital, the ninth minute, Gary was gone.

No hassle

We Com -- This Far-ar-ar -- By Faith, dum, dum, dum, dum, Lean-ing ooonn the Lord -ord'. Trusting in his Holy word, He never failed me yet.

Alycia closed her eyes and sung out loud with the W & E Gospel Choir on the radio. Though she loved gospel music, she never went to church. Every Sunday it would be her, her gospel music, her cleaning and her cooking. Now it was time for 'The Hour of Power' and Alycia would sit down concentrating and viewing her life against the given sermon.

"Ya friends, May not know." the rough voice began to preach in his own rhythm.

"I said!" he paused.

"Ya friends, may not know!

"You can keep it from ya husband," he paused then whispered.

"And you can keep it from ya wife. And then back in his rough voice.

"But I'm heah to tell ya," he exploded.

"God knows everythang!

"He knoows what ya takin' and what ya fakin".

He knoows when ya sleepin' and who," he paused, while Alycia imagined him pointing and looking around the congregation.

"Ya sleepin wit. I said . . . God knows everythang!"

"He . . .

Annoyed, Alycia jumped up and turned off the radio, every time she wanted to do something exciting, the Reverend would start preaching about it. It was almost as if he selected the sermon just for her. She looked on top of the stereo and noticed her WOW Gospel CD was out and played it to return to her good spirit. Alycia was excited, today was the day that she invited Jeffrey over for a home cooked meal, hoping to snag his behind.

Let her tell it, she was the best cook in Manhattan. Her cozy attic apartment on Dyckman Street was kept spotless. She was anal about her white carpet, vacuuming it several times a day. She did a fine job in showcasing her exotic African art throughout her home. She had an expensive used bar and stool set that separated the kitchen from the living room, that was neatly kept with a set of plates, two long stem wine glasses, and black napkins saluting out of the wine glasses. Her bar was also used as her dining table, her ironing board, her desk and of course her bar. Her bedroom was small, her king sized waterbed was the only thing in it. She had sophisticated window treatments at every window including the kitchen. Bamboo sticks, eucalyptus bunches and dry flowers were perfectly arranged throughout the apartment.

The cinnamon from her candied yams filled the three-family house. She was tickled at the thought of her perfect dinner, in her perfect home, for a perfect guy. She had some seasoned chicken waiting to be fried, fresh collard greens, smothered beef tenderloins, potato salad and rolls. She even brewed some fresh ice tea and made a six-layer apple jelly cake for desert.

Jeff had called earlier, confirming that he would be there at 2:00, and that he couldn't wait to eat at 3:00. He also made a couple of sexual gestures, like: I'm bringing dessert I hope that you're good and hungry, and how he missed the way her gravy poured. She knew exactly what he was trying to say and she loved it. All the years that they had not seen each other or talked she never stop thinking of what might have became of their relationship if either would have taken what they had serious. So when he made those gestures she just, said "believe me, I'm hungry." She was not planning on losing him again.

Alycia got on the carpeted floor with her too short jean shorts, a black tank top and no bra. She could get away with not wearing a bra, she had, if you will, perfect breasts.

Everything was just right, the house was spotless, dinner was done and Alycia was in heat. She closed her eyes and smiled as she sat there fantasizing about the treats she was in store for.

It was 4:30 when the complaining sound of the doorbell woke her up.

"Oh shit, it's 4:30." She said looking at the stereo's clock. Not bothering with the intercom, she just ran downstairs hoping that whoever it was wasn't gone. It was Jeff and he appeared to be running for his life. He was dripping wet with sweat, tired and out of breath. He certainly didn't look like he had an invitation for dinner.

"What happened to you?" she said frowning.

"Hey baby." He said leaning in the doorway, reaching to kiss her face, "We've just won the West 4th Division championship 96 to 88." He said still panting, trying to catch his breath. "I scored 22 points!"

Alycia wasn't impressed. His odor choked her, his soft curly hair looked like stiff curly dreads and his skin had a coat of dirt and oil making him two shades darker than she planned on seeing. The ground had ripped his orange and black team uniform and his sneakers were covered with mud.

"Don't look at me like that baby, invite me in. I bought my bag." He said lifting the almost new looking black back sack. "Give me a couple of minutes and I'll be the man you're looking so sexy for." He said plucking her breast with his dirty fingertips. Alycia grinned. His white teeth were still the same and that smile of his would make any woman blush...

"Come on up, silly." She said trying not to smile to hard. Climbing up the stairs behind her, Jeffrey was pleased at what he saw. He made a naughty comment about her cheeks peeking out of her shorts and began licking the back of her thighs. She tried to ignore it but tripped two stairs from the landing in front of her door. He leaped over her body caging her, she turned to face him, and he pulled up her top and covered her breast with his mouth. His funky perspiration dampened her skin, forcing her to accept him the way he was. She gave in immediately and started to moan. With ease he unfastened her shorts, ripping them so they would just fall. He separated her legs and gave her a gentle yet firm stroke with his tongue. Alycia went nuts. She grabbed his head and pushed it in as far as it could go. He remained there, pleasing her until he could feel her hands drop releasing his head. Sharing the taste in his mouth, he kissed her, giving her his tongue. He was famous for that, 'if it's good enough for my tongue its good enough for yours.' Now it was time for act II, he motioned for her to turn around, placing her in her favorite position. Pinned against the uncarpeted stairs, Alycia's knees were begging to be set free. But did she complain? Oh no, she wouldn't dare, remembering his favorite saying, 'Hassle-free pussy is the best pussy.'

"You've got the best." he said taking off his weighty condom.

He took a shower, changed his clothes and ate like there was no tomorrow.

Sucking his fingertips he said, "Baby, you sure could put a hurtin' on some pots. I wish my lady could cook like you."

What? Back up. Alycia's face said.

"Your lady? I thought you said, you didn't have a lady." Alycia said with the knife she was about to cut the cake with.

Jeff was picking his teeth and talking at the same time.

"I thought you (ssdthck, ssdthck) knew. I'm still with the same honey I was (ssdthck) with when we used to swing. You remember (ssdthck) Cheryl? She used to be at the Club too."

Oh yeah, how well did she remember Cheryl. Pretty Cheryl people used to call her. Whenever someone would refer to her it was never Cheryl Coolidge it was always Pretty Cheryl. Cheryl got big respect from all the brothers and was accused of intimidating the sisters. There was nothing she couldn't have or do. Everyone bowed at her feet as if she was some kind of queen or something. Alycia hated Cheryl; it was Cheryl that opened Jeff nose while it was still supposed to be opened for her. It all started coming back, why she and Jeff never made it. She was the one he loved to fuck and Cheryl was the one he loved to be seen with. She was too cute to get on her knees for a deep screw.

"Yeah, I remember her, but I don't remember you telling me that y'all were still together!" Alycia said pissed that she had already given up the goods.

"You never asked." He said sincerely.

"Never asked?!" Alycia voice broke. "Jeffrey, I would have never invited you over here, if I thought for a minute that you were still with her or any other woman for that matter, but especially her. I've changed I don't want someone else's man. It's not right. Get your shit and go!"

Alycia was too through with herself and with him.

"Aw c'mon baby, don't go there on me. I want to spend the day with you it's not even six o'clock. What's the big deal? Shit happens, just because you grew out of it doesn't mean that I did. I don't want to hurt you or anybody else, but I'm still young and I'm enjoying my life as I see fit. It's not like I'm married. I don't even live with her. We just have a daughter together, and I still think she's pretty special. Is that a crime?"

Alycia couldn't concentrate. She had just been fucked literally and mentally, and she didn't want to hear his 'It's No Big Deal' speech. She heard it so many times in the past that she knew it by heart.

"Jeff, please leave." She said slowly, as if she was about to lose her mind.

"I would if I really thought you wanted me to, c'mon admit it, what we just did was great and it only gets better. I know I want some more, don't you?" He said, walking toward her with a set of devilish eyes. She lowered her head, hating the whore inside of her, the one who could never say no to quality meat. Tears filled her eyes as she thought about Jeff's outstanding performance. He was right; she didn't want him to leave. She did want more rounds of pleasure. Damn, it was just like old times.

Jeff applauded himself inside, *'Good show Jeff'*, it was just like old times, she wants it, she don't, will I respect her in the morning, all that bull that women go through, should they follow their hearts or their pussies. He's been through this scene a thousand times and it always turns out the same. He kissed her until he reached the place where he could eat again.

The make up

"Next stop Pavonia/Newport." The Path conductor announced as Maya ran down the escalator onto track 2, just in time for the doors to close in her face. She was late for work again. Her date Saturday with Gary really got the best of her. Sunday, she didn't even get dressed; she turned the ringer off her phone and let the machine pick up all the messages. Gary called four times. He sounded so pitiful. "Maya, are you there, pick up/Hi Maya, this is Gary please pick up/Maya, Gary, in case you lost my number here it is again, I hope everything is alright/Maya its 11:00, goodnight."

She was angry and confused at what happened all she knew was that she let him know that he could have gotten just about anything he wanted from her that night. She hated the fact that he didn't. He vanished so quickly she didn't even get a chance to tell him that she would be glad to pick him up, or that it was alright to get a cab back to her place. She stayed up until 5:00 am hoping that whatever he had to do was over and that he would call to say he's on his way to pick up where they'd left off. But he didn't. Something's up with him she thought, fuck him!

She knew she was being childish, but she hated taking chances. She wasn't about to let him make a fool out of her like Perry did.

It was 9:22 when she sat at her desk. There was a phone message on her answering machine, it was Arthur: "Ms. Taylor, I won't be in today, it's my sinuses, they're flaring up again, please handle all urgencies on my desk. Also it is 9:12 where are you?

"Hallelujah!" she rejoiced when she heard the message. "Just what I need a day off from Arthur. Thank you Lord." She said closing her eyes with her arms stretched and her face to the ceiling. Maya made up her mind to just relax and do nothing but her nails. Unfortunately, the phone rang so much she didn't even get them done.

"You whore." Roz snapped at her over the phone.

"Whore? What are you talking about?

"C'mon Maya, I haven't got all day. Was he good?"

"Was who good? My vibrator? Yeah, he was good. Good and patient." Maya joked, but didn't laugh.

"Oh, that's how you're going to do this. Not tell me anything. Okay, be like that."

"What do you want to know? Gary turned out to be Captain Pediatrician, that damn beeper went off just when things got hot. He didn't waste one second, we were at the hospital in a blink of an eye and then he disappeared."

"Wait, hold it. You mean to tell me that he had it out and was about to put it in, when his beeper started beeping?"

"Who said all that, I said when things got hot, not on fire? We weren't even in my apartment. We was walking through Hamilton Park, kissing under that big tree, everything was perfect. He kissed me a hundred times and I felt him rise. Then he asked could he make love to me. I said yes. His beeper went off, end of story."

"No girl! That's too bad. Who ever heard of a man asking? It's supposed to just happen. He sounds corny. Is he? Did y'all eat?

"He's not corny. And yes we did eat, he took me to this classy soul food restaurant called Okras, you would love it. The food is out of sight. And the atmosphere is like home, jazz and blues."

"Ooh, that sounds nice. What made y'all go there, I thought he was cooking you dinner at his place."

"Me too, I don't know what happen to that, all I know is that I didn't see the inside of his place. He didn't explain and I didn't ask.

"What? What's up with that? I smell a rat. He could have at least explained the change of plans. But just to pretend that everything was normal? How bizarre. I bet its nothing, his place probably wasn't clean. You know how men are. What happen when you talked to him after the emergency?"

"I didn't, I just listened to him beg me to pick up the phone. Girl, I don't have the time to be bothered." She told Roz, knowing that all she had was time. "Let me go girl, I need another cup of my morning boost. Mondays are the hardest."

Maya was blue. Let Roz tell it, she and Lance were doing fine. Yesterday he invited her over to his place -- they rented a movie, ordered Chinese, traded secrets and made love. Lance was a nice catch, well to do with real goals and accomplishments. She's so lucky she never seemed to have problems catching the good ones. Then she wondered, was it luck? Or, was Roz more open minded than she? Roz was a very attractive girl, but Maya felt when it came to beauty, she had her beat. Roz was also very smart. She made more money then any of her girlfriends. But Maya made an impressive penny too, so what was it? Maya questioned herself knowing the answers. She knew after Perry she wasn't good in any relationship. She would always find a reason to dismiss a man. It would be because he didn't go to college, or he eats with his fingers, or he's too easy, too stubborn, too tall, too short, too dark, too light, too friendly, too selfish, you name it -- it was a good enough reason for her to get rid of him. Now it was Gary's turn. *Maybe I should have answered the phone, why am I so embarrassed? So what if he knows that I wanted him? What's wrong with that, why do I always have to take everything so personal? He knows I'm human.* "Damn, I need to grow up." She decided out loud.

As Maya sorted through her thoughts, the buzzer buzzed. It was the receptionist.

"There's a package out here for you to sign for."

"Okay. I'll be right there."

She didn't feel like getting up, so she didn't. She wanted to remain blue, in her office with the door shut. An hour later, she got up, slipped into her pumps and took her time down the hall. She knew that it was just some new children's designs that just came out. They always sent her two samples of each to examine. She would later give them to her tenant sister's kids. When she reached the reception desk, she had no idea that the flowers there were for her.

"Where's my package?"

"Right there, the flowers are for you."

"Oh, where do I sign?" She didn't get excited; she thought it was a client thanking her for purchasing such a large amount of merchandise or Tyrone running up his company's tab. Every six months he would send her flowers, praising her for being a special friend and a shoulder to lean on.

She carried the large arrangement to her desk and complained about it being so big and heavy; she carefully unwrap them and was impressed at their beauty. Then she lazily opened the card, it read: Maya, don't tell me I've lost you already. Baby I miss you. Please call. -- Gary

Immediately her heart started racing. She gave the flowers a light hug, then a kiss. She pressed the card against her chest and shouted. "He missed me, he missed me, and oh how I've missed him." She opened her desk drawer, got out her purse, then her wallet and called him.

"Dr. Gady Coupas line." A heavy accented voice answered.

Dr. Gary Cooper. Could you believe it, a doctor, and to think she was ready to blow him off. "Uh yes, may I speak to him?" She was nervous.

"Eee's wit a payshont. Is it urjont?"

"No, just ask him to call Ms. Taylor at (212) 555-3593."

Five minutes hadn't passed before her phone ranged.

"Hey Baby, what happened?" He said expecting an immediate response.

"Gary." She began to lie. "I was out all day yesterday, my brother asked me to do him a major favor, I couldn't say no. I didn't bring my planner, so I couldn't call you. I hope I didn't alarm you."

"Oh baby, what a relief, I thought it was something I did or didn't do. Can I see you tonight?"

This was awkward -- she wasn't ready to pick up where they'd left off. She wanted to see him, but not the way she thought he meant.

"Gary, I would love to see you but I'm exhausted, I didn't get in until 1:30 this morning." She continued to lie. "If we meet it would have to be for a short while."

"I don't care if it's for one minute, I just want to see your face and hold you in my arms. I thought I lost you." His words were music to her ears. So she immediately changed her tune.

"Lost me, how could you possibly lose me after the wonderful evening we had together? I didn't even get to thank you. Dinner was fabulous and I enjoyed being with you. But these flowers, these flowers are breathtaking, I . . ."

"Does that mean I get to see you tonight?"

"Well . . ."

"I promise not to keep you too long."

"Okay, but you'll have to keep your promise."

The remainder of the conversation was too sticky sweet to mention. Before Maya left the building, she ran to the ladies room, freshen her make-up and added perfume. Her linen white pants and lavender blouse was perfect after work attire. Her whole mood had changed after she talked with Gary. She ran into Arthur's office and did all the things that she was supposed to do earlier. Then she called the distributors and gave them what for. She kept putting it off because she didn't feel like hearing their poor excuses for this and that. But after talking to Gary, her spirits were lifted and she told them to shape up or ship out. She took care of enough work to last the whole week.

When Toy barged in the ladies room, Maya had this big glow on her face.

"Um, um, um, don't we smell pretty?"

"Thank-you, but it's not for you, it's for my sweetheart."

"Sweetheart?" Toy said with major interest, then she grabbed a seat and said, "don't stop there girl, tell me more."

"Not now, I don't want to keep my Honey waiting."

"Sounds serious, well girl, don't worry about a thing, you look gorgeous." Maya hugged her and ran out of the bathroom. Toy just sat there shocked, she has known Maya for three years and never once did she hug her, not even on Christmas Eve.

It was 90 degrees in Manhattan; Maya was under the air so long she forgot it was hot until she stepped outside into the humid air to catch the train.

The moment Maya walked out of the Grove Street station she saw Gary standing outside his SAAB with dark shades on, and still wearing his white doctor's coat and stethoscope.

"Hi Gary." She snuck up behind him.

"Hey beautiful." He said reaching over and kissing her on the cheek. "Wow, so I wasn't dreaming, you are as beautiful as I remembered. You look lovely."

"Thanks Doc, you don't look so bad yourself." Maya replied coolly, floored that he just said what he said.

"Oh," Gary pretended to be embarrassed. "After my last patient I just washed my hands and dashed out of there. I forgot to take off this costume."

"I like it, you look so professional."

"Does that mean I get to make a house call tonight?"

Maya just smiled and got in the car.

Collecting her mail, she led him upstairs. Chase knew she was home and started barking, he always got excited when she hit the door.

"Just stand here, give me a minute to let him out."

"Down Chase!" she repeated as she opened the sliding doors to the fire escape. Chase didn't waste any time running out to litter on the paper.

"Have a seat, I'll just be a minute, I need to change my clothes before Chase ruins them. Make yourself comfortable, turn on the air if you like." Maya went behind the wicker partition that separated her bedroom from her living room and began changing her clothes.

"Your place is nice. It's almost like I pictured it." He said selecting a Courtney Pine CD to play.

"Almost? What's missing?" She asked coming into the living room with a more comfortable outfit on.

"My slippers, my robe, my books."

Now sitting across from him, Maya smiled, loving his forward response.

"Why are you sitting over there?" he asked reaching for her hand. "Come here, you know I've missed you."

Maya was suddenly nervous, somehow everything changed, she was fine on the phone but now the mood wasn't right. It was still day and she didn't know him in the daytime.

"Can I get you something to drink?"

"No, but you could give me a kiss."

She teased him with a small peck and pretended to have to check on Chase.

"Oh Gary, I don't mean to be rude, but I have to walk my dog."

"Why are you shying away from me? Is this your way of asking me to leave? You seemed fine on the phone, what's the matter baby? Come here talk to me."

"There's nothing wrong. I'm just exhausted, I have to walk Chase and I feel bad that I'm really not in the mood for company."

"Alright," Gary said disappointed and confused at her mood swing. "Is it alright if I go with you to walk the dog?"

"Oh of course." She said glad that he was still biting. She grabbed Chase's leash and led the way. When they came across their tree, he grabbed her and reminded her how sweet it was that night. But now she was resisting because it was bright day light and she wasn't under the influence of alcohol.

Maya was a very private person, she wasn't about to let her neighbors know her business, and they were all out that day walking their dogs too.

"What's wrong, why are you pulling away from me?"

"Nothing, I just don't care to kiss in front of my dog. He doesn't know you yet and he might think you're hurting me."

"I would never hurt you." he said, buying the dog story. Then he thought again and asked. "Am I keeping you too long?"

"No." Maya answered quickly. She didn't want him to leave she loved being with him, but didn't know how to act. He was so incredibly together that he made her nervous. So she said. "I mean, we can have dinner."

"Dinner? No baby, I don't need all that, I know you're tired. I just wanted to see you and let you know that Saturday night was special to me. I just wanted to feel your warm body against mine. I just wanted you to know that I want to be a part of your life."

"Gary . . . I don't know what to say. Saturday night was . . ."

"You don't have to say anything, just don't stop me. Don't stop me from making this thing beautiful. Maya, I know it's only been a few days, but girl, you're all I can think of. I can tell that you're a little more hesitant toward me today then you were Saturday. I don't know what went sour all I can say is that it can be sweet again. I'm sorry if you got caught up between the Doctor and the man. But baby, if you hang in there long enough you'll have them both."

"Gary."

"Sshh" he interrupted her. "You don't owe me anything, I promised not to keep you long and I'm not. Think about what I said. I'll call you tonight." Gary said walking toward his car.

"Gary don't leave." Maya whined before she could stop herself. "I don't want you to leave. I'm sorry if I've been giving you the wrong signals. Stay, have dinner with me."

"Whew," Gary said pretending to wipe sweat from his forehead. "I thought you were going to let me leave. Now can I have a kiss?"

They kissed, then hugged and walked to the neighborhood fish market. Gary begged Maya not to cook; he wanted them to be served at his favorite seafood restaurant in Hoboken. But Maya insisted on cooking, she said that she preferred the privacy of her own home, and she enjoyed her cooking better than most restaurants.

In thirty minutes, dinner was served, Maya made broiled fish, Caesar salad, and hot rolls. The candles were set and the wine was chilled. Gary was impressed, not only was this woman beautiful, her place was charming and she could cook. He walked over to the switch on the wall and dimmed the lights then walked over and changed the music to something softer. She was taking off her apron when he grabbed her and said, "You know, you would make a perfect wife." Then he kissed her and made a point of saying his Grace out loud so that she could hear him thank God for sending her his way and then they ate.

Gary wouldn't stop about how delicious everything was. He said jokingly, with the kind of talent she had, he may never take her to another restaurant. She just giggled and denied that it was that good. Maya was pleased with Gary. His mannerisms were so charming. He was a lot like her uncle – the perfect gentlemen; his charming manners, smooth and humble tone, straight white teeth, and those lips, soft and rewarding.

Maya didn't know what to do while Gary went out to get another bottle of wine. She picked up the phone and dialed Roz to tell her how perfect this man was, then hung-up before the first ring. Then she called Alycia and did the same thing. Then she ran back and fourth through the house talking to herself. She was nervous, excited, giddy and tipsy. She wanted to change, put on something sexy. She knew that this was it, but couldn't let him know that she knew. She warned him that she didn't want to be up too late. Now her mind had changed. It was 10:10 and she was feeling no pain. Liquor always freed the insecure girl in her. Now she stood at the window peeking out for his return.

Before he left for the store, they were sprawled out on her living room floor trading histories. After talking about his college days, Gary felt like a college boy and began touching every part of Maya's body. Maya was feeling pretty loose too and did some exploring of her own.

In addition to the wine, Gary decided to pick up a three-pack of condoms, just in case, he blushed at the counter clerk.

As soon as he reached the top landing, Maya snatched the door open and jumped in his arms. Her legs straddled around his waist. She took the bottle out of his hand and threw it on the couch and began kissing him all over his face. He reciprocated and followed her aggressive lead. Finding the single pin that was holding her hair back, he released it, and while holding her, kissing her and walking, he sloppily stumbled through her small apartment until they tumbled on top of her queen sized bed.

In flash her sexy little bra was off and he got to taste those breasts again. She exhaled at the touch of his tongue and fought to hold back her tears but couldn't. When he reached up to kiss her mouth to let her know that he was about to give her something special, he felt her tears.

"What's wrong baby?" He stopped, thinking, another first. No woman had ever cried before he made love to her.

"Hey, hey, what's with the tears?"

"Oh Gary, it's just that . . ." Maya took a long sigh.

"What baby, it's just what?"

"It's been so long." she confessed with both hands covering her face and tears streaming down between her fingers.

"Is that all?" Gary said removing her hands and kissing her tears. "Baby, you don't have to cry. I'm here to stay. I'll make it all right, I promised." he whispered. "I'll make it alright."

Six months later . . .

Too much to handle

"I ain't lying, the boy has lost his mind he came home last night and told me that Dane is moving in with us."

"I know you flipped."

"Flipped shit! I told that motherfucker, to take his shit and leave. He's the one flipping. He's forgotten whose name is on the lease. I took his ass in, and I'll put his ass out! If he thinks I love his ass enough to let that skunk live with us he's crazy."

Tyrone was hurt and Maya knew it. It was the first time she ever heard him use foul language.

"Look, meet me after work, we'll have a few drinks and talk about this some more." She offered.

"Thanks babe, I really need to talk. I'm sorry for hitting you with this shit, but . . ." Maya heard him breakdown. "I gotta tell somebody."

"Cut it out Tyrone, after what you did for me? You're not hitting me with anything. You're my brother, and I love you. Don't ever feel that you can't come to me. Now dry your face and meet me at Roscoe's for drinks."

Maya was drained after speaking with Tyrone. She didn't know what she could do or say that would make him feel better. Wesley had been abusing their relationship for months and things had only gotten worse. Wesley would spend two and three nights out with Dane, telling Tyrone that he would be out of town on a business trip; meanwhile he would be seen in restaurants and at the movies with Dane under him. He would have the audacity to come home and deny it all. "Who saw me? People need to mind their business, everybody has a twin, I told you, I was in Atlanta doing a show, now why are you tripping?/Look Tyrone, Dane is just a close friend, he hasn't done anything to you, so I don't know why you don't like him./What do you mean, 'are we screwin'?/I'm not even going to respond to that."

That's all Wesley would say, knowing full well the damage--the truth would cause. Poor Tyrone was shot out over him, he didn't want to let go and Maya knew better than to suggest it. She would just sit and listen and give compassionate nods. But basically she was going to stay out of it.

As planned they met at Roscoe's run down establishment down the street from Macy's. Tyrone was already there drinking heavy by the time she arrived. Since the last time she saw him he had lost at least 20 pounds. No shave, no cologne, no manicures and his clothes weren't even matching. He was clearly going through something.

"No Tyrone. Ahn, ahn." Maya said pointing her finger and nodding her head. "I know this isn't you. You know better than to come out of the house looking like this. No." She kept nodding her head.

"I knew you were going to scream on me when you saw me. I can't help it. I can't eat or sleep. Drinking is my only outlet."

"Look Tyrone, I'm going tell you straight. If you plan to deal with this thing right, you're gonna have to take care of yourself. Who do you love more, Wesley or yourself?"

"I know your right," He broke into tears. "But I hate to let go." Now his tears were bigger and his cry louder. "You don't know how badly this hurt -- he's supposed to be mine. This is just not fair, oooh." The tears in Maya eyes began to spill as she watched her friend fall apart.

"Sshh, sshh, it's alright, it's alright, I'm here." She said lightly. Maya hated seeing Tyrone this way, he was really taking it hard.

"Why won't he just let me off the hook, confess, tell me that it's not me he loves?" This really bought the gushes of tears down. Maya was speechless. She knew she could offer no relief. She just held Tyrone in her arms like he was her child after his first fall.

Guess what?

It was Saturday, 2:30 am, when Maya woke Gary up with her decision.

"I'm gonna ask Tyrone to move in with me for a while."

"What?!" Gary thought he was hearing things. He sat up and looked at her. "Maya are you crazy? I know that he's your close friend, but . . . baby."

"I know, and believe me I'm not too excited about the decision, but Tyrone is starting to scare me. He's not eating or sleeping and every time we talk, he sounds suicidal."

"Maya, slow down. What about me? I don't think I could handle another man living with you. Watchin' my goods pass by, and eating my dinner."

"I am not your goods and nobody is gonna eat your dinner!" She said insulted by his surprisingly chauvinistic words.

Gary got out of bed and walked around to her side and sat in the chair facing her. He looked at her hard and her expression didn't change. After realizing that she was more than serious, he got up and took a shower. When he returned his socks and pants were on.

Maya was surprised to see him half dressed.

"Where are you going?"

Gary didn't answer; he just reached for his t-shirt.

"Maya, tell me something," he said with his t-shirt covering his head. "Haven't I given you 100% of me since we met?"

"Yeah."

"Do I send you flowers all the time?"

"Yeah."

"Do I bring you special gifts every time I travel and every time I come over here?"

"Yeah."

"Do I make sure you're satisfied when we make love?" his voice deepened and he stop dressing for a moment to make sure she confirmed he was putting it down right night after night.

"You know you do. But Gary why . . .?"

"That's right Maya, why!" he snapped. "Why do you think I do all that?"

"Because you love me?" she said in a low voice.

"That's right Maya, because I love you, at least I thought I did. The girl I love wouldn't ask me this."

"Ask?" Her tone changed. "Who's asking you? I wasn't asking you anything, I was informing you."

"Oh, so your mind is set?" He said buttoning his shirt so fast that he buttoned it wrong.

"If you would just calm down we could talk about this."

"Make up your mind, a minute ago you were telling me, now you want to talk to me!" he snapped again.

Maya was thrilled. His anger turned her on. He was always so sweet to her, so giving, loving and warm. The man that she'd dreamt about and prayed for was there but now she realized that she wanted a more aggressive man, a man to put his foot down and speak to her with authority. She blushed at his angry face and continued to upset him.

"Look Gary, I sat up all night trying to figure out a way to help Tyrone. He's in a lot of pain and needs a good friend right now. This is something I have to do; I couldn't live with myself if he did something to hurt himself." Now Maya was standing on the bed behind Gary with her arms around his neck. Feeling her soft silky skin on his neck calmed him down. He turned around and faced her, he could see that she was serious, and she could see that he was hurt.

"Okay, you win." He grumbled softly, hating the push over he's become for her.

"Before you say anything else, there's more." She said kissing him and unbuttoning his shirt.

"More! Maya what more could there possibly be? You already convinced me that he should live with you. Now what?"

"Weelll," She made a Lucille Ball face and started easing his shirt off. "I'm going to take a week's vacation and offer him a little retreat to the Islands."

"Islands!" Gary shouted. "Maya, what is this, a test?!" Now he was fuming. "All I wanted was a little romantic evening with you. That I didn't get because you have too much on your mind and now you're telling me that you're about to move a man in and take him to the Islands?"

Gary grabbed his shirt, this time not buttoning it at all; he pulled his sweater over his head and snatched his overcoat. Maya felt the frigid air as it whirled through her apartment and wrapped her half naked body as she stood by the door calling after him only to hear the front door slam shut.

Cramping my style

"Yo, what you doing here?" Dice whispered. "I thought you were out for the night?"

"Yeah, I thought so too." Gary said sitting on the couch holding his head down.

"So what's up?" Dice asked impatiently.

"What do you mean what's up? I'm tired all I want to do is go to bed."

"Yo Gary, you can't go to bed man," Then he lowered his head and voice as if he was standing before his father. "I got company."

"Company?! Man how many times do I have to tell you that this is not a hotel?

"Yo man, lower your voice. Don't blow this thing out of proportion. You know how things happen. I was hanging out, had a couple of drinks and this babe was all over me. You know after a couple sips of wine women want to get laid."

"Then you should have laid her on the floor. What did I tell you about going into my bedroom? Damn man, you ain't shit!" Gary was pacing frantically around his sofa waving his hands in the air. "This has got to stop, I don't mind you coming over every now and then to watch cable or play music. I understand that you need a break from Queetha, but Man, I can't get with this cheating shit. What about the commitment you made?"

"Man don't bring up Queetha, we had a big fight. I hate being around her, she's so mean. The girl stays mad 24-7. I'd leave her in a minute, if it wasn't for my baby girl. I refuse to let another man raise her. And you know Queetha, she so fine, she's sure to get another man. I hope she do, whoever wants her can have her mean ass. She'll trick them just like she tricked me. She's the devil in disguise."

"Yo man, I don't care to hear that, all I know is that Queetha is special and that you are going to lose her if you keep this mess up."

"Special? I'll be lucky to lose her. You try living with her you'll see just how special she is." Dice said taking a seat, realizing that he had major problems. "The fox I got in the room, now she's special. She's soft, warm and inviting." Dice said with a big grin on his face, fantasizing about what was in the room waiting for him. "And just like me, she lives with a nut. See Gary, you're naive, your head have been in the books so long that you don't realize how fucked up relationships can be."

"Yeah okay." Gary said dismissing Dice's bull.

"I'm serious man, if you knew the deal you would know that all I'm doing is seeking therapy. I need this babe to help me release my tension and she needs me to do the same. After a couple of drinks she let me know that she wanted to be alone with me. So, I brought her up here."

"Why here?"

"Yo man, you know I have to take care of home first. I didn't have any money to take her to no hotel. Check it out, I kissed her once and right after that she opened up and told me everything. She cried about how her man is sleeping on the job, how he complains night and day about petty shit. She explained how she didn't mean to come on to me so strong, but what she needed, her girlfriends and momma couldn't give her. Man it's the same thing all over. Good women be having those fucked-up men and fucked-up women be having us good men."

"Okay, okay, you've made your point. But I'm not leaving -- I'm going to sack out right here on the couch. And do me a favor man -- control the passion. I don't want to hear it."

"You don't have to worry about that, the main event is over. I doubt that she wants more, I'm sure she's done for the night." Dice laughed nudging Gary. She's been asleep for the last hour I have to wake her up before five he comes home at seven."

Gary was amazed at Dice's cool. "Tell me something, where does Queetha think you are?"

"Man, you know that my moms been sick, I told Queetha that I was going to stay with her tonight. Queetha hates my mother so she doesn't call, I doubt it if she knows the number. Man that's what I'm trying to tell you, shit is fucked-up. How can she be my girl and not love my momma? She could at least pretend but she don't and man that hurts. You know Mom's the one. Troy's over there tonight, I told him that I'd see him in the morning and he said cool."

"I gotta hand it to you man, you think of everything. Hey, I'm sorry if I came off a little strong it's just that . . ."

Just as Gary was about to get into his thing about Maya, Dice's new honey stumbled into the room.

"It's not polite to leave a lady waiting." She said licking her lips while staring at Dice's handsomely carved chest instead of his face.

Dice jumped up as if he was caught doing something wrong. He didn't want Gary to see his new honey. It had nothing to do with her features, because she was pretty enough. It was her age that made Dice uncomfortable. His new honey is just twenty-four. He's thirty-seven and Queetha thirty-nine.

"Hey uh, um." Dice could not remember her name so he called her Honey. "Hey Honey, this is my brother Gary. Gary this is my Honey." He said kissing her on the cheek.

"Hi, how are you doing?" Gary smiled at the sexy, short lady.

"I'll let you know, if you're still here in, oh about a half an hour." She said pulling Dice by the elastic in his pants into the bedroom.

Gary's mouth flew wide open, Dice had it going on. It was hard for him to contain himself knowing that a sexy young lady, that appeared to be in a good mood, was in his bed. He loved the way she looked when she came out of his room wearing his t-shirt, her hair all messy, eyes all dreamy and lips that were in the mood. Then he laughed, Dice said that the main event was over, he told the wrong person because evidently she couldn't tell. Then Gary began thinking about something else that Dice had said, about how one side of the relationship is good and the other is fucked-up. He thought about how mad he was at Maya and how he would rather be in the room making love to a nice, soft, warm body that understood him. He came to the conclusion that Maya was definitely headed for the sides with the fuck-ups. Then he cancelled all thoughts and went to sleep.

Don't be a fool, fool

"Yeah, girl, we leave tomorrow."

"For where, the electric chair? Loosen up girl you're going to the Bahamas!"

"I know it's just that . . . I haven't made up with Gary yet."

"Maya! That was two weeks ago. Don't tell me you haven't called him yet?"

"Nope."

"Why? What's the problem?"

"I don't know, every time I call him I get nervous and hang up. I think its best if I don't call until Tyrone's problem is over."

"I know Tyrone is your friend, but come on, your man is priority. Why are you jeopardizing your relationship with Gary? It's not like he's an ordinary guy, he's got it together."

"Tyrone is going through hell, its only right that I stick with him through this. I'd do it for you."

"At what expense? Help is one thing -- going to the Bahamas is another! How would you feel if Gary was taking one of his supposedly gay female friends to the Bahamas for a week? Don't even bother to lie about it -- I know the answer. You wouldn't like it. Now Tyrone may need your help, but your relationship with Gary is still new, it's at a fragile stage, you shouldn't even want to leave him. That's probably why he's pissed, he can't bear to be without you and here you are with plane tickets and suntan lotion in your hand."

"Oh shut-up Alycia, I don't want to hear it."

"Yes you do, that's why you called me. You're just looking for a reason to fuck with Gary. That's how you are, always wanting your ass kissed. Well keep on playing games. I can guarantee you one thing's for sure, if you board that plane without talking to Gary, you can kiss his fine ass good-bye. Now tell me I'm wrong."

"You're wrong, Gary loves me. Why don't you take some of your own advice and call Jeff? Let him know how you feel."

"Jeff? Where have you been, I talked to Jeff this morning, in my bed, thank-you very much. He may not be my man, but there is no confusion in our relationship. I know we're just friends and that he's my occasional lay." Then Alycia added a lie and said "I wouldn't have it any other way."

For a second Maya was jealous. She always wanted to have flings, but at the same time the thought of it made her skin crawl, it was disgusting, it was low, different men in her bed. No, never!

"Alycia, I don't understand you."

"What don't you understand?" Alycia snapped defensively. She was ready to let Maya have it. She knew that Maya thought it was disgusting and degrading to have several lovers in a month's time. But Alycia felt like hey *to each his own.* I need what I need and it ain't yours, your mommas, and nobody else's business what or who I do.

Why do you have to be a whore? Maya thought but didn't have the nerve to say. She knew that Alycia was going to tell her exactly why, so she just changed the subject.

"So you think I should call?"

"Definitely!"

"Do you think I'm wrong for going with Tyrone?"

"Wrong is not the word I would choose. I think you're stupid. I wouldn't go, but that's me. Tyrone is your friend and you have to make up your own mind. If you feel that the boy is suicidal then yes -- help him as much as you can, but don't get caught up, you have a life too and most importantly, don't let him move in, he may never leave."

Maya was laughing, "Thanks, I'll send you a postcard, now let me call Gary.

Indecent proposal

"Where's my stethoscope? Anna I can't find my stethoscope anywhere. Who's my next appointment with? How come there's no one in the room for a check up? Anna what's going on, where is everybody?"

"Dr. Coopa, it's late, you do not halve entymore appoin-ments. The office has been closed for now twenty minutes. And your stethoscope, you gave tit away. You gave tit to the littu gurl that look like the picha of the womin on ya dess. I tink you call ha Maya, no?"

"Oh, oh yeah, I hadn't realized it was so late. What time did you say it was?"

"Dr. Coopa vhat tis it? You have been acting so strange lately. I vould be glad to stay a vhile and talk vith you."

"Vhat are you, I mean what are you talking about Anna?" Then Gary lowered his eyes sat down and said. "I guess its apparent Anna, I love this girl so much."

"So vhat's the problem? Vhy don't ya juss call ha?"

"I can't. I have to know that she feels the same way I do. If she doesn't call soon then I'll know that she doesn't and that she's not the right one for me."

"Oh, I don't know Docta Coopa, sounds like you should call. I mean if you don't vant to lose huh?"

"If I have her, I can't lose her, it's only if I never had her that I could lose her."

"You're the docta."

"Believe me Anna it makes sense, it just doesn't feel good."

"Good night sir."

The office was too quiet after Anna left so with nothing better to do, Gary began dialing the phone.

"Judy?"

"Gary?"

"Yeah, how are you?"

"Gary!" Judy screamed delighted to hear his voice again. Right now I couldn't be better. What happened to what's her name? The mystery queen, did she tripped over and broke her crown?"

"What mystery queen?"

"Oh, so y'all broke up?"

"Look Judy, I called because I wanted to know how you were doing."

"It's been months and you're just getting around to calling me?"

"Well I was contemplating on whether or not it was a good idea."

"What is there to contemplate about? You know we fit like hand and glove and like I told you when you left, I was going to be right here waiting for you when you get back and I still mean it. So, are you ready to come back?

"Look Judy, don't start. You know that it's been over the minute I left Georgia."

"Sure Gary, so what is this call for? Tell me again."

"I told you I wanted to check in and see how you were doing. That's all. I may be coming home for a week to handle some business and thought it be nice to stop by and say hello."

"For real Gary! You're really coming home! I'll be ready."

Why am I doing this? Gary thought to himself.

"Now Judy, don't go getting all excited. I'm just stopping by for a minute, nothing major. So make sure it's alright with your man. I don't want to cause any problems."

"Gary, you are my man and you know it, I've been waiting for this call and now its here. Baby when you come home, I'm going give you that good Georgia style poon-tang, I know you missed. I'm going to whip that thing until its red. I'm going to remind you what good sex is and how much I love you. Day and night I dream about you. You know that you were my first. I'll never forget that day behind the . . ."

"Wait a minute Judy, just wait a minute. That's not going to happen. I have to take care of some business and I thought it would be nice to see you. Please erase all thoughts of us making love. I'm committed."

"It's amazing. You haven't changed a bit. Who's going to know? Besides once you get here I'm not going to give you a choice. If I have to strip you down in the restaurant I will. And you know I will. That's why you called me. That little miss special is getting on your nerves. She probably don't know what she wants. She probably whines during sex instead of rejoice. I can't stand her already."

"Judy, you don't even know her, so how can you say all these things?"

"Oh please don't defend her, what is there to know? If you're calling me, she has you upset. Am I right? Also, you would never come home unless you were lonely. Your family can handle any business that you have. Gary, its time you admit that you still love me. I know you still need me. And now you're telling me that you're committed? To who? Not Ms. Ungrateful. She's sitting on a gold mine and still begging for money. Drop her. Let her sink."

Gary said nothing.

"Alright, I won't say another word about her. I'm sure she's nice." Judy lied just to break the silence. "Let's talk about where I fit into all of this."

Gary still said nothing.

"Oh I get it." Her voice became enthusiastic. "You need me now. You want to have phone sex. It's alright baby, you don't have to ask. You know how it goes. First adjust yourself, lay back, close your eyes and let me take you where you want to be."

After a few moments of silence, Gary heard Phyllis Hyman's *Meet Me On The Moon;* the song reminded him of the passionate love making he shared with Judy. His mind eased into the days in the fields behind the old mill.

Judy started sucking and slurping an ice pop for effect and began to moan. "Let me take you there." she faded in and out in a luring voice. "Are you holding it?"

"Yeah." The word came out of Gary as if he was in a deep spell.

"Good boy, now with the other hand, unbutton your shirt and message your hairy chest. Pretend it's my hair, let your fingers go between my legs until they reach my hairs."

Gary sucked in his breath and did as he was told. "Put your finger in your mouth," he whispered. "Let me hear you suck it loud. Yeah, just like that, suck it, yeah, suck it louder." he cried.

After a long period of moaning and sucking Judy asked still in her sultry voice.

"Are you where you want to be, did you make it?"

It was too soon -- she interrupted and broke the trance too soon. When Gary opened his eyes and found himself sitting behind his desk jerking off, he dropped the phone. Quickly tucking his penis away and zipping up his pants as fast as he could. Unfortunately, he caught some hairs.

"Ouch!" Judy heard him scream over the phone.

"Gary." She called. "Gary what's going on? Are you alright? Are you still there?"

"I had you on hold." he lied. "A patient just kicked me -- I'll have to call you back."

Click.

The phone rang six times the first time and ten times the second. Gary paced and paced, hoping that it would stop. Judy did take him where he wanted to be, but he didn't want to thank her. He regretted letting her know. *Why did he call her?* He questioned himself. How could he be so careless as to let her, out all people, know that he needed someone? Then he convinced himself to answer the phone, get it over with, confess that he used her and apologize, promising that it won't ever happen again.

"Look Judy," he answered the phone ready to set her straight.

"Gary it's me, Maya. Who's Judy?"

"Maya? Maya baby." he cried delighted to hear her voice.

"Gary, I'm sorry. I should have gotten your opinion first. I didn't mean to be so forward. I love being with you and I don't want to lose you."

"Where are you?"

"I'm home."

"I'll be right there, I need to be next to you. Give me a few minutes, I have to make one call and then I'll be right there."

It wasn't long before Maya was buzzing Gary up. The minute she opened the door he grabbed her and squeezed her tight.

"Tell me you love me." He insisted.

"I love you Gary." Maya said slowly looking into his eyes.

"I love you too." he said smothering her with a long passionate kiss.

"Gary, before we get into anything, I just want you to know that I'm leaving tomorrow." After saying that Maya quickly closed her eyes as if to protect herself from the explosion Gary was going to make.

"So you're still going?"

"Yes, also I've decided not to let Tyrone move in. Just the trip that's all, six days and five nights." She was still prepared for fireworks.

"All right Maya." Gary said with a very serious face. "I'll make a deal with you. If I promise not to be upset about you leaving me, in return, I want you to promise me . . ."

Before Gary could finish his sentence Maya started jumping and kissing him all over, "Oh Gary, yes, yes, anything you want, just as long as you're not upset."

Gary's whole face was smiling. "Wait, wait, let me finish."

"Oh, go ahead." She returned to her seat and looked up at him like he was her teacher giving out homework assignments.

"As I was saying." He got serious again. "I want you to promise that when you come back . . ." he hesitated then repeated "when you come back, promise me, you'll marry me."

Maya's eyes stretched and her mouth fell open. She grabbed her heart. "Oh, Gary."

"Is that a yes?" He was looking at her with hoping eyes.

"Oh Gary, thank-you but, I can't."

"You can't? What do you mean you can't? You can't marry me?" He was upset. "Maya what's wrong?" He demanded.

"Nothing's wrong. Gary I love you, but . . . this is too sudden. I didn't see it coming this soon. I mean we just had a terrible fight, we haven't talked for days and now a proposal?"

"That's right Maya, a proposal. I don't know about you but those days were hard for me to make. There wasn't a second that you weren't on my mind. I love you girl -- don't you know that? I couldn't eat, I couldn't sleep. All I could do was imagine that you were there with me. Baby it was hard. It's even harder to face the fact that you don't feel the same. I don't know how this could have happened to me and not to you."

"Gary, don't say that. It happened to me. I do feel the same. It's just the timing, Honey. You caught me by surprise. This is not the proposal I imagined that's all. I mean, tomorrow I'll be on an airplane. I don't want to be away from you after saying yes to you. I want to celebrate, wrap my arms around you and celebrate. Do you understand?"

Gary was confused. Why the games? Her call said please be mine, stay mine. But once I get here its like, well we really don't know each other that well and I didn't plan it this way.

"Alright, Maya, I'm sick of guessing. Where do we stand?"

"Oh Gary, don't get like that. You know where we stand. You're the only man in my life and that's the way I like it. I love you, and I want to be your wife, someday, but . . . right now I just want to enjoy you and discuss this at another time.

Gary exhaled. Because he missed her and wanted some real loving he tried not to show his bitterness to her response.

"Fine, would you like to go out and get some dinner?"

"Actually, I thought it would be nice if we stayed in." Maya smiled, because she was due too and wanted to get her fill before boarding the plane.

"We could order, or we could eat yesterday's dinner." she continued with her behind extended from the refrigerator as she bent to look for the available. "There's enough rice, peas, yams, and steak. How does that sound?"

"Just fine, is there any wine?" Gary said, still uptight and wanting to take the edge off.

"Yeah, I put some in the fridge last Saturday night and never opened it."

After gulping down two glasses of wine Gary grabbed Chase's leash.

"I'll be back." He said already halfway out the door with the dog.

Maya released a deep breath and slumped down in the chair. She was glad Gary gave her a 10-minute break. She wanted so badly not to hurt him -- she wanted to say yes, but not like this. She wanted it to be romantic she wanted to spend days with him afterwards. She didn't want to say yes and then be on an island with Tyrone, she wanted to be with Gary, and now she wanted to tell Tyrone to go fly a kite, that Gary was more important. But that wasn't her style, the commitment was made and she was going to keep it.

Gary too, had made a commitment. Now feeling how he imagined Judy, must have felt when he called her back to apologize. Before crying and telling Gary she understood, Judy was screaming all kinds of foul words across the phone, wishing Maya dead and forgotten. She vowed to have Gary in the end and regain her title as his women. But with sensitivity and pity, Gary calmed her down. He took the blame for dialing her number and getting her excited about something that could never be. He reassured her that he could never be her man but always be her friend. He told her that he wasn't sure why he called her then explained that he didn't enjoy it and that it wasn't the same. He promised her that he would take it slow with Maya. Let her lead the way. He circled the block four times to blow off steam then decided it was time to go back up.

When Gary walked in Maya already had a perfect speech prepared.

"Gary . . ."

"Shhh" He stopped her. "Don't say a word."

"But,"

"Ssh, it doesn't matter." He said leading her to the bedroom.

For a minute, Gary had forgotten who he was with, after pushing Maya on the bed he sucked her neck until it bruised. His little exercise with Judy made him horny; he wanted to have some kinky sex. It was the only kind that Judy liked. She never said *make love to me* it was always *let's screw!* She liked it rough, hot and heavy. Gary grabbed Maya's legs and held them up on his shoulders and plunged. To his surprise Maya loved every second of it. She giggled, moaned and complimented his style.

"What's my name?" -- *Gary*.

"Who has the best? -- *You do Gary, you do.*

"Who does this belong to?" -- *It's yours.*

"All of it?" -- Yes, yes all of it.

"Say you'll marry me?" -- *I'll...*

"Say you'll marry me?" -- I'll marry you Gary, I'll marry you.

In Maya's mind, each stroke was better than the last. Working her muscles, she tightened up gripping him to stay deep inside. Then she motioned to change position, to be on top.

"What's my name?" -- *Sweet Maya*.

"Who does this belong to?" -- *You baby.*

"All of it?" -- *Every inch.*

"Who's Judy?" -- *Whaat?*

"I said who's Judy?" -- . . . please don't take it out.

"Do you want her?" -- Naw baby, I don't want anyone but you.

"Who's Judy?" -- Stop playing Maya don't take it out.

"Will you do me a favor -- Yeah, baby anything, just don't stop.

"Tell Judy I said thanks." -- *Whaat?*

"Tell her I said thanks for warming up *my* motor."

"*I Love You*". -- "I Love you too."

Concerned jealousy

"I think Maya is crazy, going away with that fag."

"C'mon, Roz. Tyrone isn't a fag. Not that I really know what a fag is, but I do know that Maya loves Tyrone like a brother and from what she's told me, he's pretty special."

"Maybe, but honey, let me tell you, I wouldn't leave my meat hanging around loose while I worried about somebody else's meat. You get what I'm saying? I mean really, would you?"

"I hate to admit it, but you're right, I wouldn't have gone with him either. I think she paid for the trip."

"Yeah, she paid for it. She told me she was going to pick up the tab because he deserved it. Now you tell me what brother, not to mention a soft one, but what brother is going to get that kind of service from me? None in this lifetime. Not from me. The ones who didn't get over when I was young, damn sure ain't getting over now."

"I heard that. I think Maya is just trying to be superwoman, trying to prove that she can come and go as she pleases. You know her, Ms. Independent, always on the move."

"Yeah, but is she happy?"

They laughed.

"I don't know girl, but what I do know is that she better snap out of it and let Tyrone wash his own draws before somebody stains Gary's."

"It's true, you know I don't like gossiping, but Gary puts up with a lot of her shit. You would think she was the only girlfriend he's ever had."

"I doubt it, he's too perfect."

"A city brother would have disappointed her so often that she would know how to appreciate a man like Gary."

"For real." Roz said agreeing.

They went on and on about how stupid Maya was and how Tyrone was just using her and how Gary was going to leave her, and how they would never be that stupid, only to reach the conclusion that they wished that they were going on a trip to the Island, and that they could have a close male friend like Tyrone and that they could have a loving, understanding man like Gary.

Bahamas

"Girl, I can't believe we're here. We should have thought of this, months ago."

"We?"

Tyrone and Maya were relaxing on the white sands of the Bahamas, sipping on the famous Bahama Momma drinks. Maya had on her right fitting two piece teal bikini set, with her teal lens shades. Tyrone was showcasing his fake looking bulge through a stingy black bikini-type pair of briefs. Afraid to miss anything he let his shades rest on top of his head.

It was 98 degrees and the water was blue and warm. They laughed and talked about the people around them and ordered drink after drink. Tyrone took a couple of swims and Maya just cheered him on and rubbed oil on her body.

"Girl this is too much fun." Tyrone said blotting his skin with a thirsty white terry towel.

"Oh yeah, I just love it, I can stay in this spot forever." Maya said closing her eyes and stretching her arms out toward the sun.

"Maya, I don't want to shock you, but I think I'm going tipping tonight."

Maya lifted her shades up enough for Tyrone to see her eyes and said, "Tipping?"

"You heard me. I think I'm going looking tonight."

"Down boy, down. Just calm that horse down. We did not come down here to whore."

"Speak for yourself, Sugar. I'm in heat. I have been holding out for months and I can't take it any more. I came here to enjoy myself, to find a new love and if not a new love, at least a new lover."

Maya didn't say a word she just looked at him thinking to herself, *he's drunk.*

"Besides did you see that tight hunk of meat over there with the yellow trunks on like mine? Well girl, he already let me know the deal. Asked me where the party was. You know what I started to tell him, right down here baby, right down here." Tyrone was dancing and pointing at his bulge, then he fell back laughing, but Maya didn't find anything funny. She'd never seen Tyrone behave like this before, (like Dane). But then she realized that for months Tyrone had been crying and losing weight over Wesley, he had not been eating or sleeping, not working or hanging out. He was right, this was the reason they had come, to take a load off his mind. So she started laughing and said, "Go for it."

"Check it out, Maya." Tyrone said as he took imaginary steps toward her. "First, I'm gonna make boyfriend beg for me." he bragged. "I'll wear my white silk jumper, with my soft leather sandals and my ivory bracelet and anklet. That'll have him drooling. What are you wearing?"

'A bag over my head,' Maya thought to herself. "I don't know, I don't think I'll go partying with you tonight, I'm beat." Maya lied. She did not want to be seen with Tyrone acting this way, drunk and careless with his body and mouth.

"Whatever girl," he threw his limp hand toward her. "I don't mean to be rude but I came here to party." Tyrone did some kind of ballet kick and quick switched toward his new friend.

For a minute, Maya felt like a fool lying there watching Tyrone and his soon to be lover act like teens. But after watching him in pain for months, she was relieved that he was letting himself have fun. So she just laid back, re-adjusted her shades and allowed the hot sun to rest on her long, beautiful, brown body.

TKO

"Will you put that back!" Wesley snapped.

"But I like it, Ty won't miss it." Dane whined, as he helped Wesley pack.

Wesley was pissed; he didn't see why it was necessary for him to leave Tyrone. He loved Tyrone, and didn't want to add to his pain by leaving him. But Dane's sexual abilities had overruled Wesley's love for Tyrone. Dane gave him pleasures that he, at thirty-six, never dreamed of having. When it came down to sex, Dane was an artist; Wesley had never experienced such talent before and was in over his head. He loved the thick, long, beige rod that awaited him on call. The rod that never went down, the rod that danced long after the music stop playing. It was the rod that Wesley often craved before falling off to sleep at night. And now it was his, to have if he wanted it, but the catch was that he had to leave Tyrone. Dane would dangle his heavy, lanky rod in Wesley's face and say, "if you want to continue enjoying this, you betta tell Ty you're leaving him". Then he would ram it in Wesley's mouth before he could complain why it wasn't possible for him to do it. Wesley would then stop trying to explain and enjoy the sweet taste of his lover, for he knew what followed.

This was not part of Wesley's plan, his plan was to 'hit it and quit it'. Use Dane for pleasure and then throw him back in the dumps he came out of. His plan was to never be seen with him, and definitely never to eat him. But the tables turned. The first night they were intimate, Wesley took control, he flipped Dane's small body over like it was a piece of fish. Then he did what he thought was turning Dane out. Little did he know it was an act, Dane could adjust his body to do whatever the situation called for. Wesley was good but Dane was professional. So when the second time presented itself, Dane whipped something on Wesley that had him begging for more.

With all that, Wesley was still upset and unsure about the move he was about to make. As he stared at the two-year old, 8 x 10 photo of he and Tyrone that sat on their nightstand. He felt confused, weak and ashamed. Tyrone had given him so much when he needed it. It was Tyrone that first told him that he had designing talents, and that he should pursue the industry. It was Tyrone that encouraged him to do fashion shows, displaying his collection. It was Tyrone that got the business cards, called the newspapers, set up the appointments, creating the website, hired a photographer, etc. Tyrone was the guts behind the scene. He was the one that made the first call and got the show on the road. Now as he stared at the picture, with pain choking his heart, he didn't have the strength to leave. Why should he leave? Why couldn't he just see Dane on occasions, get screwed, and go about his day? Why? Because Dane said he couldn't. Dane wanted all of him. He wanted to be the one on everyone's lips when the gossip spread. He wanted everyone to know that it was he who turned Wesley, yeah, the designer Wesley, out. He was already being praised for opening the celebrity's nose. But to turn him out was more than he ever imagined.

When they were seen together, all of Dane's friends would run up to them and act out long hellos, then blush and bat their eyes at Wesley. Doing the nasty with Wesley Jones was like winning the academy award. Before they got together, Wesley was often talked about amongst Dane and his friends. He was the ten on the top ten list and often in their fantasies.

Now looking at the photo only brought back more pain. It was a New Year's Eve shot. Thanksgivings' and Christmas's was spent with their families. Halloween and New Years' Wesley and Tyrone spent together.

Tyrone made Wesley promise that they would stop in Booties for a drink or two, before they went to one of his boring $200 a ticket fashion industry engagements. Wesley didn't want to go; he was above the crowd at Booties. He knew that young, wanna-be-gay-men would be there making everyone look bad. He hated un-established gay men. Men who just got out of the closet and didn't know quite how to act. It reminded him too much of how tacky he used to look. Tyrone, on the other hand, loved Booties, it was his old hang out, and the only place he truly enjoyed partying. He was sick and bored with Wesley's high nosed friends. They were so boring and stuck up. The food and drinks were the only part of the evening Tyrone enjoyed. He always complained that the music sucked, the crowd sucked, and everyone got drunk and wanted to either fight or get laid. Last year something about a-woman-really-being-a-man fight had broken out and the supposedly upscale crowd started throwing fists, throwing food, and throwing up. Someone called the police and the newspapers. No one was arrested, but for some strange reason the only face that got printed was Tyrone's. A shot of him with white cake icing all over his black tuxedo and somebody's gloved arm around his neck.

Tyrone warned Wesley that if he wanted to be with those designing bitches again this year, he would have to first go to Booties with him. Little did Tyrone know -- this was where his nightmare began.

Even though Wesley agreed to go to Booties he held his breath when they entered the dark funky club. The outfits they were wearing looked to good to be in a dive like Booties. Tyrone was too happy, kissing and hugging the owner, bartender and all of his old friends. They all knew Wesley, but thought that he was a snob and Tyrone deserved a more exciting partner. Wesley motioned for Tyrone to take a seat at the table in the corner but Tyrone rolled his eyes and motioned for Wesley to come and sit at the bar.

They sat at the bar and drank for about an hour before Wesley started to unwind. He started popping his fingers and admitting that Booties had an excellent deejay and the crowd seemed live. Tyrone hugged him; they made a toast and exchanged their Happy New Years greetings.

Dane and his horrible looking boyfriends were on the hunt that night, cruising for established meat (older gay men with money). They all had the same type of outfit on; skinned-tight pleather pants with matching vest and they all smelled like they had too much of some old lady's perfume on. They were grinning and whispering the whole time. Whenever someone decent passed by them, Dane and his friends would reach out and feel their behind. If the person responded by turning around, they would just smile and say 'Happy New Years' and then throw a kiss from their greasy Vaseline lips.

After a while, Tyrone's heard his favorite record, *'I was born this way'*. He went nuts. "Oh Wesley, that's it. That's my side-- we've got to dance off this one!"

It just so happened to be everybody in the club's favorite song. As a matter of fact, it was Booties anthem. Every time the place was packed Larry would blast it, mix it, cut it and blast it some more.

- I'm - happy, - carefree, - I'm Gay, - I - was - born - this - way.

While everyone was on the floor stomping, jumping, humping, kissing, and rejoicing, somehow Dane got close enough to slide his rod up on Wesley's cheeks. "Whoa," Wesley leaped to his toes, then turned around hoping to see something he liked and to his disappointment there was this thing, this little, yellow, tacky, thing with big greasy lips throwing kisses at him. At first he chuckled and then continued dancing with his baby, Tyrone but then Dane gave him another stroke of pleasure and slipped a note written on a Booties napkin into Wesley jacket and disappeared in the crowd. After dancing, Wesley excused himself and went into the bathroom to read the napkin. It said, *would love to lick your fudge stick*, and then there was a dripping wet curved tongue, drawn between the cheeks of the Booties logo--a tasteful picture of a raised behind. After examining the tongue on the napkin several times, Wesley zipped down his suede pants and released his king. At first he yanked it, and then he slid his hand tunnel around it. Concentrating on what he wanted to achieve, Wesley closed his eyes as his grip got tighter, choking it, while his other hand massaged the two soldiers that stood at the king's sides. Tugging up and down, breathing hard and moving fast, Wesley quickly erupted. His breath was heavy as he leaned against the stall wall until his pleasure had eased. After he cleaned himself up, he read the note again and memorized the number on it, then flushed it down.

When Wesley came out of the bathroom, he found Tyrone against a wall whispering with an ex-lover. Wesley was walking toward them when Tyrone spotted him. Tyrone gave his ex-lover a quick Happy New Years kiss and sashayed toward Wesley. Tyrone could see in Wesley's eyes that he didn't like it and that he wanted to go. Tyrone was partly right Wesley did want to go, but not because of the ex-lover, he didn't want to face that little yellow tacky thing again tonight. He was exhausted from what he'd achieved in the bathroom and wanted to disappear to a quieter setting. So they left. Wesley was relieved that he got out of there before Dane could find him again. Although Wesley wanted to take him up on his offer, he was not ready to let it be known.

"Look, nothing in this apartment belongs to you." Wesley said angrily.

"Check again boyfriend, I think you overlooked one very important item." Dane said staring between Wesley's legs.

"Hey, I'm not in the mood, you know what I mean?"

"No, I don't think so. What do you mean?"

"Look Dane, don't start your shit."

"Uh, uh, baby you're the one starting. I know just what's going on in that pitiful head of yours. You don't want to leave him, do you?"

Wesley held his face in his hand as if he had a major headache.

"Look I asked you not to start, I need to think."

"Think! Motherfucker, I know you're not going sit up there and tell me you need to think! Just get your pitiful ass up and let's go!"

Wesley didn't budge; he just sat there holding his face.

"I said come on! Don't make me leave without you. I really don't think you want me to do that, because if I do, it will be over!" Dane announced like he meant it, but was getting a little unsure about his powers. Wesley stood still, hoping that Dane would just leave. But Dane wasn't going without a fight.

"You mean to tell me that you're going to stay with this bitch?!" Dane said snatching the picture out of Wesley lap and slamming it to the floor."

When Wesley heard the glass break he jumped up as if he intended to save it. He got on his knees and said, "Why'd you do that?" His voice was strange, sort of quiet. "Why'd you break my picture?"

"Fuck that picture!" Dane shouted picking up the photo and ripping off Tyrone's head.

"What are you doing?" Wesley shouted. "I know you didn't just do that" He roared as he flung Dane's frail body across the floor. Dane loved being man-handled, so he came back for more, but what he didn't realize was that he was in danger. Wesley had flipped right before his eyes. Ripping Tyrone's head from the picture was a huge mistake.

Before Dane could get his claws into Wesley's face -- Wesley grabbed him throw him against the wall and beat him senseless, it wasn't just for the picture, it was for everything that he could think of. Wesley blamed Dane for turning him out, for making a fool out of him, and for sending Tyrone on a mental merry-go-round. Every punch was for something -- the shows and engagements that he missed, the pills that he had to take to remove some itch that he got, and most of all for the embarrassment he carried.

He hated Dane for bringing out the selfish dog in him. Dane was like a bad germ that he couldn't medicate away. After beating Dane, Wesley didn't know what to do. He wanted to push him out of the door with his feet, but was sickened by the madness he already committed.

Dane laid still, blood oozing out of his mouth and the side of his eye. If it wasn't for his chest slowly rising up and down, he could have passed for dead. Wesley wanted to help him up but didn't want to touch him. Wesley felt suffocated and suddenly vomited over Dane's body. He then grabbed a towel and rushed out the door.

Two days had passed when Wesley finally returned home to find everything gone, the jewelry, the VCRs, the TV's, the computer, the gun, the stereo, the microwave, the juice machine, and the luggage. All of their pictures were slashed. The king-sized mattress was knifed and pissed on. The white walls were now streaked with blood-red paint. Dane had written on the bedroom wall: the next time you get your period bitch, take Midol!

The arms and legs of their expensive clothing where cut off. The leather couch and expensive rug was gone. The bar was empty, every last one of their fine wines. Dane took everything and what he didn't take he messed over. Oh he was still going to be the name on everybody's lips when it came down to Wesley!

Although everything he and Tyrone built together was destroyed, Wesley was relieved. He was relieved that he didn't have to put up with Dane's boisterous personality any more. He was relieved that the grueling hours of sex, that he used to love, were over. He was relieved that he didn't make the mistake of leaving Tyrone and hopefully it wasn't too late to ask for forgiveness.

We're in the money

"There, right there, that's where I want the vase. No not there, I didn't say hang it there, I want that in the bedroom. This one belongs in the bathroom. Yes, hook up cable to all four TV's including the one in the bathroom and no," In a flirty voice, Wesley pointed at the telephone man. "I don't want a phone in the bedroom, the living room and kitchen is quite enough."

Buying the largest condo in The Beverly would no doubt persuade Tyrone to forgive him. For years Tyrone fantasized about living in the The Beverly. He always talked about moving there when Wesley struck it rich. The Beverly was a lavishly designed hotel-styled condominium for the wealthy gay. It stood overlooking the city and all that could not afford to live or mingle there. It was a polished resort that supplied every desire under the sun. Most residents there didn't work, so unless they were planning on visiting someone, there was no reason to leave the premises. Wesley too, fantasized about living there, but refused to put himself in a position where they would be struggling to pay the bills. Wesley liked living comfortably, a place where he could pay bills, buy clothes, shoes and drinks when he wanted to. But Tyrone saw things differently he told Wesley a long time ago that his designs would earn enough money to buy The Beverly. He knew from one look that the designs were worth millions and that they would be living on easy street once they were sold. Tyrone was right. Fortunately for them, while Dane was on his mission to destroy, he forgot to look under the bed. After showing Dane the drawings, Wesley had all but thrown out the sketches, Dane told him that they were boring and that real people would never wear outfits like that. He laughed at what Wesley called talent and made him feel insecure about his work. Not being able to handle the criticism Dane had chosen to give him, Wesley snatched the drawings off the board and forced them in his drawing case, throwing it all under the bed. On the other hand, when Tyrone saw the sketches and swatches, he flipped. He told Wesley, "this is it -- this is our ticket to paradise." Tyrone oohed and ahhed at the designs, dancing in celebration, "I'm in love with a genius." But Wesley never saw his work the way that Tyrone did. He thought that the pieces were good, but never the way Tyrone saw it. He just sighed and said, "Yeah, maybe." When Dane destroyed everything, Wesley had no other choice but to take the quickest route he knew to replace everything. He carefully opened his drawing case, pressed out the wrinkles, and headed for the company his designs were made for. The designs were sold within hours of his presentation. Wesley was in a state of shock and could not believe the figures on the first of six checks he was contracted to receive.

Proud of their new designs and excited about the money it would deliver, the president of the company invited Wesley to a celebration lunch where he would be their guest of honor. Wesley agreed and stayed less than half an hour. He also offered Wesley a contract to do designs for them on a seasonal basis, but Wesley turned down the offer. He didn't want to commit himself until he knew what was happening with him and Tyrone.

Even though it was part of his defense, Wesley couldn't wait until Tyrone saw his new home at The Beverly. He didn't know what would make Tyrone happier, living in The Beverly or the fact that he was right about the designs. Wesley couldn't wait to tell Tyrone that he could quit his job if he wanted to. He couldn't wait to thank Tyrone for believing in and loving his work.

Wesley also depended on *So Natural,* the $14,000 painting of what appeared to be: attractive men of color bathing one another on the beach of a deserted island, to help him make his case. The condo was stocked with all sorts of pleasures and entertainment that Tyrone had oohed at one time or another.

"What do you mean? You can't be here until 4:00? If my furniture is not here by noon tomorrow, you can cancel my order!"

Wesley had less than forty-eight hours to complete everything. He smiled as he saw everything coming together. He was impressed at the bad ass designer in him. Everything was new and flawless. The only thing in the apartment that was old was the picture that Dane tried to destroy. Along with his impressive check, Wesley had taken the picture to one of his buddies at the studio and had it refinished and framed.

It was all planned out, he would be at the airport waiting to pick Tyrone up, and then he would take Tyrone to their favorite restaurant, eat and try to apologize. Then they would go to a cozy bar and Wesley would ease into why they couldn't go to their old apartment. As soon as he caught Tyrone feeling uneasy and confused, he would spring the fact that he had bought them a new home in The Beverly. He went over his speech a thousand times, and every time he was pleased at the smile he imagined on Tyrone's face.

Narrow-minded

"Wait Gary, back up. What was that fag doing here?"

"Shut up man. That brother is real cool. He wanted to know when Maya's flight was coming in."

"I asked you to back up. Start from where Maya went."

"Man, I don't have to explain anything to you, that's my girl!"

"Oh, so you think I don't already know. You know you can't tell Dice nothing, besides he was getting you back for the incident with him and his new honey."

"Getting me back? That loser should be paying me for the last couple of nights I let them use my place. I knew I shouldn't have told him anyway."

"Yeah okay, leave me hanging. All I want to know is why Maya would go to an Island with a fag, that's all."

"Man, what's your problem? I bet you wouldn't call him that to his face. Maya went to help out a friend. So what, he happens to be gay."

"You said it yourself, he. Man, Gina wouldn't go!" Pookey said like his word was law. "My man probably was soft when he left, but if he's with the Maya I've seen, he won't be soft when he comes back."

"You know what your problem is Pookey? You're narrow-minded, you think that everybody has to be in it for something. I trust Maya, if she wants to be with her friend on the moon, I would trust her. Why did you marry Gina if you don't trust her?"

"Trust ain't got nothing to do with it. I'm talking about common sense. No man in his right mind is going to let his girl go away to the Island with another man. No man!"

"Oh, so now I'm not a man?"

"No, you're a man. You're just slipping."

"Pookey, I didn't know you were so pathetic. All you're proving is that you're insecure about your manhoood. You think if Gina has the chance, she'll take it. That's poor thinking. Gina has the chance everyday. She doesn't have to go all the way to the Islands and neither does Maya.

"Say what you want, but right now everybody is laughing at you."

"C'mon now, I'm grown. Let them laugh, Maya will be back tomorrow and nothing else matters."

"Yeah, alright, so who was the other fag? Your friend? Is it your turn to take an upset softie on a trip?" Pookey began laughing alone.

"I'm glad you find that funny. That dude was Maya's friend's friend; he wanted to know all the details about the arrival time since he's picking them up."

"You're gonna let him pick Maya up too?"

"What's wrong with that? He's doing me a favor. I don't even know how to get to Newark Airport."

"Man, you better learn. Maya's not going to want to see them fags kiss. She's gonna want to see you."

"Make up your mind. A minute ago you said she would be kissing one."

"Come on Man, I was just messing with you. You know you're the man. I just hope Gina doesn't hear about this mess, next she'll be wanting to go to the Islands with some friends. You know what Eddie Murphy said, Dexter St. Jock will be waiting."

Gary shook his head and laughed.

Yeah, you still got it

The tapping on the window outside of Alycia's fire escape alarmed her. She grabbed her can of mace and eased out of her bed on to the floor. She crawled into the kitchen and grabbed one of her sharp knives. She sat still under the table not knowing what to do next.

"Alycia." She heard a male voice whisper. "Alycia open the window, it's me!" she heard the voice again. Puzzled she wondered. *Who would be on her fire escape at 2:30 in the morning calling her name?*

"Alycia, it's me, Jeff."

"Jeff?!" She jumped up hitting her head against the table, running to the window without turning the lights on to let him in.

"Jeff!? What are you doing out there? What happened to your face?"

"That Bitch."

Alycia smiled. "What happened? Don't tell me you and Cheryl had a fight."

"Yeah," He said still angry. "She had some chump over her place when I rolled up. When I asked her who he was, she choked up, and before I could kick his ass, he ran. Fuckin' punk!" Jeff said bruising Alycia's wall. "She couldn't even look me in the face! It was clear that she'd already waxed him! The bed was tangled and she had on a big t-shirt with no bra or panties. Oohw," he scowled. "I could just kill her."

"Jeff, don't say that." Faking sympathy, Alycia was delighted as she wiped his face with a cotton swab and alcohol. She grinned, thinking her prayers had finally been answered. Pretty Cheryl had turned out to be Pretty Slutty Cheryl.

"I'll say what I want. Fuck her and her new cock!" Was the last thing that he said before breaking into this fighting back the tears macho speech? "I know why she did it! There could only be one reason why she would do something like this. She just wants me to marry her. Yeah, that's it. That's why she's screwing around. She's trying to get me jealous so I would marry her. That has to be it. What other reason would she have to be screwing around on me?"

Alycia tried to hide the face she wanted to give him. The face that would have said, "You don't really want to know." But she didn't, she didn't want to give him the impression that she wasn't satisfied with him.

"Well Jeff," Alycia began in this take-it-from-me voice. "Sometimes women feel that they are being taken advantage of. This sometimes makes them seek outside attention. It's a feeling of needing to know that they still have it. "

"Have what!? Cheryl is not like you! She knows she has it." Jeff built a laugh while placing Cheryl back on her pedestal.

"What do you mean, not like me? She sounds exactly like me -- unsatisfied! That's why she's taking new applicants -- the last guy left the job undone!"

Jeff took the truth like salt on an open wound. He moaned, groaned and shouted.

"Cheryl is not like that! She's not even hot. Half the time I have to beg her for sex!"

"That's because she doesn't want to do it with you." Alycia matched his tone and then began to back down.

"It's not because you're not satisfying. Cheryl knows you in and out, she knows if you're paying the bills, if you're an alcoholic or a drug user, whether you're a real man or whether you hit women. She knows if you're jealous, petty, selfish, or a liar, she knows if you brush your teeth once, twice or at all. She knows all about you, and that can be a turn off. If you did something really screwed up, she might not hold it against you, but her pussy will. Although one part of her will be forgiving to your games and the crap that you constantly pull. Another part will be disgusted by it and turned off when it comes down to making love. Because she knows the real you and that may mean knowing that you're full of it. It may be hard to sleep with you especially if she knows you're fucked-up."

Jeff just sat there dazed by reality. When did Alycia become so smart? How did she know everything that he thought was a secret? On a roll, Alycia found it hard to stop; she could have gone on for days about why women do the things they do.

"Whatever Alycia, that's probably why you do the things you do, but I know Cheryl and that's not it, she wants to get married."

Alycia could tell that she won that argument but didn't want to push it; Jeff was in a bad mood and refused to admit that Cheryl was no different than her.

"Jeff, why don't you take a shower, lie down, and relax for a while? I'll make you some apple-ginger tea and give you a massage." Alycia offered letting him know that his problem with Cheryl didn't matter to her.

"Tea? Did I ask you for any damn tea? I need something strong, where's your liquor?"

Duh, Alycia thought. "It's in the bar." Then she walked over to the bar and recited her menu. "I have some Alize, Tanqueray, Cognac and Henney . ."

Before Alycia could finish, Jeff grabbed the cognac.

"Jeff, before you get started, why don't you take a shower." she pleaded.

"I don't want to take a shower!" he growled kicking off his Timberlands and loosening his belt.

Alycia questioned herself as to why this turned her on. She would have much preferred for him to shower and meet her in the bedroom, but the pain and anger that was beneath him promised her a night of passion and excitement, a night too good to tamper with. She weakened as he grabbed her by her hair, bringing her lips close to his. Instead of kissing her, he directed her to fall on her knees. He escorted her head to go between his thighs and moaned the second her wet lips touched him. Alycia closed her eyes and concentrated on satisfying him. After peeking at the gratitude on Jeff's face, Alycia went to work to move Cheryl out permanently. But her thin teddy wasn't enough to keep her warm on the cold kitchen floor. She pulled out all her tricks to make him come so that she wouldn't have to interrupt his good feeling, but she was too cold. Finally she stopped and offered to continue on the carpeted floor in the bedroom, but the grip Jeff had on her head tightened, forcing her to complete the job she started. Feeling used and abused, Alycia began to cry and as he came, she choked.

"Swallow dammit!" He yelled pushing her head down on him. Alycia's so called night of passion and excitement, turned into a night of pain and disappointment.

"I said swallow it." He forced her head down again. Alycia swallowed hard, and got up as Jeff released the hold he had on her. She ran straight to the kitchen sink and rinsed out her mouth. Jeff laughed.

"I thought you wanted to know whether or not you still got it. Well," he laughed. "You got it now." Then he fell over laughing, "You definitely got it."

"Get the fuck out!" Alycia screamed as the tears raced down her face.

"Gladly." Jeff plucked at his shirt like her words bounced right off of him. He snatched the fifth of cognac off the counter, drank it all down in one take and wiped his mouth with her dish cloth, then let out a loud burp.

"I hate you! She screamed at his back. "Don't ever come back!" She followed behind him with the empty bottle in her hand.

"You want me back now." he turned around and smiled at her. Then he continued to skip down the steps and laughing. "Don't worry baby, you still got it!"

Let's get one thing straight

"Hey Selina, girl there's a scandal brewing."

"Hold on Roz, you know how much I love scandals! Hey Alycia, you got a minute?"

"Yeah, what's up?"

"Roz has something scandalous to tell us. Hold on."

"Roz, Alycia are you both there?"

"Yeah, we're here."

"Okay Roz, shoot."

"Get this, Maya and her fairy friend's flight comes in tonight and . . ."

"Hold it Roz." Selina interrupted. "His name is Tyrone, he's a real person and I don't think he deserves the criticism."

"Excuuuse me." Roz sang. "When did you become Pro-Fag?"

"Grow up Roz, everyone has a right to be, feel, say what ever lives inside of them, especially when it comes down to something as personal as sexuality."

"Oh Selina please." Alycia joined in.

"Mmmm" Roz moaned. "I don't know how to take you."

"It's simple, take me the way that I am." Selina finally said, ready to set them straight about her sexuality.

"What are you trying to say?" they asked, knowing the deal but waiting to hear a lie.

"I'm not trying to say anything, I'm saying that I am gay, lezzy, bi, whatever label you prefer to use."

"Selina!?" Alycia gasped.

"That's right, hold your heart, go ahead, fake it, like I did for so many years. Hey it's alright. I know the situation I put everyone in. I heard the whispers, the jokes, the comments. That's my fault. I should have been honest, but first I had to be honest with myself." Then they heard Selina's tough exterior crack. "It was so hard for me to be honest, I was so ashamed. You don't know how it feels to want someone who is the same sex as you."

"You got that right." Alycia said not feeling any sympathy.

"Hey Selina, I'm sorry," Roz apoligized. "I didn't mean to play games. I've always wondered but never had the guts to ask. But that doesn't change anything, I still love you the same. And as far as the whispers and comments are concerned, it was never harsh it was just fear, fear of not understanding. And the only reason I say those thing about Tyrone is because I'm jealous, I don't have a unique friend like him. Maya has this cool gay friend who is like a brother yet a girlfriend, I think I would enjoy a relationship like that. I really could care less about his sexuality. But I have to admit I wouldn't mind hearing some of those stories he tells Maya."

Alycia, still blurting out the wrong words, said. "I can't wait until Maya comes back she is going to flip when I tell her that you're bisexual."

"Maya already knows, besides if she didn't I wouldn't want you to tell her."

"Maya never mentioned anything to me."

"Me either, but trust me, she knows. Remember we grew up together."

"So, that doesn't mean that she knows."

"Well there's more." Selina continued.

"One night we got pissy drunk, laughing and bullshitting with men. I convinced Maya that she should stay with me because it was dangerous for either of us to go home alone. I wanted to make a move on her so bad. But instead I gave her a quiz. I asked her did she see that woman checking her out. I wanted to see her reaction but she was cool and said of course I noticed and I gave her an ugly look. That was enough for me. It was an obvious "no" so basically, nothing happened and we both fell asleep."

"Selina!? You mean to tell me that you would have made love to Maya?" Alycia kept digging.

"Yeah and you too," she laughed waving her hands no. "I'm just kidding, that was years ago, I was never really into her just like the comfort of her company.

"So it's over between you and men?"

"No, I like them too, women are just better lovers."

"How can you say that? They don't even have a you-know-what."

"That's exactly it, they don't have one, you'd be surprised at all the things you can do without one. I was."

"So is it like you're the man and your partner is the woman?"

"No. There is no man. That's the whole objective. Women know exactly where they want to be touched. We know where our needs are and its easier to direct a woman into that spot than it is to direct a man. Men are always so aggressive, they think with their dicks. They don't know how to use their hands, feet and tongues."

"Feet?" Roz came back to life, but said no more.

Alycia took a deep sigh, shook her head and changed her tone.

"Honey, I can't see it. I'm the type that thanks the creator for men, especially the ones with the long tongues and the long you know what. I can't imagine a woman satisfying me. You can just pass all those handsome men on over to me. I'll be glad to have their aggressive mouth wrapped around my breast and my you know what. I love men. Oooh, just thinking about them makes me feel like singing."

Then she stopped, remembering how insensitive Jeff had just been and how she didn't like it.

"Look I'm not trying to sell you on women. I'm just enlightening you on why I'm sold on them. Men have their moments."

Realizing that Selina had a decent point about her man, Alycia listened quietly.

"Well, I'm glad that I got that off my chest. It was easier than I thought only if everyone would take my news the way you two did."

It was Roz's turn again.

"Girl you are thirty-six years old and holding your own. What do you care about how people respond to your lifestyle? I say don't worry about it."

"Thanks Roz, that was so easy to say. Now try wearing these shoes."

"It's not about wearing your shoes. I had a tight pair on every since I discovered men. I use to get hell because I liked to party with them, had two and three boyfriends at a time. I use to care, hide and be ashamed of what I was doing. But girl it hit me, nobody was doing a damn thing for Roz, but Roz. So if I wanted to see Derrick in the morning, Kareem at lunch, and Jamal for dinner, who's to stop me? Later for what people say, I talked big shit on Maya for going away with Tyrone, but if you check her out thoroughly, girlfriend did what she wanted to do. She made a commitment to her friend and didn't care about what I, Gary or anyone else had to say. She held her own and she knew that if we were really her friends that we would be her friends when she got back. So get up off of your behind and let's go out and celebrate, my treat, 'cause girl there are so many questions I got to ask." Roz ended with a big laugh.

"I knew that was coming, I'll pick you two up in twenty minutes."

"I can't make it." Alycia lied, feeling that she had nothing to celebrate.

"Alright, I'll just pick you up Roz."

"Bye Alycia." The two women sang.

"Enjoy."

Here's to you

After receiving their first drink on the plane coming home, Maya decided to get into Tyrone's business.

"Tyrone, I don't mean to pry, but um . . . uh, did I hear you and your friend last night?"

"I hope so honey, I was trying to let everybody know I was having one."

"Tyrone!" Maya responded by hitting him.

"Don't act surprised, you know what I had planned."

"Yeah but . . ."

"Oooh," Tyrone frowned. "Please don't say that word."

"What word?"

"B-U-T-T." Tyrone spelled out.

Maya gasped and said, "OK enough, too much information."

"No. I'm glad you asked cause honey, you are with the new Tyrone. As a matter of fact call me Roni."

"Roni?!"

"Yeah, that's what Eric called me all weekend."

Maya looked at Tyrone and laughed. "Boy, I think you need to take a nap. There is no way I'm calling you Roni." She laughed holding her stomach.

"Maya," Tyrone got serious. "I'm just trying to soak up these last few hours away from home, away from my problems. Don't laugh at me."

"Oh, I was just kidding, I would never laugh at you."

"I know honey, I was kidding too. You better not call me Roni, that's for Eric to do." And then in a flash he said.

"Wait a minute, enough about Eric, close your eyes, I have a surprise for you."

"Tyrone, I told you to take a nap."

"No seriously, I have a surprise for you."

Maya closed her eyes thinking that Tyrone was going to give her a pack of Bahama condoms or the sexy Bahama men calendar she saw him buy. She closed her eyes, preparing herself for a prank.

"Okay now you can open them."

When Maya opened her eyes she could not believe the beautiful tennis bracelet inside the slender velvet navy box.

"Oh Tyrone!" Maya screamed, grabbing his neck, knocking the bracelet to the floor. "It's beautiful. It's the most beautiful thing anyone has ever given me. Oh thank-you." she said kissing him and hugging him.

"Hold on." He said blushing at his good taste, he knew she was going to die when she saw it, it made him die just trying it on. "Hold on, let me fasten it." Then he grabbed her hands and looked into her eyes and said. "This is for taking time out for me. I know that you got a lot of shit for taking this trip, and I know that you had second thoughts, but Maya, I want you to know that this trip was successful and it did me a lot of good. I feel much better and I'm sure I can handle whatever is waiting home for me. Plus I met someone special that I think I'll always have as a close friend. I also had a chance to think clearly. While spending intimate time with Eric I told him all about Wesley and he gave me good advice and the opportunity to believe in me. He made me feel loved and gave me what I needed to come home and face reality, but if it wasn't for you, I wouldn't have gotten this chance. You were the first to pull me up. You are a special friend and I'll always love you." Then he buried his head in her shoulder as she wrapped her arms around him. Then Maya looked at Tyrone, smiled and said. "I love my bracelet."

"Hey, special gifts for a special friend."

"So Eric gave you advice, what did he tell you? I mean do you know what you're going to say to Wesley?"

"Eric said that the best thing for me to do is to lay all the cards on the table, give Wesley a do or die. If Wesley prefers to die, I could see him on occasions or I could meet the many single friends that he has. The bottom line is that I refuse to be unhappy, and to tell you the truth, it doesn't matter whether Wesley do or die because, honey I plan to see Eric anyway. Even though he made it clear that he was spoken for, he also made it clear that we could get together anytime either one of us needed to."

"How are you going to do that? Oh, I forgot, you said that he lives in East Orange. When is he coming home?"

"In two weeks, he's doing a photo shoot. Isn't it ironic the way I attract models."

"You attract handsome men. I mean Eric is just gorgeous. He has a nice personality too, I enjoyed hanging out with y'all at the bar the other night, he had me in stitches. What's his sign?"

"Scorpio. Just like Wesley."

"Yuck" Maya interrupted looking out of the window, frowning. "Look at how filthy Newark is, we're home."

Aunt Moo

"Leena! Gal is dat you? Come heah and give ya Aunt Moody a kiss. Lawd, where ya been?" The unattractive, heavy breathing woman with sideburns and a mustache asked Selina, kissing her in the mouth. "Chile ya know you bin mist around heah. We ain't bin havin' no fun wid outcha. Herd you flipt to da ahdda side, how is it?" Moody hollered showing off her last four teeth.

Selina faked a smile, and never answered. She never liked Aunt Moody. Aunt Moody -- Trudy's adoptive mother, the one who turned Trudy -- and everybody she could get her lips on -out, was nothing more than a child molester, a sicko, and alcoholic. She used every trick in the book to persuade kids to skip school and spend their days with her. She would take the best years of their life and ruin them, leaving them hooked on drugs and alcohol. When concerned parents would complain, she would explain that the kids weren't happy and that they would rather be with her. Shortly after she got them hooked, she would begin charging them rent, using the money to keep her liquor stock full in case of emergency. She didn't care about her own two daughters, both grown, on drugs and living on the streets.

Trudy loved her Aunt Moody, but Selina despised her. Back in the days when they were just leaving their teens, Aunt Moody would supply them with alcohol, drugs and a place to lay up, she was cool, but when she started joining in on the fun, her coolness became annoying.

Aunt Moody would wait until the girls got good and high, then she would storm in with a deck of cards. '*Alright now, who wanna play scrip poka?*' The girls would look at each other and and giggle, thinking that Aunt Moody would give them the cards so that they could play. But Aunt Moody would grin a "move over" grin and take a seat. At first Selina didn't mind, so what if Aunt Moody saw her tits, it's not like she didn't know what was going on. But when the game developed into more than just stripping, Selina got nervous. Every time one of the girls would remove their bra, Aunt Moody would steal a suck and Trudy would laugh. *'How ya like da game so far?'* Moody would tease. When it was Selina's turn to take off her bra, she hesitated, hoping that the roof over Moody's head would cave in and kill her. Knowing how Selina felt, Trudy intercepted and beat Moody to the taste. Selina was relieved but Aunt Moody got mad. *'Go in da back, look in my chess, and get my corn!'* She would demand. Trudy knew exactly what that meant, Selina was in trouble and whenever Moody wanted her way she would drink corn liquor to build her mental strength. Trudy's heart raced, *'Aunt Moo, you know what that corn does to ya. I'll get you another beer.'* is what everyone heard Trudy say, but what Moody heard her say was *'Aunt Moo, please don't get drunk and take Selina, I promise I won't interfere next time you want to taste her.* Moody smiled, accepting the offer. Besides, she didn't want to take Selina yet, it was too soon. She just wanted it to be clear that she was running the show.

"Where's Trudy?" Selina asked still faking her smile.

"I haven't seened dat heffa, in a while now. You know afta you leff she done up and find huh self some white trash up dere in da Heights. Work down dere on Wall Skreet. Posta be makin' plenny money. Besides da money, I don't know what True see in huh, long dead looking hair, no titties and no ass. Ain't it a shame da way dem white folks don't have no ass? Ya know why dey don't, don'tcha? It's because of all dat work we done done for dem. Yeah, all dat pickin, cuttin, sweatin' and such, done give us more muscle tone to our already helzsty bodies. Dey sit up on dere porch jussa laughing at us. Oh yeah they lay around day and night watching us work. All da time dey was juss flatning away. Done sit so long till dere butt flat. Had da nerb to spread, we 'ez lazy. Huh, seem to me, da proof be in da puddin'. Dey was so lazy, dat four hundred years later, dere chillun' still flat. And where do you see mose of dem today? Right up dere in the helz spa, trying to shape dere flat selfs up. Ain't it funny? But dis heah one, True got, she's flat, uglay and look like she useta be a man or somedin'. And ya know she wheres dem glasses, dey all do. Have dem pull close to huh face, like she can't see wid out dem." Moody shook her head and laughed real loud, this time showing off her brown gums as well.

Selina's smile was gone as she thought about the time she caught Trudy kissing a white girl at Washington Square Park. Trudy was just like her father. She thought all races were beautiful.

"Don't juss stan dere lookin' scrumptious, come on up and give ya Aunt Moody somedin' she can hole to." Moody was out of her chair scratching the elastic mark around her belly.

"No, I'm in a rush." Selina said sickened by the thought. Selina rushed away, afraid to look back. It amazed her how Moody still frightened her. It was as clear as yesterday the way she cornered her in that room and threatened to kick Trudy out on the street, if she didn't do the right thing. She remembered how close she was to being raped. *'Go ahead kick her out.* Selina said escaping the strong hold the manly woman had on her. *'You'll be sorry, you fake lesbian!'* Moody shouted throwing down the piece of blouse that ripped off of Selina's back..

"Hee, hee, dat chile was always scared of a real woman." Moody said taking her seat and shooting spit onto the street.

Just let me explain

"Flight 213, flight 213 from the Virgin Islands is boarding on level B6," the airport intercom repeated.

In his sexy fitting black jeans, black boots, tight black t-shirt, and an arm full of yellow roses, Wesley snatched long masculine strides down the corridor looking for level B6. He ignored the women, stares and pointing fingers as he passed by.

"I thought you weren't coming?" he said shaking Gary's hand.

"I had a change of mind, I figured you and Tyrone had a lot to talk about, besides I can't wait to be with my baby."

Wesley shared an understanding smile and the two men stood quiet, watching as the plane landed.

"Gary!" Maya screamed.

Gary ran over, grabbing Maya and swinging her through the air. Wesley's heart sunk, he was so afraid at the scene Tyrone had every right to cause.

"Oh Gary, I missed you so much!" Maya said not letting go of his neck.

"Welcome home, Maya" Wesley interrupted. "These are for you." He said handing Maya the perfect bunch of yellow roses. "Thank-you." He whispered in her ear instead of kissing her on the cheek.

Trying to hide the shock he felt seeing Wesley at the airport, Tyrone snatched Gary's hand, shaking it. "Congratulations, Maya told me the good news."

"That's right, she promised that she would be all mine when she got back and I'm going to hold her to it."

Maya blushed, taking Gary's extended hand. "I guess this is it."

"It was great." Tyrone said still not looking at or saying anything to Wesley. Gary and Maya began to walk, and then suddenly Maya stopped, put her roses down, ran back and gave

Tyrone a big passionate hug. Then stepped away walking backwards, not taking her eyes off of him.

"If you need me just ca--"

"Good-bye fellas." Gary waved with his left hand while he covered Maya's mouth with his right.

"He'll be alright." Wesley winked at Gary and grabbed Tyrone's bag.

****

Nothing was said as they walked to the leased, red, convertible Jaguar. Wesley neatly situated the luggage in the back and opened Tyrone's door.

"Where's your girlfriend?" Tyrone finally said before he got in the car.

Wesley took a deep breath and said "I have no girlfriend, what I did was a mistake and it's over."

"It's over! Just like that you're going to tell me it's over! Am I supposed to be happy?"

"Please Tyrone, don't do this, hear me out!"

"I'm listening." Tyrone said, now leaning against the car door paying close attention to his perfectly manicured nails.

"There is so much I have to tell you, but right now I just want you to trust me, get in the car and let's take it slow."

"Look Wes, I took that trip to get focused! I refuse to let you waltz back into my heart so that you can tap dance on it when you feel like it."

"You have every right to feel that way, but please give me a chance to explain. We need to talk. I've made reservations at your favorite restaurant." then Wesley hesitated and said. "Tyrone, believe me when I say I love you. What I did was wrong, but a lot of good has come out of it. I've learned a very valuable lesson."

Tyrone's heart was beating as fast as it could. What happened while I was gone? He wondered. The way that Wesley talked to him was all too familiar. He remembered that patient yet desperate tone -- the one that Wesley used when they first met.

Seven years ago while Tyrone was sitting in the shoe repair shop, Wesley walked in took off his shoes and sat next to him. Right away Tyrone notice what they had in common but chose to let this one pass. He was in a brand new relationship and didn't have any room for another friend. Tyrone checked him out thoroughly as he handed the counter clerk his shoes. "*Hmmm, Johnston and Murphy*" Both men shoes were made by the same company. When Wesley turned around, Tyrone quickly pretended to reading the leather wear magazine in the chair beside him.

"Excuse me, don't I know you?" Wesley asked.

"I doubt it." Tyrone answered almost rudely.

"That's too bad." Wesley said knowing he would get a better response. Tyrone turned around to face the well dressed chocolate coated man.

"What did you say? I mean what do you mean?" Tyrone softened.

"I'm new here and you're the first man that caught my interest."

"What about me, is so interesting?"

"Is that a joke?"

"As a matter of fact it was. But I can't help you. My friend is across the street waiting for me. It's a new relationship, I'm sure you can understand."

"New? That's what I want, a new relationship. How long have you been seeing your friend?"

"Two months."

"Two months? That's hardly any time to call him your friend. Look, why don't you give me your number and let's set something up for this weekend. Would that work for you?"

"You're serious aren't you?"

Wesley batted his eyes and smiled.

"Okay, take my number down, but remember call me before six, I like to know what I'm doing with my evenings before six."

"No problem, you'll get your call nice and early."

The next day at noon Wesley was inviting Tyrone to a sushi bar on 96th Street. Tyrone explained how he only agreed to go out because Wesley said that he was new in town and that he had a friend and really couldn't afford to start any new relationship. Meanwhile, that's exactly what was taking place.

The evening of the date, Wesley patiently insisted that he was the man for him. He told Tyrone that he had an eye for good happenings and they were good for each other.

Tyrone sat there avoiding Wesley eyes as he remembered their first date, their first kiss. He wanted to just grab Wesley by the neck and scream I forgive you, but he was afraid to, afraid that Dane was around the corner some where waiting for Wesley to come back.

"Fine but I'm not making any promises."

After they ate dinner and had two drinks Wesley began telling Tyrone why they couldn't go home. Tyrone's response went something like this:

--"Whaat? I know that dog didn't ruin my place."

--"Don't shush me, I'm grown."

--"Why couldn't you beat her in the streets?"

--"What picture?"

--"Calm down my ass! I want to go home."

--"Why would you leave her there?"

--"Where did you go?"

--"Yes it matters!"

--"That trifling tramp, I'm going to kill her. So help me, I'm going to beat her yellow behind until its black."

--"What do you mean it's not necessary?"

--"What good came out of it?"

--"A new place? Wesley please, I'm in no mood for your shit!"

"The Who? The Beverly? Yeah right Wes, and I didn't have sex while I was away. That dog has you loosing your mind too."

"Get your hands off of me, I'm not waiting! I've heard enough."

"What designs?"

"Maxi!?"

"You sold Maxi?"

"They already gave you the check?"

"Let me get this straight. You and that dog were in my apartment, you had a fight over our New Years Eve picture, you beat her half to death, left her in my apartment for two days, came home and found the place destroyed, felt that you were doomed because I was going to kill you so, you had to get some money fast and replace the damages, the only thing you could think about was to do some quick designs, but instead you remember Maxi, the designs under the bed, sold them in less than two hours, received a check in less than four, and bought me a new apartment in The Beverly?"

"That's right."

"Well, why are we sitting here? Let's go home."

Baby I'm back

"Oh Gary, it's so good to be home." Maya grinned, throwing her arms around his neck and sliding her tongue into his mouth.

"Hey, that felt good. Do it again."

"Chase! Mommy's home." Maya said opening the sliding doors to the fire escape letting Chase into the house.

"How's mommy's baby? Yeah, yeah, mommy was gone. Did daddy give you lots of love?"

"Come here man, good dog. You know Maya, we never had a dog when I was coming up. My mother didn't trust them. I was disappointed that you had a dog when we first met. I thought that he would have complicated things. But Chase is special. He is such a smart dog. Do you know, everyday last week I walked him without a leash? He didn't give me any trouble, he listens well."

"Thanks. You hear that honey, Gary loves you."

"C'mon on Chase, back on the fire escape, daddy has some business to take care of with mommy."

Maya smiled as she watched Gary led the dog out. She knew exactly what business he was talking about and couldn't wait to negotiate.

"Come here you."

"Sorry, I'm dying to take a shower, if you want to discuss business you'll have to wait or join me." She laughed as she ran into the bathroom locking the door.

"Let me in."

"Just a second." she said as she quietly unlocked the door allowing steam to escape.

"Where are you?" he asked knocking over the spray, then the powder.

"Yoo-hoo, Gary, I'm over here."

Apricots and peaches filled the steamed room and led him to the rich lather all over Maya's body.

"Oh, there you are. Girl, you know how to drive a man crazy." he said kicking off his shoes and pulling off his clothes at the same time.

"You said you wanted to discuss business?" Maya teased.

"Yeah," she heard him trip against the commode. "I uh, need you to help me."

"Help you what?" Maya asked laughing, while putting piles of suds inside of his shirt. Then she heard him fall again.

"Maya, stop, before I break my neck."

"You better not. What are you doing? "

"Right now? Trying to get out of these tight jeans you got me."

"Climb in and I'll help you get them off."

She laughed playfully.

Gary hesitated but fumbled his way in.

"Ahh, it smells so good in here. Mmm, it feels good in here too."

First the shirt went flying out of the shower, then the t-shirt, a couple of minutes had passed and then his jeans, boxer shorts and one sock landed on the floor.

"See how much easier it is to take off your clothes when you have help?" Maya said lathering the bath gel into his chest hairs.

"No, what I see is how lucky I am to have a special woman like you. Thank-you baby, you couldn't have come up with a better way to say you missed me."

"I know." Maya said closing her eyes as she went to work on her man.

Yeah, I'm feeling this

"I can't believe all of this is mine." Tyrone said examining his new hand carved African marble art. "These pieces are fascinating, where did you find them?"

Wesley just smiled, pleased at what he saw in Tyrone's eyes: forgiveness.

"I got them from Afrique's Treasures on 73rd."

"Afrique's Treasures! I bet Rashida could have died when she saw you in there with all that money."

"She did. You know how greedy women are? When I told her about my good fortune she tried to lure me into the back room. It amazes me, how women try me, knowing that I'm gay and sexually uninterested in them, they still try. They always think that they're powerful enough to make me want them instead of men. Don't they get it?"

"Don't be so hard on Rashida you're every woman's dream and every man's reality."

Tyrone laughed forgetting that he was not supposed to seem too friendly.

"Not every man, just yours." Wesley said in a serious tone, and then disappeared down the hall into the bedroom. "Let me show you the check."

When Tyrone read the figures on the check he just passed out. Mouth to mouth resuscitation was the procedure Wesley chose to wake him up.

"I've been dying to kiss you every since you got off that plane. Who knew that it would have happened this way?"

"Are all those zeros for real? Wes, we can retire!"

"You can if you want to -- Bakari offered me a two year contract. This is just one of the six checks that I'll be receiving for this season alone."

"Bakari! You sold Maxi to Bakari! That's who you had in mind when you designed them. Wes, I'm so proud of you!" Tyrone threw his arms around Wes hugging him and then kissing.

"Even after what I did?"

Tyrone eyes left Wesley's. "I'm not ready to talk about it."

"We don't have to. As a matter of fact, I prefer if we just start all over, me loving you and you loving me. I've missed you so much." The third kiss followed.

"Look Wes," Tyrone jumped out of his seat. "You have to slow down. First the car, then the place, you haven't stopped giving me gifts and you tell me that I have a new wardrobe. It's all going too fast. You really hurt me. I'm not ready to give into you. It's too soon, too crazy. I need time to let all of this to sink in. I need to go to sleep tonight and find you still here. I mean, if part of your plan was for us to exercise our rights then maybe I should sleep somewhere else. I'm not ready for that kind of relationship with you yet."

"Ty-baby." Wesley said walking towards Tyrone with open arms. "You don't have to feel pressured. I just got a little excited. You taste so good. I could kiss you all night. But please, understand that this is your home, I ruined your other one and now I'm giving you this one. If anyone sleeps somewhere else it'll be me. I understand that you need time I want you to take as much as you need. Just tell me that you still love me and that you don't want to leave me. That's all I need to hear from you tonight."

"Wes, stop! All that will come out on its own, besides there's something else."

"Anything."

"I want you to take another AIDS test."

"No problem. I'll take any kind of test you want me to take. But I think it's necessary for you to know that I didn't break our agreement. We agreed that if we ever made stops outside of our home that we would always use a condom, and I haven't broken that promise. I've never been bare without you."

Tyrone believed Wesley, he wanted to just jump all over his chocolate coated honey and ride until the morning came. But he knew that it wasn't time. He didn't want Wes to get too comfortable to soon. He loved being pampered like a queen. He wanted to live like this forever. He knew the minute they made love things would have gone back to normal. No sweet talk, no candles, no gifts.

"That's not the point, things happen. As a matter of fact, I plan to take one too."

"Are you saying that you've been intimate with someone?"

"What do you think?"

"I guess it doesn't matter. I'm just glad that were back together. I mean that we're together now."

"Wes, I still think that this must be a dream. If everything is still here tomorrow, I think that I will just go crazy."

"You can start now, because this is real and nothing is going to change, except my love for you, it'll be growing stronger each day."

Don't be late

"Hey Roz, guess who's home?"

"You're late, Maya called me for a hot second last night. All she said was *I'm back* and hung up. I took it to believe that Gary was there and that she couldn't really talk."

"Well anyway, she wants us to meet her at Sylvia's for dinner, she's treating."

"She still has money?"

"Does she? Get this, Tyrone's friend sent her a check covering all the expenses she made on the trip."

"What friend? Not the one that was cheating on him."

"Yeah, chile! Turns out, he made some big deal with some big magazine people about some fancy designs he did and got paid a whole lot of money."

"Get out of here!"

"Yeah, he sent Maya some expensive chocolates and . . ."

"Chocolates? I wonder who started that. If you ever want to thank me, don't do it with chocolates, unless it's a chocolate man." Roz laughed out loud by herself.

"Anyway . . . Maya said the check almost triple what she spent."

"Damn, as much as I hate to admit it, that girl is special, something good is always happening to her."

"It's true. Anyway, be on time, she paying and it's rude to be late if you're not paying."

"Wait! Did she call Selina?"

"Please, Selina was with her this afternoon when she called me. Anyway she said that she has a surprise for us. She swears its going to knock us off of our feet."

"Oh good, I love surprises."

"Who was that baby?"

"Oh that was Alycia, Maya is inviting all the girls out for dinner."

"Are you going to tell them?"

"I guess so."

"You guess so? It doesn't sound like you're too proud about little Lance."

"Little Lance," she cooed. "They're not going to believe it. I can hear Maya now, *Crazy Roz having a baby?*"

"And Roz is getting married. Don't forget that Honey. We're having a baby and getting married, right?"

"Of course we are, but when I get back from dinner, there is something I'd like to talk to you about."

"Why don't you cancel and tell me now. Lance said very concerned. What is it? I hope you're not having second thoughts."

"It's not second thoughts, and now is not the time to talk about it. I have to shower and get ready to meet the girls."

"Roz, don't do this to me. Don't leave me hanging. I need to know what's on your mind."

"I'm sorry I said something, I don't want to cancel with the girls. I'm looking forward to seeing them. I promise you have nothing to worry about."

And it's on

"Maya!" Alycia screamed.

"Girl, look at you!"

Maya dropped the bag of gifts and gave each a big hug and kiss.

"You look like a million dollars, look atcha, you're glowing and shining and grinning and ya smell good too! Welcome home Girl!"

"Thanks Alycia."

"Oh my God," Alycia said grabbing her heart. "Maya, where did you get that bracelet?"

"It was a gift."

"Gary has outdone himself. This is gorgeous. You mean he gave you that just because you were away for a week? Damn, how come I never find those kinds of guys?"

"Who said Gary bought it? This gift is from Tyrone. He bought it here in the diamond district and gave it to me on the plane on the way home."

"Girl it is gorgeous. What did Gary say?"

"Just like the trip, he didn't like it, but he pretended to."

"That's a good man."

"Where's Roz?"

"I don't know, she was so excited about us meeting, I'm sure she'll be here any minute."

"Well too bad for you girls, because y'all are just going to have to wait until she gets here to hear my news."

"Now Maya, you mean to tell me that you don't think we had enough sense to figure out your news?"

"Oh? What's my news?"

"You screwed Tyrone while you were away."

"Yeah," Alycia added. "You couldn't help yourself, you got drunk and the romance of the water, sand and air became your excuse for being horny and not knowing what you were doing."

"Go on admit it, you screwed Tyrone."

"Well actually it was the other way around, Tyrone screwed me."

They hollered, and then blushed over the thought.

"Y'all should stop, Tyrone barely spoke to me -- he was too busy with his little boyfriend to give me a second thought."

"What?" Alycia responded with her ears and mouth wide opened, wanting to hear every detail about Tyrone affairs.

"Yes honey, he met this nice guy, he had a ball."

"You mean four balls." Selina corrected.

"You should stop, as a matter of fact, lets get off of him. Tell me what's been going on? You're first Alycia, who's the lucky man this week?

"It's still Jeff."

"Get out of here. I know your knees are sore." Maya laughed nudging Selina then stopped short.

"Why did you stop there? You don't think I get down on my knees when I'm giving head? If you would have asked me what was going on first, I would have told you like I already told Roz and Alycia. I'm out the closet."

"Wait let me order a drink before you . . ."

"Before I what? There is no more. I'm out the closet period!"

"Hallelujah! Hallelujah! I thought you were never going to come out. Give me a hug girl. You know, I knew for years."

"So why you didn't say anything?" Selina asked bitterly.

"It wasn't my place, like my aunt use to say, if you wasn't there holding the light or beating the drum you don't know what was going on."

"Light? Drums? Maya I don't understand what your aunt meant." Alycia gave a puzzled face.

"It's was just her way to of saying that if you weren't there holding the light on the lovers and beating the drum while they made love you can't be sure about what was going on. Look it doesn't matter."

Everyone just kind of gave Maya a funny stare.

"Anyway, Selina, what made you finally come out?"

"A lot of things, but I guess the main thing is that I want Trudy back."

"Shit and I thought I had something juicy to tell! Who's Trudy?"

"You don't know her. But if I get my way you will. As a matter of fact everyone will." Selina blushed.

"Mind if I ask a question." Alycia raised her hand to interrupt.

"Go ahead." Selina regretted, knowing the kind of questions Alycia asked.

"When you first told me, I was a little hesitant about asking questions, but now that Maya's here, you seem so free about the whole thing I thought it would be a good time to get some information."

"Information? What, you writing a book?"

"No, I'm just curious, anyway, are you like a lesbian?"

"No. I'm like me. I like women, yes, I like men, yes. Who do I prefer the most, I would say women, but it has a lot to do with how I'm feeling that day."

"Like lunch? You know, how you don't know what you want to eat for lunch until its lunch time?"

Selina closed her eyes and shook her head.

"Maya, where did you find this girl?"

"I mean like, don't you feel funny with a woman?"

"To be truthful, I feel funny with a man. It's hard to explain, but they seem so awkward sometimes. I guess you can say it's like cats and dogs. Some people like dogs as a pet and some like cats. They're both pets, but they're very different. Dogs are more like men. They're always jumping all over you barking loud just to get attention, you know, they like you to pay close attention to them. Wherein cats are frisky yet sophisticated, they play and pounce lightly. Most of the time they're just lying around in a clean spot meditating on life."

"So you like cats?"

"No, I hate cats! They're too sneaky, I don't trust them and I really hate it when they arch their backs up in the air."

"But you just said . . ."

"Hey there goes Roz! Roz, over here." Maya signaled.

"Perfect timing." Selina whispered under her breath.

"Maya!" They exchanged hugs and kisses.

"Girl you look good. I know Gary was glad to see you."

"Is Maya the only person you see?" Selina growled.

"Of course not, hi Selina, what's up Alycia."

"Drink number three and we're starving."

"Ladies please forgive me. Lance wanted to show me something just as I was about to leave."

"Oh!" They grinned, giving each other the eye.

"How is Lance?" Maya had to ask, impressed with the smile on Roz's face.

"Right now he's doing real fine."

"Doesn't look like he's the only one." They laughed.

"Are you gaining weight?"

"Dog Maya, you took the words right out my mouth." Selina rolled her eyes. "Roz your face does seem to be bloated."

"Damn, y'all good! I'm only five weeks."

"Five weeks what?!" They shouted in harmony.

"Pregnant. Sillies. Now let me see I think I'll have the Fisherman's Platter."

No one said anything they all just stared at Roz like she just landed from the moon.

"Stop staring at me, I'm not the first person y'all know that's pregnant."

They still stared. Then finally Alycia broke out of the trance.

"Whose is it?"

"Girl don't let me have to get up and kick you across this room! What kind of funky question is that suppose to be!?"

"Calm down Roz, I didn't mean to upset you -- it's just that I know you have a lot of . . ."

"No! I *had* a lot of friends, alright, that's in the past, the night I met Lance changed all of that. I'm not like you I don't need to jump from Rick to Nick, just to get Dick."

"Ooh, I heard that!" Maya agreed, not meaning to take sides.

Selina still was too shocked to move.

"Now that Alycia got me started, I might as well tell y'all the rest."

"Oh no!" They all sang.

"Lance asked me to marry him."

"Me too!" Maya shouted.

"Lance asked you too?" Alycia scream.

"Alycia, do me a favor, don't order anymore to drink, okay."

Selina and Alycia sat and watched pitifully while Maya and Roz hug, kiss, dance and sing.

"We're getting married! We're getting married!"

"Will you two nuts sit down" Selina barked. "So, I guess that was the news you had to tell us, huh Maya?" Selina said not hiding her disappointment.

"Yup. Gary asked me the night before I left. At first I was scared, I told him no. But then we made love and honey, I took a U-turn and said yes. You know how I love Gary."

Selina rolled her eyes, and then said. "Okay mommy, tell us your story."

"Well, once upon a time there was this big dick . . . and the big."

"Never mind, Maya just told us that story." Selina noted still rolling her eyes.

"I'm just playing Lance had been asking me to marry him for months now. I kept telling him that I wasn't the marrying type and that he didn't know what he was getting himself into. When I found out that I was pregnant, I didn't tell him about the baby right away, because I knew that he was going to feel that we had to be married. So that weekend we went to the mountains, I prepared everything story book style and waited for him to ask me the way I always dreamt I would be asked. And he did, and I accepted. A week later I told him about the baby."

"Wow," Alycia sighed, fantasizing that this was her and Jeff's story.

"Guess what else I did?"

"What?"

"I made a video tape."

"You didn't?"

"Yes I did, from the moment he walked into the cabin, he was being taped. I would let y'all watch it one day but it's X-rated. That tape caught more than I wanted it to."

"Oh, that is so romantic, a 'before' tape." Alycia wanted the same for her and Jeff.

"Roz that was really smart. I just love the thought. I wonder if Gary would be game for something like that."

"Girl, you can't let him know until it's done. I don't think Lance would have been as sexy as he was, if he knew he was being filmed. He would have been all nervous and smiling at the camera. But I caught him in a natural state. Butt naked. We watched it again last night. Y'all should have seen the way he blushed. He got up, clapped, cheered and whistled like he was watching a football game or something. Of course he was cheering himself on for what he calls three touchdowns and one assist. Then he made a crack about how the woman in the video was feeling the next day. Of course I assured him that the woman was a little sore but, was able to play as much football as the man liked." They all laughed.

"Go Roz!"

"So you're having a little baby, awhhh. When are you due?

"The baby is due the first of May."

"Awhh, a spring baby."

"Maya's getting married, Roz is having a baby and getting married, and Selina is out of the closet. Everybody has something going on but me."

"Now, now Alycia, don't start tripping, you could be getting married if you wanted to, shit, I know you know what to do to have a baby."

"That's right, leave that married dog alone and get your own man."

"Jeff is not married and I love dogs, thank you very much. Besides I love Jeff, I don't want anyone else, is that so hard to understand? Jeff has it going on. He satisfies me like no man ever has. The fact that he has a daughter and a piece of a woman is not enough reason for me to leave him alone. When he says that it's over then I'll stop, but only when he says so!"

The women looked at each other, shocked by Alycia's tone. She's drunk, they all decided silently.

"So you don't mind sharing him?"

"I'm not sharing him. They live together but, they don't sleep in the same room."

"Alycia!" the three women groaned. "Girl wake up, Jeff is using you. You just said that he was a dog, now you expect us to believe that this dog sleeps in the same apartment with this pretty woman and never asks to touch? Be realistic. He is having his cake and eating it too."

"I don't care! He satisfies me! Don't y'all get it! He turns me on and then out! It's Jeff that I think about 24-7! Now if he's using me, then all I can say is thank-you Lord, this kind of abuse, I love."

"She's sick." Selina said blowing air out of her mouth and rolling her eyes away from Alycia.

"Sick? I know you're not talking Selina, you can't even decide which one you want to . . ."

"Drunk or not, you're going to pay for that remark."

"Ladies, ladies," Roz jumped in before it was too late. "Come on now, this is supposed to be a happy occasion. What's good for one is simply not good for the other and there's nothing wrong with that. We're sisters and we have to stay true to that. So what if she loves a man that has someone else, if he has someone else, and so what if she loves men and women. Who really cares?"

Alycia and Selina still appeared to be upset. So Maya added what she could.

"I care. I care whether or not you are happy or in pain. The two of you are long time friends of mine. I love you both like sisters and you both know that. I can't pick and choose what's right for you, only you can do that. But I do care. Whatever makes you happy makes me happy, so don't be upset with each other, it's not worth it. We all have different needs."

"Maya, you're right. Alycia, I'm sorry for saying that you were sick, I guess we're all a little sick sometimes."

"No, forgive me for joking about your preference. Life is about choices. Let's forget it and order some food."

"Now that's a good choice!" Roz concluded.

Now that everything was cool again, Maya wanted to giggle more about her and Roz's good fortune.

"Roz, I can't believe this, who would have ever thought that we would have met husbands and daddies at that club two years ago?"

"Two years, four months, sixteen days." Roz corrected her.

"Well, excuse me!"

"This calls for a toast." Alycia said.

"Here's to love and happiness."

Clink.

Double trouble

"C'mon Gary, please let me stay." Dice pleaded.

"Why should I? You deserve to live on the streets after what you did. I don't feel sorry for you."

"Damn, Gary, I don't need this shit from you, you act worse than Queetha. Fuck you!"

"That's right curse me out because of your mistake. I don't care. I told you months ago that this cheating mess was going to catch up with you."

"Man, what did you expect me to do? I fell in love."

"You already had someone to love. Why would you chance falling in love again?"

"Look Gary, I don't know how you see it, but the way I see it, you get what you give. Queetha don't love me, I really don't think she ever did. Argue! Argue! Argue! That's all she wants to do. She treats me like shit. She won't even let me feel like a man in my own home. Yeah, it could have come out in a better way, but fuck it! Fuck Queetha!"

"Just listen to you. How long are you going to pretend it doesn't hurt? Your walking around here like you did nothing wrong. You got your wife and your lover pregnant at the same time. I don't feel sorry for you, I feel sorry for them. They're the ones that will have to carry the babies for nine months. They're the ones that will have to wake up in the middle of the night for feedings and changing. What will you be doing? Let me guess working on a new woman."

"You're wrong Gary I plan to be there for my babies. And please, don't worry about Queetha, she filed for support the morning after the bust. You should have seen her she was smiling and gloating like she just won the lotto or something. The situation couldn't have been more perfect for her. She was dying for another baby, but she didn't want to make love. Every time I touched her she would snatch her body from me and roll her eyes like she hated my guts. It wasn't until I started loving Sharice that Queetha saw something she wanted in me. I would come home beat tired from getting my Jimmy waxed by Sharice and Queetha would be in the bed waiting for me. I mean, my girl would be butt naked. I would try to play it off for about an hour, eating dinner, then reading something I wasn't interested in. I would even turn on the TV. Man it takes a while to build up your strength from Sharice, plus I had to act like I hadn't had it in months. Shit, that was a job. But you know me, I'm greedy. Queetha was giving it up, I was taking it. Having the two of them back to back made me horny as hell. Man I surprised myself. I played it smooth though -- I would get in the bed and turn my back to her, because her back was always to me. Then I would feel her hands on my ass. Then she would call my name. *Dice man,* she would say in that voice I don't hear often. I knew what she wanted, but I would ignore her until she climbed on top of me. I would let her do her thing until she demanded that I do mine. Again, I would play it off doing easy shit like tasting her body all over. I even got away with giving her a passion mark on her thigh last time."

"So you think that's enough reason to be careless with both of them? You knew Queetha wanted a child. What about Sharice, did she want one too?"

"Sharice wants me. Having my child would be like having me, those were her exact words after she fount out she was pregnant. Man, you know I don't believe in abortions, but Man I have to admit, when Sharice first told me she was pregnant, I thought about asking her not to keep it. I was so scared that Queetha was going to kill me."

"So that's why you've waited six months before letting Queetha know."

"Let her know? Man if it was up to me, Queetha would have never known. I told Queetha that I would take her baby-shopping Saturday morning over in Jersey. Just so happened Sharice wanted to go to the same mall in Jersey. Middle Creek or something, anyway, I told Sharice I would take her Friday night when I got in from work. Well, we drove over there, and you know Sharice, she's all happy and lubby dubby, she has my hand and she's pointing at cribs and things. She's all dressed in her soft pink maternity jumpsuit looking like she's eight months instead of six. And you know me, I'm chilling, she's carrying my baby and she's looking fine, everything is merry. Well, we get in the store and go to the back to check out the crib she saw in the window and who is checking out the same crib but Queetha and her mother. Man, I liked to pass out. The first thing Queetha did was look down at our hands then she aimed for my balls. Sharice started screaming, and then Queetha tried to choke her. Man you talk about belly dancing. Queetha and Sharice were at it. I was scared to take either side, so I pushed Queetha's mother in between them. She broke her glasses, lost her wig and popped her bra. Man, I was never so glad to see a police officer in my life. They broke up the three women and escorted Queetha and her mother to their car. Sharice wasn't mad at me, she just cried for about two hours. She said that she was disappointed that I didn't tell her that Queetha was pregnant too."

"Man its amazing that you're still alive -- two pregnant women fighting over your sorry ass."

"Like I said before, Queetha is happy. All she wanted from me was my seed and my money. She don't want a man -- she's too busy trying to be the man."

"What about Sharice? What are you going to do about her?"

"Sharice, now that's my baby. I'm going to take care of her. Man, that's my future wife. You know what she calls me?" Dice said smiling. "She calls me Daddy. I'm telling you Gary, she makes me feel like a king. I mean she's just a beautiful, sweet, loving person. I love that girl. I'd do anything for her."

"Please, you've done enough."

"Look, I'm not asking for much, all I'm asking is for you to understand. You don't have to let me move in, just understand. Imagine being treated like you wasn't worth a dime, and then someone comes along and treats you like you're worth a zillion dimes. Can you imagine that? Sharice makes me feel like I can do anything. She talks to me and tells me what she likes and what she doesn't. Man, that's beautiful, and it has nothing to do with a new relationship, Queetha was never rewarding like Sharice."

"Dice you don't want to remember. You said those same things about Queetha when you first fell in love with her. Don't you think that Sharice is going to turn into the nagging, arguing wife just like Queetha?"

"Hell no! Nobody can be like Queetha, she's too selfish. Everything has to be adjusted to her liking, which is impossible. I learned a lot about love being married to Queetha. Love is not selfish or demanding. It's free. But as long as you're with Queetha, you're gonna have to pay a price. You're gonna have to be stepped on and lonely."

"But wait a minute Dice, isn't Sharice already married?"

"Yeah, she's still married to Queetha's brother."

"Queetha's brother?!"

"That's what we call him because their descriptions are so much alike. It's like their twins."

"She's still married and she's having your baby?"

"Well, he's not around, hasn't been for about fourteen months now."

"Fourteen months? Where is he, in jail?"

"Yep."

"For what?"

"Trying to make a dollar out of fifteen cents."

"What?"

"All I know is that he robbed the wrong person. A judge or somebody, him and another guy, they broke into one of those fancy houses up there on the hill. The other guy had a gun, shot the judge's daughter. I don't think we'll be seeing him around anytime soon."

"Does he know that Sharice is pregnant?"

"Yep. I went with her to the jail house last month to tell him. I wanted to make sure she was showing when she saw him, to let him know that it's really over. He was cool, shook my hand and asked me to take care of her. He told me that he didn't love her. She was too simple for him. Then he told me to get her to divorce him so that he could take her name off the visiting list. He said that his girlfriend wants to come and have those visits where they could have sex, but she can't until Sharice's name is off the list."

"So is Sharice going to do it?"

"Man, haven't you been listening, I told you she's having my baby, and she wants me. The papers were in the works before she conceived my child."

"So are you going to divorce Queetha?"

"Gary you haven't heard a word I said. Where do you think Queetha went when her and her moms got in that car? Straight to our lawyer's office. She didn't think twice about what she was going to do. You know how some women go through the crying stages first? Not Queetha. No she didn't waste not even a minute. Divorce is not a choice for me it's another order from the evil Queetha that must be filled. But that doesn't matter. All I want is to be able to see my kids. These next couple of months I have to watch my step, I don't want Queetha to try to set me up on some bullshit charges so that I can't see my kids."

"Man, I don't think you have to worry about that, she wouldn't deprive the kids from seeing their father."

"Yeah okay, keep believing that. Oh yeah, I almost forgot, I want you to be the children's godfather."

"The children's Godfather? I'm already your damn godfather, get out here."

"No Man, I'm serious. Queetha is going to have another girl and my sweet Sharice, she'll probably have my first son."

"How do you know that Queetha is having a girl?"

"Because I want a boy, whatever I want I don't get with Queetha."

"Tell me something, is the day ever going to come when you don't need me for something?"

"I doubt it." Dice laughed shaking Gary's hand to thank him for saying yes.

Just beep me

It was dark as Alycia climbed up to her attic apartment.

"Damn, another light shot out." she cursed.

Still tipsy from all the drinks she had with the girls, plus feeling down about all the good news they had to share. Alycia dreaded opening the door to her clean, empty apartment. How come she wasn't getting married? Where was her proposal? She sat on the top stair in the dark and began to weep. She touched the nail that stuck out from the stair and remembered how her knees had pressed against it when Jeff had made love to her. She'd missed Jeff and wanted his body against hers. Thinking about the fight they had, she kept telling herself that Jeff was wrong, that she would never call him again because he was wrong. Then she cried harder. She couldn't help the way she felt, she wanted him. She wasn't ready for it to be over, it was too soon. She hadn't gotten enough of him. *So what, he had a bad night and took it out on me. He didn't mean to. It was the liquor, that guy, Cheryl. It had nothing to do with me. He misses me too. He wants to come back but he thinks that I would never forgive him. Yeah, that's why he hasn't called. He thinks that his apology would not be accepted.*

After convincing herself that Jeff was dying to be with her, Alycia got up feeling a little better. *He just needs a little push.* She opened the door and grabbed the phone. The glow of green light from the touch-tone phone was the only light in the house. She dialed his beeper number and left her number with a 911 code on the end, praying that he would return her call. Ten minutes after the phone didn't ring she beeped him again, this time putting in a code 69 on the end. Sure that he would return her call, Alycia kicked off her shoes and sat on her bed waiting for the phone to ring. When she woke up it was the 7:30 in the morning and the birds were outside chirping about the new day.

"That motherfucker!" Alycia cried out, throwing the phone against the wall. "I don't give a fuck. I'm going to get in touch with him if I have to go to Cheryl's!"

Alycia began snatching off yesterday's clothes and plugging up her curling iron.

"That motherfucker is going to confront me today!"

She opened her closet and yanked out a sporty outfit and stomped into the bathroom to start her shower.

"He just don't know, he's going to give me what I want! Not answering my beep like I was just another whore. Fuck that! I will go on the basketball court, his momma's wherever I have to, to get his ass back in this bed!"

Instead of taking a two-minute, splash shower like she planned, Alycia stayed in the shower for close to an hour accepting the soft, warm, water as her refuge. With a slight hangover she closed her eyes and kneeled down letting the water drench her thoroughly as if to wash away her pain. When she returned out of the shower, she found a newly burnt spot on her outfit that she had set out to wear. She was so upset with Jeff that she was careless and left the curler on high and placed it right on top of her outfit.

"Damn!" she cried. "The motherfucker's got me loosing my mind." Then she fell to the floor and cried out. "Why am I doing this to myself? What's wrong with me? Why can't I let go, and forget about him?"

Just as she was about to continue feeling sorry for herself, the phone rang.

"That's him!" she hollered. "He couldn't call me last night he wants to come over now!"

Tripping over the curling iron cord she fell, still reaching the phone.

"Hello!"

"Sorry, it's just me. I'm on my way to do laundry. Coming?"

"Roz?"

"Yeah, who were you expecting?"

"No, you told me you were going to call. Give me ten minutes and I'll be down with my load."

"See ya in ten."

Alycia placed the receiver down and headed for the hamper.

"That's it! No more crying over that tired motherfucker. It's over, it's over! Who needs him?" Inspecting herself in the full length mirror on the bathroom door, Alycia realized that she was a ten. Then she decided maybe an eight, definitely, a seven and a half.

"Look at these curves, not a blotch on my face and teeth too pretty to eat with. Hell, I can get any man I want." She pulled out her white sneakers and light blue sweat suit and said, "Go get 'em girl!" Just as she was about to put the bottle of bleach in the laundry bag, the phone rang.

"I'm going to kill Roz if she's fucking around with Lance again and wants to come later. -- What is it now, Roz?"

"Yo! This is Jeff, you beeped me?"

Alycia was stunned. She didn't know whether to scream YES! I beeped you or to say NO motherfucker I didn't beep your ass! Click.

"Yes, I beeped you."

"What do you want?"

"That was last night. I was going to invite you over."

"I'll be right there." Click.

"Jeff is on his way, Jeff is on his way!" Alycia rambled on. "Oh shit. Jeff is on his way! First let me clean up, no, I got to call Roz. Oh, Jeff is on his way!"

After canceling the laundry date, Alycia took off her clothes and put on her mint green teddy with the g-string back. Then she slipped on her sexy anklet and sprayed extra perfume on the insides of her thighs. Out of nervousness, she re-brushed her teeth and changed the sheet on her bed. The house stayed spotless but she vacuumed and sprayed just to make sure it smelled fresh when he came in.

After three hours of peeking out the window and thinking she heard her bell ring, Alycia turned off Soul Train, put her sweat suit back on and headed for the Laundromat.

That's him

"You're still here?"

"I just got here. After you said that you weren't coming, well, let's just say I found something else to do."

"I thought I heard his voice in the background when you first called."

"Yeah, he was home."

"Home?"

"Yes home. My place is his home and his is mine. I can't wait until we get rid of one, most likely it'll be mine."

"Why yours?"

"Well, actually we're getting rid of both, but were going to stay in his until our house is ready."

"Oh." Alycia said closing the subject, unable to handle more good news that didn't include her.

Roz sensed the jealousy and glowed inside. She did feel sorry for Alycia but not as much as she felt happy for herself.

"Alycia," Roz whispered. "Isn't that that fag?"

"What fag?"

"Not so loud, don't look now but the guy behind you is that fag that was messing with Tyrone's friend."

"Who's Tyrone?"

"You know, Maya's friend." she whispered making eye signs.

"Oh, that's Dane." Alycia returned the whisper. "Maya told me that he works in the salon across the street. Yeah, that's him, ooh, he's a stone fag."

"Oh my goodness, you're right. Elllk! He's a screaming fag. Elllk! Why would anyone want to sleep with that?"

"Look at those lips, there so damn big."

"No, it's the hair, look at it -- it's so . . . so . . ."

"Yellow?! Nobody has hair that color. You're right who'd want to sleep with him, uugh!"

"What does he do at that salon? Wash the towels?"

"No girl, I heard that he is the best stylist they have."

"Well you know that's a lie, the best wouldn't have time to come in here and wash out his outfit for tonight. Can you believe it, coming in here with two items: a shirt and a pair of pants?"

"I didn't see any pants. I saw a shirt and a skirt."

"Roz, you know you can lie." Alycia laughed.

"It's called exaggerating. I like exaggerating."

"Sssh, ssh, he's talking to the Laundromat lady."

"Honey, excuse me Honey, I have to go back to work, I have somebody under the dryer. Don't let anybody steal my clothes. Okaaay! I'll be back in twenty minutes, Okaaay." Selina and Roz heard the ugly woman's voice come out of his mouth, then watched as he threw the Chinese woman a kiss.

"Why did he throw her a kiss, who does he think he is, Zsa Zsa Gabor?"

"I don't know, but I remember Maya saying that he's always throwing kisses at everyone. I guess it's a big lip thing." Roz laughed. "So why are you here, I thought you said you were having a morning fling?"

"Jeff called to re-schedule, something about picking up a friend from the airport."

"Oh." Roz said, so that Alycia wouldn't have to continue her lie.

Back together

"It's eleven-thirty, when are you going to wake up sleepy?"

"Eleven-thirty?" Tyrone yarned. "I got up about nine but you were gone. Where did you go so early?"

"I called Dr. Gibbs at eight, he told me to come right over."

"Oh." Tyrone said shocked, he had forgotten all about Wesley going to take the AIDS test.

"What do you want to do today?"

"You know what I want to do. First I want to shop and then shop some more and then shop again."

"I made us an appointment with Ralph to get our hair cut. And I stopped at the travel agency and brought back some brochures for us to decide on where we want to take our celebration trip."

"Trip? Wes, I agree, we have a lot to celebrate, but I would prefer if we celebrated right here in our new home. I want everyone who doubted your love for me to see us now. I want to invite about forty of our closest friends and ten of our not so close friends. I want to make them sick. And please don't let me forget to invite Ramone, can you imagine the look on his face when he sees what you have done? Remember how he bragged about hitting the number that time. I think he won about $30,000. For weeks he walked around tipping everybody. Moved his tacky shit into the York Towne Houses and got kicked out a year later. He was a fool, didn't invest not one single dime. You know he tried to persuade me to come stay with him. Can you imagine that? And let me tell you about Nelson, his silly behind had the nerve to ask me to go out with him for drinks. Yuck! I would die first."

"That's what I don't understand, why would you want to invite them into our home? This is a new start for us. I don't want to confuse things by stirring up things with them. Jealousy can be dangerous."

"I'm not trying to stir up anything. Do you think I was jealous of Dane? Never! I was embarrassed for the two of us. The gossip about you and It tore me apart. They were saying all kinds of ugly things about you. It was said that Dane was using you. She made a bet that she could control you and she did. One night I went to Booties to try and ease away some of the pain and I heard Harold and Tommy talking about you and Dane. They said that she had you whipped. They laughed at me and said that it was evident that I didn't have the right tools for the job. That shit pushed me over the edge. I couldn't take it anymore. I wanted to fight. Carl asked me to leave the bar. He said that I was drunk and hallucinating, that no one had mentioned my name. I felt so betrayed. Carl had been my friend for years. Why didn't he ask Harold and Tommy to leave?" Tyrone stopped there not able to talk about the two suicide attempts that he and God only knew about.

"I don't know, but if you feel that it's important for you to invite them here, fine. I'll do anything to let you know that I regret what I did. Just name it."

"Then it's settled, the party will be at the end of this month. I have seventeen days to prepare. Now what about breakfast? Did you eat? I'm in the mood for some buttery croissants."

"I thought you would be. There's a half dozen in the breakfast nook waiting for you. You're going to love the food The Beverly kitchen prepares. They have the best of everything. French, Italian, Caribbean, Thai, you name it, they have it. The two nights I was here setting up everything for you, I ordered lunch and dinner. The rice, the salad, the meats and the sauces are all delicious. Their bakery, they have the best pastries and breads. Umm. What's nice about The Beverly is that everything is included. We can order breakfast, lunch and dinner 24 hours a day. If were having guests over, they will come up and cater it for us. They do our dry cleaning and laundry. They come up and clean the apartment daily. They even have car maintenance downstairs, the cars stays cleaned and shined."

"Yes, sounds like we're in the right place! Last night when I went to sleep, I took a long look around this room and convinced myself that I was dreaming. I said no way could this be true. It's still hard for me to absorb. You sold your designs and now we're living well. How could you stand it? This kind of money doesn't fall into anyone lap, Wes, you're gifted!"

"Thanks. But, I still say that I would have never known it if it wasn't for you. When I made those designs, I thought they were good, I liked them a lot. But when you saw them, you flipped. You told me that they were the ones that would change my life. You're the gifted one. You have a good eye. You're the reason I went to Bakari, you said that they would buy it in a second and they did. You should be as proud of yourself as much as you are of me."

Tyrone smiled, he was so happy to be with Wesley again, to be with his man. Their conversation was just like old times, battling over who was the gifted one.

"Why the smile? What are you thinking about?" Wesley asked, puzzled about the look on Tyrone's face.

"Nothing just thinking about what I'll wear today."

Give me some shuga

"Sho' nuff, dat gal come round heah lookin' for ya. Said she wants to see ya."

"I wonder what she wants, it's been years now, don't tell me she finally got out de closet." Trudy pretended not to be happy about the news.

"I doubt it. She was just as scared of me as she ever was. I was juss tryin' ta be nice and invite ha in for somedin' ta drink. She got all scary and dissapeered lak I was gonna eat ha or somedin. Hee-hee."

"Did she leave her number?"

"Naw, dat chile ain't leabe nothdin'. Tolcha she was a-scared. Where's frog eyes today? How come she not heah witcha? Ya a-scared I might laff and make ya shame? Or is it dat you two mad?"

"I wouldn't say mad. Aunt Moody you know how it is when you are just putting time in with someone?"

"No. Da only time I put in is da time I wants ta."

"Well, I don't want to be there, I ain't feeling her like that anymore."

"Anymore my ass, ya neber did want ha. You was juss greedy, ya knew she would eat ya toenails if ya asked ha to and dats why you went wid ha, ta git ebee ding you could git from ha. Ya dink I don't know ya by now? Dat chile Selina is da only one you eber did love. Well make dat me and Selina. Hee-hee. When ya come strollin' home wid dat white heffa I said to mysef: she eider is a good coochie eader or got money. She look lak da type to do boff. Much as I lub me somebody dat knows what dey doing, dey hasta look bedda dan dat ding ya had. Um hmm, I refuse to let anyding uglayier dan my coochie, eat my coochie. Hee-hee. Dat is sure an uglay chile."

Trudy laughed with her aunt.

"It's true, some mornings she scares me half to death. I'll be clearing the sleep out of my eyes and the sight of her makes me jump and scream. She wears mud packs every night and shaves her arms and legs every morning. Always asking me why I'm making faces at her."

"You shoulda toll ha, cause ya so damn uglay, dat's why. Dat is the uglayiest chile I hab eber seen. I toll Selina too. I toll her all about your uglay heffa."

"What she say?"

"Not much, she juss look at me like I belong in da circus. Heck I dought she wanted me, she was staring so hard. Anyway she'll be back. I see it in her eyes."

Trudy wanted Aunt Moody to be right, she wanted Selina to come back. Selina was the real love of her life. Her best times were with Selina. *How could I have let her go?* Trudy asked her heart.

"True, are ya lisnin' dat chile'll be back for ya. Now come on up heah and give ya Aunt Moody some shuga."

Watch your mouth

"You lying! For real? No, you lying! I love it! Are you certain? Honey, if you were a man I would kiss you." Dane said hugging the pitiful looking patron that looked more like a patient. "Who told you?"

"My brother."

"Your brother? I don't think I've ever met him, I mean I didn't know you had a brother that was . . . " Dane cleared his throat. "Friends with my friends."

"So! Mr. Jones has big dollars and is living in The Beverly, I did a job there once." He reminisced for a second then dropped the subject when the patron didn't quite understand and requested a house call visit for her grandmother.

"Mmmm, he does have money if they moved into The Beverly. It just kills me that Wesley is such a pussy, going back to that tired Tyrone. And planning a party no less, well that's yet to be seen. You see, I'm planning a party too, the only difference is mine will be in court, and of course Wesley's invited."

"Huh?"

"That's right! Wesley Jones will split his little fortune with me whether he likes it or not. I will tell the court that he gave me the ultimate package."

"What'd he give you?"

"Don't make me spell it out E.T."

"Now Dane, I told you before don't nobody should ever call me that."

"That's what your family calls you."

"I know, but I don't want ever you calling me that. What package did Wesley give you, a gift?"

Dane asked himself. How could anyone be this pitiful?

"I've got the package, the virus, AIDS."

"You've got AIDS!" Edith asked with a scowl on her face and eyes stretched.

"Who don't?" Dane replied turning his lips up and staring at Edith as she crawled out of his chair. "Go ahead run," he pointed at her. "That won't save you. Most likely it's too late!" he continued at her as she stumbled to the door. Its to late E.T., you should have thought about running instead of kicking your bony, ashy legs up for all of those closet men that had me."

"I hate you Dane!" she said like she was using her last breath.

"Tell me something I don't want to hear, you smelly fish bitch." he laughed, signaling for his next customer.

"Dane! What in the world is wrong with you? Why did you turn on Edith like that? Boy don't you know she's been coming here for years?"

"And she still looks like shit." Dane said cleaning off his work station, barely paying Sarah any attention."

"Look Dane, every since you broke up with that man, you've been acting crazy, I think he knocked you in the head once too many."

"I'm glad you said that, because I've decided to take his ass to court. That's right, that motherfucker just came into some real money and I plan to get mine. Who does he think he is, planning a party and not inviting me? I hope he doesn't think he's going to make a fool out of me, cause he just don't know Dane always gets the last laugh. Ha!" he laughed in Sarah face.

"Oh Lord!" Sarah closed her eyes and asked Jesus for help.

"Call him all you want, its not going to change my mind. I'm going to take his ass to court and I'm not doing another fucking head until I do."

"Wait a minute Dane. Next week is Palm Sunday and you know how busy it is on Easter, don't do this to me. I've always treated you right."

"Yeah, you have, but I never liked your ass. I can't stand the way you're always staring at me and the minute I turn my back you're nudging one of your customers. Fuck you Sarah, this shop ain't shit without me and you know it! So don't give me that I've always treated you right bullshit. And another thing, even though I've made good money here, I've stolen from your ass left and right. That's right bitch, I took money out of the drawer every time I felt like it. I did all the boys hair for free and I over charged all your ugly dog looking friends, you know the ones I'm talking about, the ones that look like you. Now tell me, do you still want me to stay?"

Sarah didn't move but her hands began shaking, she stared at Dane with a chill in her eyes, cold enough to kill him.

"I asked you a question, Grandma, do you still want me to stay?" Dane pranced around the shop stuffing items in his bag that did and did not belong to him. "You don't mind if I take a few extras, do you Granny?" He giggled, wiggled and winked his eye at her then grabbed his cashbox and headed for the door.

Before she knew it Sarah had taken the smoking hot curling iron and pressed it across the back of Dane's neck. Dane scream was loud and piercing and then he flipped around quickly and caught the iron right on his face.

"Help!" He screamed. Get me some water, some Dax, something to cool my skin, hurry, somebody help." No one moved so Dane ran to the shampoo bowl and let the cold water run on the throbbing burns.

With curler still in hand, Sarah walked over to her sink and said, "Get the H out of my salon!"

"Sarah cut it out, I'm hurting, call an ambulance, get me some Dax to soothe this burn, do something, my skin is burning!" Dane cried in unbearable pain.

"I said get out!" she threatened with the smoking curler.

The row of gray haired women seated on the side of wall, just watched in awe with their purses clutched to their hearts as Dane crawl his way out of the shop.

"You're gonna pay for this Bitch. I swear you gonna pay." Dane declared.

"He got what he deserved!" One woman bravely stood up and said.

"Yeah, who do that chile think he is calling somebody a dog? Sarah chile, you was nice, you coulda burned his you know what. That's what I woulda done."

All the women agreed like they were in church agreeing with the preacher. Another woman got up and said something funny, but before the women could get out a good laugh, they heard the glass crashing down. It was Dane. He had gotten his baseball bat out of the trunk of his car and was smashing all of the salon windows.

"You're next bitch!" He said charging at Sarah thru the broken glass. Sarah was scared. She hadn't stopped shaking since he called her out of her name the first time.

"Boy, I know you ready to die now." she said with no weapon within reach. When Dane went to swing the bat at Sarah, the woman who said she would have burned his thing grabbed his burnt neck and squeezed it until he dropped. Sarah wrestled to snatch the bat out of his hand then she stood over him in a threatening way.

"Boy, she just saved your life, cause if you woulda hit me, you'd betta hada kilt me, cause son, you was only going get one hit, the rest woulda been mine." The woman cheered another Amen.

Dane stay on the floor as still as he could, then as if he had just awakened from a deep spell he questioned himself, why is my Sarah standing over me with a bat? Then he broke out into a passionate cry.

"I'm sorry Sarah, I love you like a mother. You know I do. I don't know why I said all those horrible things to you I didn't mean any of them. I swear I didn't. Please Sarah help me, I need help. I don't want to lose you, forgive me. Please Sarah, forgive me."

Sarah studied Dane for a moment then said.

"Dane, I'ma tell you straight, I would never, ever, forgive you for what you did to me and to my place. When the police get here I want you to leave and never come back, you hear me? I mean never come back. I haven't been this mad since I don't know when. I don't believe in people saying things and not meaning what they say. You meant everything you said. I don't know why you feel that way, but you meant it. I know I'm not the best person on earth, but I took you in when you was just fourteen, I let you sweep up and then when you turned sixteen and showed me you could curl that mannequin's head, I let you shampoo. Yeah, you're the star of this salon, but that's with your friends and some of the younger people. Most people come to Sarah's for Sarah. I had this salon for thirty-four years you've just been here a little more than nine. Nobody else would have given you the chance I gave you. Yeah, I found out about your ways, but hey, *to each his own*. Who am I to put you down? My main concern was this here salon. And that's going to be my last concern. That's right, I will die for this salon. And tonight you made me feel that I might have to. So, there's no way I could ever forgive you. No. No way."

"Sarah the police is here." One of the women announced.

"Took 'em long enough. Bye Dane, good luck with your life, and don't forget what I told you. Don't come back here no more."

"I'm sorry, Sarah." Dane said turning back as the police escorted him out the door.

After the police pulled off, Sarah fell into the arms of one of her friends.

"Oh Lord, I was so scared." she cried.

"You did good. You know the Lord would never put more on you than you can bear."

"I love that boy like he was my own chile. Lord why, why did he have to go fool and turn on me?"

The crowd outside of Sarah's took a while to break up. Everyone from the area stood around the broken glass. Roz and Alycia ran out of the Laundromat and went across the street to find out what was going on.

"What happened?" Roz asked a girl that was telling the story to everyone.

"I'm not sure, but something about him quitting his job at the salon and the owner burning his face with a hot iron to keep him to stay."

"No that's not what happened." Another woman offered. "I've known Sarah for years, she just found out that her son was gay and told him to leave. He wouldn't, so she burned him.

What? Why was he quitting, I thought he was famous here, isn't he suppose to be the best?"

"I don't know about all of that, all I heard was something about his boyfriend has a lot of money and he's suing him for half of it. That's why he was leaving, cause he got money. I think."

"Alycia, did you hear that?" Roz whispered, grabbing Alycia by the collar forcing her to walk away from the crowd. "They're talking about Tyrone's friend he's the one with the money."

"Get off of my neck. Of course I know who they're talking about. Poor Maya, she might as well pack her bags, looks like she'll be going on another trip soon."

The letter

"Phone bill, light bill, credit card bill, church newsletter, BodyWorks Magazine, travel brochure, sales circular, newspaper -- same junk, different day." Selina complained as she collected her mail off the lobby floor.

"What's in this green envelope with no return address, I bet its one of those chain letters, I hate them." Selina carelessly ripped into the envelope tearing the letter.

Dear Selina,

How are you? I couldn't be happier.

Aunt Moo told me that you came by the house asking for me. Is everything alright? She also told me that she told you about my new friend -- Trish.

How's life treating you? Right now my life is very hectic and crazy. I've just got laid off from my job, but Trish has me involved in all sorts of things I never thought about being involved in.

I'm going to be in your neighborhood Monday night. I have to pick up some Opera tickets for Trish. I plan to stop by, if you're not home, I'll understand.

Trudy

Selina balled up the letter and threw it on the floor.

"Bullshit letter, what was I suppose to get out of that? Who cares if she going to be in the neighborhood tomorrow night? I got a wrestling class. Sending me a letter telling me that she's very happy, she knows the rule: if you're happy you don't have to say it. She could have just ignored the fact that I came by looking for her. She could at least let me come by two or three times before she had to write me about how happy she is. Opera tickets -- next she'll be buying slaves."

I hate to brag

"Is it all that he said it was?"

"Yes girl, wait until you see it, you are going to scream."

"Oh Tyrone, when we were coming home on the plane I have to admit I felt so sorry for you. I just knew that Wesley was still involved with what's his name and that you would have to just start all over."

"Me too."

"What took you so long to call me?"

"If you would have seen the way Gary cut his eye at me at the airport, you would know why. I could tell he wanted a few days of uninterrupted time with you and I can't blame him. So I wanted to give you a breather before I called bragging about everything. I'm surprise he's not there now. You know he told Wes how he feels about you and although he didn't say it, I could tell our friendship has really put a strain on him."

"It has but, you know what I've been through in the past. I'm glad that I had an opportunity to find out where he really is and he's proven to be right where I want and need him to be. We partied from the minute I placed my foot on the floor. But about two o'clock this morning there was an emergency and his job beeped him, he just got in a little over two hours now. I fed him, gave him some more lovin' and now he's out. I plan to go get my hair washed and my nails done while he sleeps."

"Sounds rewarding, you got a pen? Take my number down. In case Gary gets called this weekend in the day time we can do lunch or something."

"Why this weekend, aren't you going to work Monday?"

"Monday? Girl I never plan to go back. Didn't I tell you? Wes and I are starting our own design studio. That's my new job. He designs and I get paid. Doesn't it sound lovely? You know how much I hated working for Maude. The only thing about that job that I liked was meeting with you once a month and now we can meet as much as we please."

"Now Tyrone, I know that you are all excited and everything but what if something goes wrong?"

"Like what?"

"I don't know but I don't like the fact that you're depending on someone else's money. I mean, what happens when you two fight? Is he going to snatch back all of his gifts and goodies?"

"Maya, Maya, Maya, girl you know I wasn't born yesterday, before I showed off these teeth, I made sure he fattened my savings account. Honey, the teller looked at us like what bank did you two rob? Yes, Wes made sure that I had six figures in my account. Plus we have a handsome joint account."

"Whaat? Tyrone, is there anything else? First, The Beverly, then the car, the wardrobe, jewelry and now bank accounts. Wesley must have really gotten paid a lot."

"He did. Speaking of the devil, here he comes now, let me go I don't want him to know that I'm bragging about him, I'm still playing hard to get."

"Oh okay, I'll call you soon."

Maya hung up the phone happy, talking to Tyrone made her feel like she got all the things he received. Then the phone rang again.

"Hello."

"Maya! Guess what just happened!"

"Hey Roz."

"Maya you are going to fall out when we tell you what just happened."

"Alycia? What, another three-way call?"

"Yeah, anyway guess what happened."

"I don't know. What happened?"

"Your friend's friend was just in a fight at the salon."

"Slow down, what friend's friend."

"The fags." Alycia blurted out.

"What?!"

"Tyrone's boyfriend's lover just had a fight with the owner of the salon and was taken away by the police."

"Dane?"

"Yeah, that was the name on everyone's lips."

"He started acting wild, he was kicking people out of the salon and calling them names so when the owner questioned him, he went off on her."

"Why was he throwing people out of the salon?"

"That's the juicy part. He heard about Tyrone's friend's money and said that he was going to take him to court for half."

"On what grounds?"

"You tell her Roz."

"Tell me what? Will you two get on with the story? Roz, I can't hear you, speak up."

"I said Dane is going around telling people that Wesley gave him AIDS."

"No!"

"Yes."

"Oh my goodness, Tyrone just told me that Wesley was interested in taking the test. Oh I hope it's not true."

"I don't know girl but he had a crowd down there listening and taking in every word he said. He said that he wants half of Wesley's money and that he was willing to drag him through the mud to get it."

"Please don't let this be happening, I can't go through this again with Tyrone."

"That's what we we're thinking."

After the girls had spoiled Maya's afternoon, she decided not to leave the house. She wanted to call Tyrone and warn him about the threats that Dane had made against Wesley and also to warn him not to have sex just yet, if he didn't already. But every time she picked up the phone she dropped it.

"It's not my place, I'm not even sure of the facts." She told herself.

Then she got up and walked into the bedroom, looked at Gary's sweet face and decided to lie beside him. She wanted to wake him but knew that sex could be the only reason he could appreciate being disturb. She definitely couldn't wake him to ask him to listen to another episode of life with Tyrone, Wesley and Dane. So she just kissed him softly and watched him sleep.

Surprise

Alycia was out of breath when she reached the top landing with the two loads of laundry. Drinking the night before had really taken a toll on her. She placed the stuffed pillowcases down and searched for her keys. She looked in each pocket twice only to find that her keys were missing.

I know I had them when I was at the laundry mat, because I opened Roz's root beer with my bottle opener. She thought to herself. So where could they be? She began to look again, this time into the pillowcases. Just as she went to bend down to search again she heard Mrs. Reeves leaving her apartment slamming the door behind her. The pressure from the wind behind the door traveled up the stairs and that's when Alycia heard her apartment door eased open.

I know I didn't leave this door unlocked. Alycia grabbed the half bottle of bleach out of the pillowcase and took the top off. *Just in case there's some crazy fool in here.* She eased into the doorway slowly trying to be careful not to let the door make a sound. First she went into the kitchen and noticed half her cake gone, then she went into the living room and from there she could see a man lying across her bed on the phone.

"Look, what did I tell you? My mother's not here, she went to Atlantic City. NO! She asked me to paint for her. Yes, all six rooms. NO! First I have to go to the store and get the stuff. You want to come down here and help me paint? Yeah, I didn't think so. Look Cheryl, you just found out you're pregnant yesterday stop trying to get me to give you everything that you want. You're not even sure whether or not it's mine. Of course you're gonna say that, that's what I would say too. What you're saying is not even necessary, time will tell. It's simple if the baby is Spanish I know it's not mine. How could you think I didn't notice that? First you said that it was the first time, now he only got it twice. Cheryl please who do you think you're talking to? I've only cheated on you once too, okay.

Bye Cheryl, bye, I don't want to hear that, you could have at least made that cheap bastard take you out to do that shit, but up in the same bed we use? I don't think I can ever respect you again? I don't know why I lied about being at my mother's, I guess it's just a habit of respect, but you might as well know -- I'm at Alycia's. You know what Alycia I'm talking about. Yeah, that Alycia, yeah well, you'll get over it. Cheryl I'm not trying to hear that. I stuck by you when you was pregnant by me so why can't he. Look, I'm not going to be a sucker for nine months waiting to see who the baby looks like. When it gets here then I'll know. Why can't you get an abortion? Yeah well it sounds like you want to be alone for nine months. Yes you do. Look, I gotta go I think I hear Alycia." Click!

After Alycia heard the part about Cheryl being pregnant she tipped into the bathroom reached for her birth control pills and flushed them down the toilet. Then she grabbed her box of condoms and before she could throw them out she thought. *What about getting AIDS?* Then she put them back. Alycia was so happy that it was Jeff that broke into her place that she accidentally wasted the bleach on her bathroom rug causing the green to turn into a yellowy-white. *Shit!* When she came out of the bathroom, Jeff was coming in the house with her laundry.

"What's up baby?"

"This damn bleach bottle has a hole." She said going back into the bathroom and pouring the rest of the bleach into the toilet just to hide the blush on her face.

"Come here, I bought you something."

"Okay, just let me wash my hands."

Alycia heard Jeff go into the other room, she told herself to calm down, take it slow and not argue with him for breaking into her apartment.

"Surprise!"

"Oh Jeff, these are nice, where did you get them?"

"Is that all you can ask, where did I get them? Try them on."

"Size seven. That's my size. Oh Jeff these boots feel good, they're nice."

"If you really like them I can get you the matching jacket."

"For real? That'll be perfect. Thanks!"

"Thanks? I don't get no kiss or hug."

Alycia smiled. *That's not all you're going to get.* Alycia got close enough to smell his sweet breath. Then she searched his eyes for what he saw in her, his eyes revealed hunger, and he proved it by grabbing her.

"You know I missed you."

Alycia almost fell to the floor. *He missed me!*

Then he laid a kiss on her that made her body melt into anything he wanted it to be.

"Yeah, I definitely missed you." Jeff said pleased that she wanted the same thing that he wanted. Before they finished the first kiss, Alycia was naked from the waste down. He stopped kissing her, only to lay her down and kiss her where he knew she wanted it most. *Jeff has to hold the worlds record for getting right to it.* Alycia thought. From the moment his tongue touched her, Alycia began praising him, thanking him and telling him how she loved him and needed him and wanted to have his baby. She spilled her guts while he was below her and promised to give him anything and everything he wanted. She begged him not to stop. So he didn't, he just re-adjusted the position where she could serve him as well.

"You give the best head." Jeff complimented her while designing the heavy cream around her neck. Desperate for a child that he knows is his, he said. "Next time we'll put this where it counts, okay?"

Alycia answered with a big kiss. She sucked his face and left bruises on his neck and chest. *I can't believe he's letting me do this,* she thought. *He's really mine!*

"Hey Alycia I owe you an apology, I'm sorry about the way I acted last time, I behaved like a real asshole."

"It's alright Jeff, we all have our days."

"Also, I want to apologize for breaking in your place today. I saw you at the laundry mat so I went to park my car so we could talk. When I got back you was across the street with that crowd of people. I saw your keys laying on the table and thought how careless it was of you to leave your keys laying around. Then I decided to teach you a lesson and take them to meet you here."

"That's alright Jeff, it was careless of me. I'm glad it worked out."

Jeff kissed Alycia again, thinking how simple she could be.

"Did I ever tell you how beautiful your body is? You have nice curves," he fingered her. "Plump little breast, a sweet round ass all coated with the right color and texture of skin. Yeah you could have my baby. You're pretty enough."

"Thank you Jeff."

"What's for lunch?" He asked folding his arms behind his head, looking at the ceiling.

"I took some shrimps down I was going to make a beer batter and fry them."

"Shrimp and what?"

"Anything, we can have rice, fries, or salad."

"I want rice and salad. What are you going to cook for dinner?"

"I don't know I wasn't really planning on cooking anything. I don't usually eat that much. The shrimps would have lasted all night. I probably would have gotten some yogurt or something."

"Well, I want steak, yeah steak and broccoli with cheddar cheese and potatoes. But that's alright if you weren't planning on cooking I know where I can get it."

"Don't be silly, you're going to have whatever you want, right here."

"That's my baby, give me what I want. Come here girl I don't want you to get up just yet, you have to put me to sleep first."

Alycia giggled as she stuck her head under the sheets.

Pack, we're leaving

Wesley stormed into the house with his new Eddie Bauer luggage and began emptying the drawers and closets. Tyrone knew then that his six-week party was over.

"Why all of sudden do you want to go away?" Tyrone asked.

"I just need to get away. I've haven't had a vacation in two years, I need to take some time off. Are you coming or not?"

"What about my party?"

"You're going to have to cancel it until we get back. Right now, I'm not in the mood for a party, and please no more questions just start packing."

"Wes, is everything alright? What is it? What did you find out from Dr. Gibbs?"

"Nothing. The test came back negative. It's not that. I just want to get out of here for a few weeks."

"What's a few weeks?

"Three."

"Hold on Wes, sit down. Tell me what's wrong." Tyrone said grabbing Wesley by his wrist. "We've just made a new commitment to each other. Whatever is bothering you is bothering me. Now tell me what is going on."

"You don't want to know."

"Try me."

"It's about Dane."

"Why am I not surprised?"

"He's wants to take me to court."

"For what?"

"He said that I gave him the virus."

"The virus! She has the virus!?" Tyrone said holding on to a chair, feeling sick enough to pass out.

"I don't know. All I know is that he's telling everyone that he does and that I gave it to him."

"Well, you are sure that you don't have it right?"

"Yes. I've always suspected Dane wasn't clean, he bragged about to many tricks that he pulled and I've always protected myself with him. He tried to get me to go raw a couple of times but I couldn't."

Tyrone felt a little relieved, but still hated the fact that Wesley did the things he did with Dane.

"So you're leaving to avoid her."

"Yeah. I don't want to be here when the messenger arrives with the subpoena. I didn't give him any disease he just wants my money. Maybe I should just give him a couple of thousands so that he can leave us alone?"

"Hell no! Fuck her! She ain't getting shit! All that dog need is a good ass kickin' and I'm just the one to give it to her."

"No, I won't let you stoop to his level."

"Well let her take you to court, she'll lose. But I'll be damned if I jump on a plane running from her ass. I need to face that Bitch anyway and get this over with."

"That's enough already, you know I don't care for that kind of language. I hate it when you talk like that!"

Wesley stretched across the bed aggravated by the thoughts of what would come out in court. He knew how evil Dane could be and knew that Dane would not stop until he received some kind of comfort for his efforts.

"I know what you're thinking and you might as well get that idea out of your head, because you're wrong, Dane don't want your money. All she wants to do is fuck with you, either way I'm sure. She just wants to see you running back and forth like a fool over her. It's about her ego -- she wants to have anything to still be connected to you. The only way to settle this thing is in court, she'll lose and you'll let her know that it's over for good."

"You're right. She just wants to mess with me."

"Now come here and let me rub your temples, you need to relax. Just look around you, you have everything."

Wesley closed his eyes and enjoyed the tender caress of Tyrone's fingers.

"That really feels good. I miss your touch, your fingers and your love. Tyrone . . ." Wesley opened his eyes and turned around. "I'm so sorry. Even with all the good fortune that has come our way. I still feel ashamed about what I've done. No lavish home or fancy gift could ever take my shame away. I still feel that you deserve more. But I don't know what else I can do. I don't know how I'm going to let you know that I'm really sorry and that I really love you. I want to be with you forever." Holding Tyrone's hand, Wesley got on his knees and looked Tyrone in the eyes. "Will you be mine, will you marry me?"

Tyrone was stunned. He had wanted to get married three years ago, but Wesley insisted that it was foolish and unnecessary. Wesley believed that marriage was a traditional ceremony and the tradition was usually a man and a woman. He laughed at the idea and told Tyrone that he already considered them married whatever that meant.

"But I thought you didn't believe in marriage?"

"I didn't but after all that's happened I now realize what love is and what it means. I didn't know how much I loved you until I almost lost you. But now I see that without you, I have nothing. Please say yes."

"Are you sure that Dr. Gibbs said that everything was alright?"

"I have the results right here." Wesley opened up his portfolio and took out the crisp piece of paper that had and X next to the word negative. "I told you everything is fine, I never stopped loving you, I kept my promise to you."

Tyrone didn't exactly say yes, he just started making new party plans. He was all excited about the bachelor's party they would have.

"You've made me a very happy man." Wesley said pushing up on Tyrone.

Happy tears slid down Tyrone's face. He was touched that Wesley actually proposed and felt blessed that Wesley didn't contract any disease. He was tickled brown that everything was falling into place.

He's a freak

"Maya, Maya!" Toy screamed out. "Girl, did you read *Bailey's Cafe?* Gloria knows she got that off. If you haven't, you could read my copy. No, go buy your own it's a book you'd want in your library. I know you're not still reading *Jazz,* you are the slowest reader. You'll never get to *Song of Solomon* -- which is still my favorite. But you know what you got to read? *The Isis Papers.* Girl that book will change your whole perspective on the people and things around you. It was actually little intimidating but I got through it and was glad I did. It was a much needed education. But for real it was frightening. Doesn't that sound crazy, people scared of knowing the truth? I had to make myself finish reading it. But I'm glad I did. Oh yeah, and Derrick Bell has *The Faces at the Bottom of the Well.* That's deep too, his information is so compelling. But you like fiction you should read Zora's *Their Eyes.* I love Zora she's definitely my all time favorite author. For some reason I feel connected to her. Don't laugh, but it's like she's still alive, telling the new sista writers to write on. Zora had spirit, the kind that won't die. If you read one of her stories its like you could never forget it. It stays with you or should I say she stays with you. Did you know that there is a Zora Neale Hurston Festival in Eatonville, Florida? Yup, every year in January, oh yeah, I know what I wanted to ask you, did you ever finish reading Breaking Ice? My favorite excerpt in there is *The Upper Room* by Mary Monroe. I loved that excerpt it had me so curious of what Mama Ruby was up to. Don't you know I photo copied it and gave it to everyone in the office to read and give me their opinion of what they thought Mama Ruby was up to? Nobody agreed on what I thought, so I started searching for the book. At first it took me forever to track it down but since then it's been reprinted, I can get it from almost anywhere. Did I ever tell you who the first black author that I really appreciated? It was Paule Marshall. It's amazing how she changed my life. After I read Brown Girl, Brownstones, I couldn't get enough of black writers. I never was one to read those Harlequins because they didn't relate to me. Who cares if Houston found diamonds in Holly's coochie? I mean be for real? No black man is going to find diamonds in my coochie. You know what I mean? Girl, I could go on about my favorite writers, have you ever read Richard Perry's *Montgomery Children's*? That's another very entertaining one. Girl why are you so quiet, letting me go on and on? Gary's got your tongue?"

"Letting you? Toy I know you well enough to let you at least get the first five hundred words out before I join the conversation, and for your information I did finish reading Jazz and enjoyed it very much thank you. Let me see, what other question did you whirl by me. Oh, I didn't read Bailey's Cafe yet, but I did pick it up. And how could I forget about your little office excerpt of the Upper Room, I'm glad you finally got your hands on that book so that you can find out what really happened and shut up about it. As for the Isis Paper and Derrick Bell's book, I do plan to read them, but I'm not ready to read them yet. They're too political and they usually make me stressed out. Who else? I have all of Zora's books. I love her too."

"Well Girl, don't get left behind. You know we're having a literary discussion at my place two weeks from tomorrow."

"That's right, I totally forgot, which book are we doing again?"

"First we decided to do the *Third Life,* by Alice Walker, but since there are going to be men at this discussion, we didn't want to scare them away with our first session being about their brutal behavior, so we're doing *Beloved,* by Toni Morrison. Everyone agreed and Tuesday night is the night, so be there ready to battle. I hate it when someone reads a good book like that and come out with the most insignificant discussion about it. I can't wait, I know that book by heart and I'm going to make sure that when the discussion is over, everyone knows what I thought was the most significant scene."

"I'm sure you will."

"How's Gary?"

"He was fine this morning."

"This morning? How cozy."

"Cozy it was. Why are you always questioning me about Gary? How are you and your hubby doing?"

Toy's whole expression changed, she flagged Maya down to have lunch but she definitely didn't want to talk about her freak of a husband.

"Oh please chile." Toy said dismissing the subject.

"That's your answer, oh please chile?"

"Bruce is still Bruce." She said avoiding Maya's eyes.

"Go on."

Toy took a deep breath. "Well if you must know, I have a lover."

Maya placed her hands over her mouth and said, "No, not you!"

"Yes me. Don't I deserve to be happy too?"

"I thought you were. What happened to Perfect Bruce?"

"I never said Bruce was perfect, I just didn't trash him like most of these women do their husband."

"So what's he doing wrong?"

"Nothing really, Bruce is very sweet, I love him dearly, but lately he has been acting like he's weird."

"Weird? Like what?"

"Maya, you have to promise not to breathe a word about this to anyone."

Maya took a deep breath and rolled her eyes.

"Even though I'm highly insulted by your request, you have my word. Now get on with it."

"Well," Toy began to whisper. "Lately Bruce has been buying all of these X-rated video tapes."

"So."

"So, he's been watching them every night and doing himself while he's watching them."

"For real?!"

"Yes! At first I thought it was kinda cute, you know getting kinky and in the mood to give me a good time, but when it went on and on, night after night, week after week and now months. Maya I'm telling you, something is wrong with him. He will make love to me and then later put on one of his tapes and do himself while I'm in the bed with him. One night I was fast asleep, the bed started bouncing and shaking, and there was this moan and groan. I just knew that Bruce had lost his mind and brought some women in the bed with us. At first I was afraid to look, but the movements were so powerful I had to turn around. Girl, when I turned around it was just Bruce and his hand. His eyes were closed and he was getting down, I mean the man was going off. I didn't know whether or not he was dreaming but then when I looked up at the TV, I noticed that the guy in the video was doing exactly the same thing. Just going off on himself. Now, you tell me, ain't that some weird shit?"

"I have to admit, that is a bit much. I have never even heard of anything like that before. Whew! What did you say to him the next day?"

"The next day? Girl I got up and threw some cold water on that fool and put him out."

"What?"

"That's right, that freak is at his momma's, and from what I know he's still doing his thing."

"You really threw him out?"

"You're damn right! I don't know exactly what that was all about, but to me, it seemed like he's loosing his mind. Some nights I would cook a nice dinner and put on my sexy teddy, you know really in the mood to get paid, well girl, he would turn me down, then later I would hear him in the bathroom getting off."

"Damn Toy, that has to be the craziest thing I've ever heard. So how do you know that he's still at it?"

"Now you would think that when a man gets thrown out of his home that he's going to raise a fuss. Not Bruce. He didn't even ask for his clothes, he just asked me was it alright if he came by and got his tapes. Ain't that something? But it was too late. I threw that mess out the same night I threw his ass out. Ooh, it was so disgusting, gook all over my sheets, towels, everywhere. The fool was jerking off every chance he got. You want to know what really burned me up about the whole thing? It's that I didn't catch on at the beginning he's been at this for years. When I think of earlier incidents finding gook all over my towels, I thought he was just being nasty and blowing his nose. I now know that he was engaging in that madness then."

"Umph, I heard it all. Girl, I'm so sorry, are you alright? I mean how did it make you feel? Do you think that it had anything to do with you? I mean what was it? Did he need more sex or I don't know I can't, understand it?"

"You and me both, at first I was crying thinking that he was gay or something like that, but now I think he's just weird. There was a weirdness in the house when he was there, a weirdness I hadn't noticed until he left. I threw out all of his things, you know, like his recliner, all of his science books and magazines, his telescope and his stamp collections and all that creepy junk."

"Toy, why did you throw it out? You should have just given it to him."

"Well actually I did, but it was more like I threw it at him."

"Oh. What about that beautiful house? I know that it had a beautiful mortgage to match. Are you stuck paying for it by yourself? How long ago did this happen?"

"It's been five months and Bruce is still paying the bills. He was always in charge of the bills. The checking account have both of our names on it but only his check goes directly into that account. He even sends the bills off. Every month he sits down and writes them out and mail them. I usually just pick up food and house items like towels and curtains, rugs and things. That's one thing I will say about Bruce, he's a good provider. He never asked me to pay a bill and I never did. But I made sure we had plenty of soap and things like that, but most of my money was either spent on me or collecting dust in my savings account. So if someone talks Bruce into abandoning the bills I will be alright."

"That explains the always happy face."

"Yep."

"Okay so you're set financially, what about emotionally."

"Finally, something worth talking about, let me tell you about my new lover."

"Toy please, let me catch my breath, I'm still not over the Bruce story."

"Get over it. I did."

"Okay, what's his name?"

Toy began giggling, blushing and dancing in her seat.

"His name is Russell. And Maya, he is perfect for me, well almost perfect."

"Oh, but of course, what's his malfunction?"

"You're going to hate me, but he's married."

"Bye Toy." Maya said waving her hand, annoyed at what she just heard come out of Toy's mouth. "You know the rule. A real sister would not disrespect herself by dealing with another sister's husband."

"It's either going to be me or someone else."

"So let it be someone else. Just because someone is going to sell drugs to the kids in the school yards doesn't mean it has to be you."

"Oh come on Maya, its not all that."

"It's exactly like that. I would never get involved with another sister's husband or anybody's husband for that matter. Don't you think it's bad enough that we have to worry about them going to jail, being on drugs, being in the closet, and wanting white women? We shouldn't have to worry about each other too!"

"Maya, when are you going to wake up? A sister will take your man in a snap. You go ahead and walk around here with your never- never lecture. But honey, there's an old saying: Never say never."

"Well, regardless of what you say, a woman that allows a brother to jump from bed to bed is just as low as the brother, as a matter of fact, she's lower. Brothers wouldn't be pulling this mess if sisters wouldn't allow it. And I'm going to be honest with you. I can't respect a sister who is low enough to do something like that, so forget about the Diane Reeves tickets."

"What Diane Reeves tickets?"

"You were running your mouth so much I didn't get a chance to tell you that I was inviting you to the Blue Note to see Diane Reeves for your birthday. But now I've changed my mind. I will not be hanging with someone that is messing with a married man."

"Maya, you are blowing this thing out of proportion. If you have tickets for us to see Diane Reeves, then we're going. You are just going to have to get over this husband thing. You act like he's your husband."

"With you, who knows? I mean what difference would it make? My husband, my sister's husband -- you know it doesn't matter. That's what happens to women like you -- you become selfish. Let me guess, his wife is always on his back? She nags him day and night and never wants to have sex? You understand him. He wishes that he would have met you first? He wants to leave her?"

"You know Russell?" Toy asked amazed at how much Maya knew about him.

"No, I know Phil. Phil is the same as Bill, Gill, and Will. They are all the same."

"I didn't hear you mention Gary."

"Hopefully, I won't have to."

"Most likely you will." Toy snapped, giving Maya something to be upset about.

"I gotta go Toy, have a good birthday."

Maya strutted off with an attitude, but not sure why she broke on Toy. She was very disappointed in Toy, but more disappointed with herself. *What's wrong with me? Getting so upset like that? Toy is a grown woman. Who am I to pass judgment? To each his own. Besides Alycia is practically doing the same thing and I never said those words to her. Why did I break on Toy and not Alycia?* She skipped the ladies room and headed straight for her office. *I owe her an apology.*

A bad situation

Selina slipped on her one piece black cat suit and put on Dr. Dre's *The Chronic* cd. It was always Rap music for her. She studied the picture of Snoop Dogg and thought *Yeah, it would probably be fun going doggy-style with Snoop.* She did her warm ups and was ready to begin her exercise when she heard someone calling her name.

"Leeena, Leeena!" Trudy called.

"Oh shit, she came." Selina said outloud.

"I'll be right down, hang on!" she yelled.

Selina jogged down the stairs allowing her buns and breasts to bounce freely. Nosey, old Mr. Fulton stuck his head out of his door and said, "Yuummmy, yummy, yummy!" Then he called his equally old brother to come to the door to see the treats. "Come heah Paul, if you wanna good rise, come look at dis." The other gray haired man came to the door and said, "Howdy honey, how would you like to make yourself a fast dollar." Then they both laughed and quickly slammed the door as if Selina was going to take them up on their offer.

"Trudy!" Selina surprised herself and screamed. She had forgotten how beautiful Trudy was. "You're looking more and more like your father."

"Leena!" Trudy returned with opened arms. The two women held each other for a good five minutes before letting go.

"Come on upstairs."

Trudy hesitated, she hadn't been held with such warmth in such a long time that she was afraid to follow. She tried to ignore the very noticeable view of Selina's body in front of her but couldn't.

"Don't tell me that you've turned into a softie. Come on, what's wrong with you."

Trudy walked into the apartment like she was a lost child. She knew that she had a lot bottled up inside and that if her feelings were released, she would be there to stay.

"Don't you just love Snoop and Dr. Dre?"

"Who's that? I've been listening to a lot of opera music and, well, I sorta lost most of my Rap knowledge. Who is Snoopy Dog?"

Selina rolled her eyes in disbelief and disgust. Who don't know Snoop Dogg?

"Trudy, are you alright?"

"Yeah, why?"

"I don't know, it's just that you seem so distant. What's on your mind?

"Nothing." she said quickly.

"So what's been happening, do you still like going to the movies and stuff?"

"No not really. Trish usually has tickets to something and she usually plans the recreation."

"Plans the recreation? What do you do? Are you working? Do you still visit your aunt? What about your cousins do you still see them?"

"No. Not really. Trish doesn't care for them to much and she gets upset when I visit the neighborhood, so I try not to get on her nerves because she . . ." Trudy stopped after noticing that she was revealing too much.

"She what?"

"Nothing, I really shouldn't be talking about her."

"Trudy, I have never seen you act like this. I knew that this would be hard for us, but I didn't think you would be so nervous. I think you're upset about something else, what is it?"

Trudy didn't answer she balled her fists tightly and closed her eyes hoping the question would go away. Selina sensed the pressure and pain so she gently began rubbing Trudy's back. She whispered that it would be alright and watched as Trudy release her fingers slowly and then began to speak.

"Trish has put me into counseling." Trudy began with her eyes to the floor. "She says that I have a lot of problems and that I am confused."

"Confused, about what?"

Trudy lifted her head, her eyes meeting the weight bench.

"I'm not sure."

As difficult as it was for Selina not to explode, she took her time and focused on getting Trudy to say what was on her mind.

"Trudy, you must know why you're going to counseling."

"Trish says that I don't want to work, that I don't want anything out of life but a free ride. She says that I fake sickness and can't hold a job for more than three months."

"Is that true?"

"Some of it." Trudy said with her eyes now concentrating on the watch on Selina's wrist. "It's true that I haven't had a job longer than three months, but I never faked my sickness. Whenever I would disagree with Trish about something she became extra nice to me and then the next two or three days I couldn't go to work because I was feeling sick."

"Sick? What kind of sick? Are you having headaches?"

"No. I bump into things, I can't hold anything on my stomach and I feel drowsy like I'm doped up or something. Trish calls my job for me and the next thing I know, I'm fired. After about a year of this she decided that I needed therapy. She says that I don't want to work. That I pretend to be sick."

"So what is it? Why do you think you get sick so often?"

"I'm not sure, but I do have one theory."

"And that is what?"

"If I tell you, you're going to think that I am crazy and that I should get help."

"You don't know that, just tell me."

"Okay, here goes, I think that Trish is drugging me."

"Drugging you?! Trudy I'm trying as hard as I can to understand this situation. First of all you're a nervous wreck.

Second, you're looking behind your back like someone is following you and third, you haven't stopped shaking since you sat down. What's going on with you? What is this Trish person doing to you?"

"I'm not sure, but one night I left Trish, we had an awful fight and I accidentally called her white. I stormed out and came to Aunt Moo's. About two hours later Trish came banging on the door, begging Aunt Moo to let her in. She said that she was sorry and that she didn't want to lose me. You know Aunt Moo, she just laughed in her face and told her to go home. Aunt Moo called her cracker and white trash then just laughed and laughed, but Trish wouldn't give up. She pulled out a clip of money and told Aunt Moo that she would pay her if she would open the door. Aunt Moo stopped laughing and told Trish to slide a hundred dollars under the door. When Trish slid a hundred dollar bill, Aunt Moo started laughing again and said that she would open the door for two more bills like that. Aunt Moo had no idea that Trish had the money, but she did. Next thing I knew Trish was in the house and Aunt Moo was offering her a beer. I stayed in the back room and listened to the conversation they were having. Trish and Aunt Moo were toasting to a new beginning for me and her, and five minutes after that, Aunt Moo was asleep. Trish startled me when she stood at the room door and told me to hurry up and get my things. When I got to the front, to Aunt Moo, she was snoring, it seemed like she had fallen into a deep sleep. It was strange, but Trish convinced me that Aunt Moo was old and tired and that we should leave and let her get her rest. That incident bothered me for a long time, it was just uncommon to hear Aunt Moo hollering-laughing one minute and snoring the next. Also there was no way that Aunt Moo would fall asleep with three $100 dollar bills in her lap. But she did that night."

"So you think she drugged your Aunt that night?"

"Yeah, but I'm not sure."

"Did you question your Aunt?"

"Yeah, she said that whatever Trish gave her was some good stuff because she hadn't slept like that in years."

"So Trish did give her something."

"I don't know. Trish says that Aunt Moo is a big liar and would say anything to hide the fact that she's a junkie."

"Trudy, I think you know more than you care to tell me. Why are you letting this go on? What does this woman have on you that you can't even defend yourself? It wouldn't be so bad if you thought she had another lover, but you think she's drugging you. That's real serious."

"I know, but maybe Trish is right, maybe I do have a lot of problems."

"We all have problems, but when we broke up, you didn't have any problems, you were strong and you knew what you wanted. As a matter of fact, that's why we broke up. You were ready to take on the world and I was afraid to."

"Well, right now I have to deal with Trish. Because of my illness, I lost another job. Trish says she doesn't mind that I don't work. She buys me clothes and takes me out with her all the time."

"Listen to you, you sound like you're her poodle or something."

"Right now it's the best that I can do, I have no where else to go. I don't want to go back to live with Aunt Moo and my cousins, they're all on drugs. Trish is my new family now."

"Yeah, your new abusive family."

Selina's plans for her and Trudy were dead. Trudy didn't have the strength to be anyone's lover. Her situation was bad, and would be for a while. Trudy needed help--big help.

"Look, if you want you can stay here, I have two bedrooms."

"Trish would kill me."

"Kill you? She's doing that now. The first thing you need to do is see a doctor. Let him check your blood and urine. He can determine whether or not you have been tampered with."

"Trish took me to a doctor, one of her friends, and he said that I was just fine."

"If he's a friend of hers, he'll probably tell you anything she asked him to tell you. Besides, you owe it to yourself to get a second opinion."

Trudy broke into a big cry, the one she had been holding inside for months.

"Selina, I have something to tell you. I want you to know that I wanted to run away from Trish for months now. I wanted to contact you but I was afraid that Trish was right and I didn't want to make a fool of myself. Please help me. Don't let her know that I'm here. Take me to a real doctor, someone who can help me."

Selina held Trudy and fought away her own tears. *How can people be so abusive and cold?*

"It's going to be alright, I promise." Selina said stroking Trudy's silky- wavy hair."

Three's a crowd

Before Gary could get out of the shower, he heard the front door slam. He knew it was Dice and he knew that it was the beginning of something he wished he had the guts to stop. While he carefully smoothed on his shaving cream, the shower water dripped from his bare body. He shivered as he heard the boxes being stacked on his living room floor. He heard Dice's heavy breathing as he plopped what seemed like a garbage bag of clothes. Then he heard a woman's voice, it was Sharice.

"Where are we going to put my stuff?"

"Sshh, he may be home, I didn't get to tell him about you and the baby yet."

"But Diiice." She whined. "What if he says no?"

"He won't. He may mean no, but he won't say it. Anyway, it'll only be for a couple of weeks then we can move into our own place. Why don't you go back to the house and get your plants and stuff. I don't want you to be here when he gets in. I need to talk to him alone."

Sharice lowered her head as she walked slowly to the door.

"Hey, what's that look on your face? You know that whatever happens we're going to be together, right?"

"I guess." she said looking away from him.

"You guess? That don't sound like my angel. My angel is sure about how she feels, right?"

Sharice lifted her head a little and started blushing she loved when Dice called her his angel.

"Now where is Daddy's kiss? Be careful of how you kiss me now." He said caressing her high belly. "There's not that much room for me to get in there."

Gary waited through the kiss, the feels, the gooey love talk, the door closing and the car pulling off before he came out of the bathroom and sat on the couch waiting for Dice to come back in the house.

"How'd you get in here?" Dice said shock to see him.

"You can just forget it! I won't say no, huh? Well NO! The answer is NO! I mean it Dice, Sharice is not moving in!"

Dice didn't say a word. He knew that Gary rarely got mad and that when he did it was best to let him enjoy it.

"Don't even ask me, because the answer is NO!"

Dice got up and started moving their bags toward the door.

"You must be loosing your mind, I'm nice enough to let you move in and now you're going to ask me to let your girlfriend move in, a pregnant girlfriend at that? No, it's not enough that you're walking out on your family to be with a new one, I'm just suppose to pat you on your back and congratulate you. Well I'm sorry, I don't agree with what you're doing and I refuse to be a part of it."

"Who's walking out? I was thrown out, remember? Queetha had my stuff thrown out all over the streets. I had to almost fight to get what belonged to me. It wasn't like I was looking for this to happen. Queetha didn't want me. She didn't care about our marriage. All she wanted was my baby - my seed. She don't love me, never did. Now how many times do I have to explain that to you? And as far as Sharice is concerned, we are a couple. Now if you can't respect what's going down in my life, then fine. I'll still love you, but me and Sharice will be together even if it has to be in a shelter, we'll be together."

"I know what you're doing, but it's not going to work. You're trying to make me feel guilty."

"Gary, I am not trying to make you feel guilty." Dice turned his head to wipe off the smirk that said his plan was working. "I just don't want to be apart from her. Is that so wrong?"

"Dice you've been apart from her all this time. Why all of a sudden do you need to be up under her now? Where's her family? You've only known her for a year there must be someone else she can live with."

"Sharice doesn't have any family here. And she's too ashamed to ask her girlfriends because they're going to question her about me."

"And."

"And she already told them that I was a great guy and that we are going to get married after the baby's born. She don't want to tell them the truth about me and Queetha. And Man, you know that Queetha controls my money, I can't just snap my fingers and have Sharice a place to stay."

Gary took a deep breath. "What happened to her place?"

"Man that was with her in-laws. They know that the baby is mine. They have been threatening to kick her out for months. Finally they did it. She has until tonight to clean out her apartment."

"So why did you wait so long to tell me what you had planned to do?"

"Gary, do you think I want to do this? Man I'm tired of running. I want to lay my head on my pillow for a change. I thought that I would have had things straight by now. But it didn't work out that way. The minute I found my shit laying on the streets I started looking for a place. I couldn't go to Sharice's because of her in-laws. So this was my next stop. Gary, you're like my brother, I wouldn't come here if I didn't have to. Yo man, I promise, I'll be off of your hands after they finish checking my background. I'm sure to get one of those newly renovated brownstones. Just give me a few weeks."

Dice held his hand out for Gary to shake in agreement to his plea. But when Gary motioned to shake Dice's hand, Dice grabbed him and hugged him.

"I'm scared man. I'm really scared."

Keep ya head up

Roz kept moving her hair extension braids out of her face as she paced the floor.

"I can't believe this is happening, they said that they would be laying off in June, not November. I can't make it off of unemployment. And who is going to hire a pregnant black woman? Damn!" She cried, slumping down in her recliner chair, her braids falling in her face again.

"What will I tell Lance? We can't afford a wedding now. And what about the girls, this is so embarrassing. And forget mama, she's going to want me to come home. She's going to say that I'm not working so I could be down there with her. Oh Lord, please don't make me stay with Mama."

"Laid off, I just can't believe it. I have never been laid off in my life. Why couldn't they wait until I had the baby?"

Roz talked to herself that whole evening, until the phone rang. Waiting for Lance to come, she was too upset to do anything else.

"Hello."

"Roslyn? Honey this is your mama. I'm glad your home. I got some good news to tell ya."

Roz mother's voice was an instant headache. She wasn't prepared to tell her mother her news yet, she knew that it would only have made her feel worse.

"What's the good news Ma?" Roz pretended to be interested.

"I've joined the Senior Citizen Group."

"Oh really, that's great." This is good new Roz thought, now she won't be calling me every chance she gets. "So what goes on in this group?"

"Well, there's dancing, aerobics, swimming, sewing, movies, bingo, you know, all sorts of goodies to keep the old-timers busy."

"That sounds great, how did you here about it?"

"I wasn't going to tell you that part but, well now that you've asked, you know old Mr. Winston, well he is always sitting behind me in church. I don't care where I sit, there he is behind me. One time he even asked me would it be alright if he stopped by for some soda pop. I told him NO, but he still sits behind me in church. Well last Sunday he tap me on my shoulders and smiled. I smiled back but he tapped me again, this time, I gave him a mean look, and he said, *"Excuse me Ms. Mae, did ya hear about the new recreation building they put up for us?"* I tol him that I didn't hear about no sech thing but he wouldn't stop. *"It opens this here Sat'dy and if ya don't mind I can come by and we can walk to the opening together. Spose to be plenny freshments and music for the seniors in this community."* I told him I would think on it. But don't you know that high strung ole' devil come knockin at my door early Sat'dy? Well, I didn't forget my manners so I asked him in, fixed him a cup of that flavor tea. We got to talking about old times and laughing, next thing I know I was putting on my walking shoes. We went and it was some kind of nice. Place so new and clean. Cushion seats everywhere. He asked me to dance and I give him one of those mean looks again. Don't you know, he sat by my side the whole night. We started talking and laughing some more, Mr. Winston is a pretty nice fella. So we sign our names and now they done send me a membership card. So I can go everyday if I feel up to it. Mr. Winston he come running over here soon as he got his card. Look just like mine 'ceptin his name is different."

"So the real news is that you may have a boyfriend." Roz allowed her problem to fade in hopes that her mother had found someone to fill in for her dad.

"I didn't tell you no sech of thing. You young folks always puttin' words in people's mouth."

"Well Ma, I'm just glad to hear that you are enjoying yourself and that you are looking forward to spending time with your new group."

"Yeah, so far it feels like its going to be good for your Ma. How you keepin'?"

"Couldn't be better."

"You showin'?"

"Very little, but yeah I guess you can say I am."

"Well, take it easy now, don't let nothing upset ya, how's my Sonny doing? Is he still working hard?"

"Yeah Ma."

"Well you watch him, these men today ain't like the ones before, they is lazy now. You make sure he gets enough rest and food to make it in everyday."

"Okay mom, let me go, I think I hear him now."

"That's him? Let me speak to him, let him know that his Ma is thinking bout him."

Now that she told her mother that lie, she had to tell her another.

"Oh, that isn't him, that's the insurance man, let me go and talk to him, I'll call you this weekend."

"Insurance man? I don't know when the last time I heard of an insurance man coming to people's house. I send them a check quarterly. Maybe you should look into the kind that I got."

"I will Mama, let me go, I'll talk to you soon. Love you. Bye."

Moving her braids out of her face Roz, hung up the phone.

"Sorry for lying. She whispered to God."

Then she picked up the phone and called the drug store to see if Lance had left. He did. She went into the bathroom and took off the clothes that she wore to work and got into the shower. She lathered up her loofah sponge and let the water run. After about six minutes of standing under the hot pressure water, she heard Lance knock on the shower door. She turned the water down and slide the door open enough for him to see her face.

"Are you crying?" he said instead of hello.

This was the thing that Roz loved about Lance, even though she was in the shower, he noticed that it was tears, coming down her face.

"I got laid off." she blurted out.

Lance offered her his black terry bathrobe and wiped her face with its belt. He helped her out of the shower and kissed her on the forehead before he spoke.

"That's no reason to cry. You're not single anymore, you have me and this little guy." he said patting her belly. "We'll take care of you." Roz's tears didn't stop.

"What about our plans, we agreed that we would move before the baby is born. What about our wedding? Lance everything is ruined, there is no way I can get work before the baby is born and I will go crazy just waiting around until that time."

"Ssshh, I promise you that we will stick with our plans. Everything is going to work out fine. And please don't cry about money, I don't like that. When I saw you crying I didn't know what to expect, I thought it was something worse than that. Besides you always said how much you hated your job. Were you telling the truth?"

"Of course, you know how much I hate that job."

"So why are you crying?" Roz smiled.

"Just because you're not working, don't feel that you're not important. I love you because you're special. It has nothing to do with your job or how much money you make. Time will fly by so fast, the baby will be here and you'll be complaining that you don't want to work. You'll see."

Roz felt much better after talking with Lance, he was right, she did hate her job. Just listening to him made her realize what was really troubling her. She was never one to sit down or shut up. But every since she met Lance it seemed like he has changed her world, her way of being. She's no longer loud and with the crowd. She's now more conservative and to herself, so the image of being home, pregnant without a job is just an image she never knew, an image that made her cringe. But what was so bad about it? It's true, she was engaged to a wonderful man, and soon she would be having their baby. Roz's heart finally stopped making tears. She smiled at Lance and hugged him.

"I'm glad you feel better."

Please leave a message

The doormen at The Beverly wore pink tuxedo style jackets, black pants, white shirt and pink bowties.

"Mr. Wesley sir, there's a letter for you, please sign here."

Wesley snatched the envelope from the doorman, ignored the request to sign and slammed the door in his face. He was angry after hearing so many rumors around town. He wished that he had followed his mind and left town like he started to.

"Is that what I think it is?" Tyrone asked peeking over Wesley broad shoulders.

"It's from Dane's lawyer. He wants me to give him the name of my lawyer so that he can contact him so the four of us can meet."

"So, give it to him."

"No, I spoke with Allen today, and he told me to forward any correspondence to him."

"Look I hope you are not trying to prolong this thing. I want to hurry up and get it over with."

"You think I don't?"

"I don't know what to think, you are acting like a mad man. And I want this thing settled before you lose your mind."

"That's what I'm trying to do. I told you what Allen said."

"Look, if you're going to take Allen's route, then take it, leave it up to him. But if you are going to be beating your head against the wall every time you think about that Thing, then you need to confront It. If you ask me, that's really what you need to do. You're not going to be able to rest until you confront that Thing."

"You're suggesting that I go meet with Dane?"

"No, I'm suggesting that we go meet with It."

"And then what?"

"And then let It know where we stand."

With a worried look on his face, Wesley started to pace.

"I already told you that I didn't want you stooping to his level."

"I won't, but I will stoop to some levels of my own."

Wesley was unsure about Tyrone's plan. Confronting Dane was definitely necessary, but risky. Wesley wanted to confront him alone. He wanted to just offer Dane some money and get him to stop the rumors. At the same time he knew that Tyrone was right, Dane would take the money and still mess with them. Wesley knew that Dane was not happy with their breakup and basically he didn't want Wesley happy either.

"Alright." Wesley agreed. "I'll call him now."

"Still know the number I see." Tyrone said grabbing the other cordless phone to listen.

When Tyrone put the phone to his ear, he heard a voice recording come on the line. It was Wesley's voice. Wesley had forgotten about the recording he made on Dane's machine over a year ago. First there was music and then these words:

> *Under where? Under here!*
>
> *Dane is busy*
>
> *under there.*
>
> *Maybe today, or sometime tonight*
>
> *He'll get back*
>
> *After taking a bite!*
>
> *If you're thirsty and like cream*
>
> *Listen close, imagine, just dream!*
>
> *If you're down and want some too*
>
> *I think you know just what to do!*

Beeeep.

Knowing the words by heart, Wesley hung up the phone as soon as the recording began. But Tyrone didn't. He heard it through its entirety then hung up. He slammed the cordless into its cradle and stormed into the bedroom, almost breaking the door behind him.

Damn! Wesley thought. *Why is that fool still using that old ass messages. Shit!* Wesley gave Tyrone about ten minutes than he came into the room.

"That was when it first started. He had asked me to say those words. He had it written out and everything. They weren't my words, they were his. Please Tyrone, let's not go into this, I can't take it."

"You want me to calm down?! Is that what you want?! Well, I will as soon as we find where that Bitch is and settle this mess!"

Wesley heart dropped again. *Find her!* He hated scenes and he didn't want to go looking for Dane.

"Are you coming or do I have to do this alone?"

Wesley grabbed his black quilted leather jacket and followed Tyrone out of the door.

It was windy down the alley where Booties was located, the music was loud and people were standing outside underneath the orange neon lit signed that read ooties. Rumor had it that someone loved the club so much that they stole the "B" years ago. The closer they got to the club, the more they could smell the exotic aroma of marijuana. Since Wesley had been spending time with Dane, he started smoking weed and enjoyed the sweet scent that now surrounded him. He made a mental note to pick up a sac the next time he had the chance. Before Tyrone and Wesley could get anywhere near the door they could see people staring, pointing and whispering. Someone ran inside, as if to tell everyone in the club that Wesley and Tyrone were on their way. After filtering through the crowd they finally reached the door, but just as Wesley touched the door knob, Dane snatched it open from the inside. He stood in the doorway with his leg half cocked opened enough for him to show off his large relaxed penis through his tight black spandex pants. Dane wet his lips with his long dripping tongue and said in a woman voice, "What do I owe the pleasure?"

"What the fuck is wrong with you Bitch." Tyrone said pushing the little thin Dane out of Wesley's face.

"Ask him, he's the one that smiled when he saw me." Dane continued in his ugly woman's voice.

The music stopped. The record wasn't finish playing but one of Dane's friends pulled the plug so that everyone could hear what was being said.

"Dane, you can just stop with the lies! Tyrone knows that I don't want you!"

"Does he know that you gave me the virus, too?" Dane said looking at everyone in the bar like it was time to applaud.

"No because I don't have it to give so you can stop your bullshit. You probably got it from one of those old white men you brag about using."

"Fuck you Wesley! You know the truth. If I got it – you got it too. Now where we got it from it's up for you to decide."

"There is nothing for me to decide. I don't have it and I could care less where you got it from. All I know is I never touched you raw and having AIDS is the furthest thing from my mind."

"Never touched me raw?" Dane replied like there was a big mistake made.

"That's right. Never!" Wesley said proudly for everyone to hear.

"I know you're not going to stand here in front of all these people and tell me that you've never touched me raw. What is oral sex?"

Wesley wanted to run out of the bar. How could he have been so stupid?

"Look Bitch." Tyrone interjected. "It's over, that shit is in the past. Leave us the fuck alone. Keep your threats and your bullshit to yourself because if I hear another word about you spreading lies on us again, I will personally . . "

"What little Ms. Tyrone, just what are you going to do? Ty me up?"

Everyone laughed.

Tyrone moved slowly not taking his eyes off of Dane. He reached in the back of his waist and pulled out his little silver shiny gun. The crowd inhaled as they watched him put it to Dane's head.

"No. I'll kill you Bitch -- that's what I'll do. Now consider yourself on notice." he said pushing the gun nose against Dane's head knocking him to the floor. "I will kill you."

No one moved they just watched as Dane tried to pretend that he wasn't scared or embarrassed.

"Yeah, sure you will." Dane replied still on the floor after Tyrone stepped over him to get to the bar.

Wesley felt like a fool and left the bar, he didn't say anything to Tyrone or Dane. He just walked out as fast as he could to his car. He was so humiliated, Tyrone taking up for him. He felt like a little punk, allowing Tyrone to fight his battles. He sat in the car punching the seats while waiting for Tyrone. Then he reached into the glove compartment and pulled out his flask and took a drink to slow down his racing heartbeat. Tyrone took his time he wanted to make sure Dane knew that he was serious. He ordered a double Hennessy, talked to a few phony friends and walked to the car.

"Why did you do that?!" Wesley went off on him as soon as he entered the car.

"Do what? Put that Bitch in her place?" Tyrone smiled.

"When did you get the gun?"

"Never mind, I got it is all you need to know."

"I don't like that kind of talk, its crazy. We can move. We don't ever have to see Dane's face again."

"I told you before I'm not running from her."

"Well, please let's leave it to Allen." Wesley said trying to control his temper.

"Okay, fine . . ." Tyrone said smiling, the Hennessy was settling in and he got to put a gun to Dane head. *Today was a good day* he thought.

Nut'n but my boots

"Jeff, are you just going to lay there forever?"

"Why, are you getting tired of me?"

"No. It's just that you've been here for three weeks now, I thought you said that you had a job?"

"I do."

"Well when are you going to go to it?"

"I'm at it right now."

Alycia was near her breaking point, she had just come in from work only to find him hanging around doing nothing. She tried to be nice to Jeff, gave him any and everything he asked for, but day after day he seemed to be taking advantage of the situation.

"How are you at work right now?"

"I'm a hustler." Jeff said with a proud grin on his face. "This is my new territory. If you look outside you'll see two dudes standing across the street on the corner. They work for me. Why do you think I left you three hundred dollars on the counter this morning? One reason is because I got it like that and the other is because the fridge is getting low. But regardless of any of that stuff, you deserve it. You sure know how to make a man feel good."

Ignoring the compliment that would have made her feel complete just a few weeks before Alycia questioned. "A hustler?!"

"Yeah, come here." Jeff said patting the empty spot next to him.

Although devastated by his answer, Alycia came to him and allowed him to suck her face.

"Jeff, you mean those guys out there are dealing drugs?"

"Yeah, why are you whispering? They're taking care of things so that I can spend all my time with you. Unless you want me to leave?"

"No!" She blurted. "I don't want you to leave, but I . . ."

"What?"

"I just didn't know that you were into that."

"You didn't? Shit, I been dealing now for six years. See, I know when to move out. Some brothers stay on a corner for years. That's stupid. They don't know that you have to keep traveling. This is a perfect spot because no one deals in this neighborhood and so I get all of the business. You see that box over there, bring it here and open it."

Alycia couldn't believe her ears, but went to get the metal box.

"Count the money."

She didn't want to touch it but she did. She separated the hundreds from the fifties, and the twenties from the tens, there was only four fives and ten ones.

"Forty-two hundred dollars."

"Now ask me how long it took to earn that much money."

Alycia didn't want to ask, so she shrugged her shoulders.

"Six days!" Jeff bragged. "The first week I was here I grossed close to three thousand dollars. The people around here were skeptical since they didn't know me. The second week thirty-five hundred and now forty-two. Baby this area is a gold mine."

Jeff grabbed Alycia and kissed her breast through her blouse.

"How much do you want? Anything you want, name it. This is my extra. Those knuckle heads downstairs make their own profit. I don't pay them, they pay me. If I give them five hundred dollars worth, that's what they bring me back. I don't care how they fix it on the streets, just as long as I get mine off the top, but they're doing good. I make sure that they make at least a hundred for every three hundred I make. So how much is that?" he asked out loud. "If I made forty-two hundred how much did they make? That's about fourteen hundred dollars for them right? That's not bad, fourteen hundred a week tax free."

Without Jeff's attention, Alycia excused herself and went into the bathroom, she felt like she had to vomit but couldn't. *He's a drug dealer,* she cried to herself. Alycia wanted to ask Jeff more questions but she knew that the answers would be to painful to bear, she knew the answers to her questions were: *The drugs are stashed here, right under your bed and the gun is under the pillow. What am I getting myself into?* Alycia asked herself. *Will he fly off the handle if I confront him about how I really feel? Or am I making too much of this? I am.* She convinced herself. *After all he's been doing this for years and I never would have guessed. He's been doing it for three weeks right under my nose and I didn't have a clue. He must be smooth, yeah he's a professional. I can live with that.*

"Alycia! What are you doing?"

"I had to clean the bathroom."

"Girl take a break, this house is too clean, you don't want to get bags under your eyes do you? I bet you can't guess what I want for dinner?"

"I can guess." She said smiling and rubbing up against him.

"That's not dinner, that's dessert." He rubbed her back.

"So what is it tonight, I've cooked every meal I could possibly think of. What does the King want tonight?"

"Ox tails."

"Ox tails?"

"Yeah, don't tell me your momma never made y'all no Ox tails."

"I guess she did once or twice but I don't remember them being good."

"Then she never made them, because their damn good. I like mine trimmed and cooked with garlic and tomato sauce. Do you think you can handle that for me tonight, baby?"

"Sure, but where am I going to find Ox tails?"

"I'll get them, they're not hard to find. Anyway, I have to make a run. What time is it?"

"It's six thirty, I should be back by eight, if I'm not back by then, call one of your girlfriends and you two go out to dinner on me."

Alycia didn't like the idea that Jeff was leaving. She didn't trust him anymore. Something warned her that he may not come back, that maybe he was going to see Cheryl.

"Jeff, try and hurry back, I don't want to go out, I want some Ox tails."

Jeff laughed as he tied his boots. "Oh, all of a sudden you want Ox tails." Then he looked her in the eye and said. "I know what you really want and you don't have to play games to get it."

"What are you talking about? What I really want is to know why you're tying your boots when you haven't even put on your underwear or pants?"

"Ah ha, I was hoping you would ask me that question. Girl, don't you know that you make me horny? Every time I see you, I get hard as a rock. You bring out the sex beast in me. Its like I want to do all sorts of things with you, and right now, I want to get loose with just my boots on, nothing else, just me, you and my boots."

Alycia went crazy with excitement. *I knew I still had it*, she giggled to herself. She loved that she made him horny. She wanted him to let go of everything and make love to her every minute of the day. She wanted to marry him, to have his children. She wanted anything that had to do with him, anything.

"One second." Her naked body escaped from him, walking toward the bathroom.

"Where are you going?"

"The condoms are in the bathroom cabinet, we've been sloppy, we already did it twice without one and the last one, we used popped."

"Yeah, that's because they make them to small. Besides, I said just me, you and my boots. I didn't mention any condom."

"But Jeff, I thought you said that condoms were mandatory?"

"They are with women I don't love. I love you."

Alycia just collapsed. I love you, were the last words she heard him say. When she finally opened her eyes it was 6 am the next morning and Jeff was coming through the door with an armful of grocery bags.

Let it rain

"Hey baby, you got thirty minutes to get it together or you'll be late."

Alycia was embarrassed that he caught her right where he left her, but she ran to the bathroom and showered thoroughly. When she got out she ran into her room and started pulling clothes off the hangers.

"Hey slow down, I was just kidding, it's Saturday."

"Saturday? Are you sure? Damn that was some night, what do you have in them boots?"

"Naw, it's not the boots, its something else. You know you can't handle this." he said grabbing himself.

"What?"

"Girl, I been wearing you out several times a day. Last night was it, you just collapsed. But don't get mad, I had to get mine, I know it must be getting around that time. And since you've been running around here like a chicken with its head cut off making sure that everything was right for me, I'm going to do the same for you. Look what I got us."

Alycia's frowned as she stared at the bloody Ox tail bones.

"What's with the face? These are good pieces. I took the liberty of going food shopping for you or should I say for us. After I strip this bed down and put on some clean sheets I want you to get back in and relax. I don't want you catching that PMX thing you women get. I even went out and got you some movies. I got three: Across 110th Street, Superfly and The Mack."

"Jeff that was real sweet of you, but I'm not in that way yet."

"That's ok, I still want you to take it easy and relax unless you have other plans, maybe with your girlfriends or mother or something. I don't mean to crowd you, I just thought you might enjoy what's happening, since I am." he kissed her.

"I am enjoying it. The only plans I have are to be with you."

"Great, just give me a minute to change the sheets and then I want you to lay back and enjoy these movies or one of your books or some music. Anything you want, just holler and I'll get it for you."

"What if I want you?"

"Baby please, I don't want to knock you out again. Believe it or not I like looking into those sexy eyes."

Alycia laughed then blushed.

"Oh Jeff, today is a perfect day to stay in, listen to how hard it's raining."

"Yeah, its supposed to rain like this all day. I love rainy days they remind me of how sweet life is. Rain is like food, it feeds the earth -- keeps it moist, clean and fresh."

Jeff got all dreamy eyed, sat on the edge of bed and started reminiscing about when he was young.

"I'll never forget the time my father took me and my brother, Jinks to the carnival. We were so excited, see my parents were separated and my father was the one that always took us out for fun things like the movies, pizza and the carnival. The minute we got there, my brother saw the cotton candy man. Even though we just ate, he begged my dad to buy us one. Shortly after I ate mine I noticed that my hands were sticky and getting dirty. No matter how I tried to remove the sugar, my hands were still sticky. I asked my dad to take me to the bathroom so that I could wash it off, but my brother insisted that the lines were too long and that we should just get on every ride and forget about my sticky hands. So we did and my hands remained sticky and nasty feeling through each ride. It was like the cotton candy spoiled my fun. I couldn't really let go and enjoy myself because of the way my hands felt. And then it started to rain. It may have been my first time ever talking to God but I thanked him for the rain that day and since then I've been in love with rainy days. I held my hand out and let the rain wash away the stickiness. My father and brother started running for the car, but not me, I held my face to the sky and just bathed in the cool drops of rain. I love the rain."

"Aw, that's such a sweet story. I don't think I've ever heard you talk about your childhood before."

"That's nothing, I could tell you stories about my father that would have you cracking up."

"So tell me one."

"Naw, I got to put on these Ox tails." He said hoping that she would ask again.

"Just one more -- a short one." Alycia begged with one finger up.

"Alright, I'll tell you me and Jinks' favorite one. But its not short." he gleamed with excitement. "One time, my father and his girlfriend, Ms. Cindy picked us up to take us to a drive-in movie with them. We liked his girlfriend cause she was real pretty and smelled real pretty. She had these long red finger nails and always chewed gum. My mother was the total opposite. She is attractive but on a much different level. Mom kept her nails trimmed short and she wouldn't dare put on red nail polish, or lipstick. Loud perfume was out of the question. Forget it you only smelled soap and deodorant on moms. And unlike my father's girlfriends, my mother wore her own hair. Anyway, after my father parked way in the back, he told us to switch seats with them and get up front. Then, he went to the refreshment stand to get us sodas, popcorn, hotdogs and candy, Ms. Cindy had a talk with us. She was so close to our face we could taste the gum in her mouth. She said that she wanted us to promise her that we would behave and watch the movie. She said that if we behaved, she would tell our dad to take us out more often. So my brother Jinks who's older than me said that we would be good if she lets us touch her. Ms. Cindy started laughing and said *touch me where?* So my brother pointed at one of her breasts. She said *is that all? Go ahead.* So my brother reached back and grabbed her breast and squeezed it real hard. After he was done he bounced up and down in the front seat laughing. She laughed too. Then she said, *C'mon Jeff don't you want to feel it too?* I said no, I want a kiss. That really made her laugh then she said, *C'mon give Ms. Cindy a kiss.* I closed my eyes and went to kiss her cheek but she grabbed my head and stuck her tongue right into my mouth. It seemed like a real long kiss, it was wet, taste sweet and I liked it. Then she said that I looked just like my dad and that I will break some girl's heart one day. When my father got back, me and my brother couldn't stop laughing, we didn't want our goodies or want to watch the movie, we just wanted to play with Ms. Cindy some more. But my father barked real hard at us and told us to turn around and watch the movie so we did. After we finished our hotdog, wasted our popcorn and drank all of our soda, we heard dad and Ms. Cindy kissing. First Jinks turned around, I was waiting for him to tell me what was going on but he never turned back. So, then as quiet as I could I turned around. Ms. Cindy's blouse was down by her waist and dad was sucking her breast. She had pretty breasts just like yours. Maybe hers were a little bigger but they were pretty. They just stood in the air like they were at attention. Crazy Jinks tried to touch one even while my dad's head was on the other. Anyway, when dad looked like he was about to stop and Ms. Cindy eyes started opening we both turned to the front quickly. They couldn't have noticed because they started moving around in the back like they were trying to get comfortable. Jinks pretended that he was sleep, so I did too. We waited until they seemed comfortable and then we turned around again. Well actually we didn't have to turn around because dad's legs were in the front seat with us. Ms. Cindy had her legs wide open and dad pants were down. We laughed at the site of dad's butt. It was right between our heads. That's when I first saw dad's thing. I never thought mine would ever grow as large as his. I couldn't believe the size of it. I was so proud of my dad. It seemed like he was a strong man because he had a strong looking thing. At first I felt sorry for Ms. Cindy, she cried out like he was hurting her. But a little while later she began calling my dad's name and saying that she loved him and she didn't want him to ever stop. Jinks and I were amazed. After that incident we started misbehaving with girls at school, we stayed in trouble, but the girls, they liked it."

"I can't believe your father did that."

"My father? What about Ms. Cindy?"

"Yeah, she had a lot to do with it but y'all were his kids."

"Yeah, but a lady is supposed to be a lady. That crazy girl would have let the three of us have her if my dad would have said so."

"How old were y'all?"

"I'll never forget, I was eight and Jinks was ten."

"That's big. They should have known better."

"My father was crazy like that. He always did things in front of us that he wanted us to pick up on. He never did anything directly towards us, always indirect. Like when I turned sixteen, I told my father that I remembered what happened and he said *I thought y'all was asleep*. He knew we wasn't sleep, but that's how he did things. Most times he would blame my mother for something that we did instead of just blaming us. Everything was in earshot but nothing direct. Even though when he yelled at mom we stopped. I love my parents."

"So where is your father now?"

"He got married and moved to Virginia."

"Did he marry Cindy?"

"Hell no! We never saw her again. My father was a lover, he was considered fine and had plenty women. We would get crazy gifts at Christmas time. My mother would laugh and say that the women were stupid. At the same time she was happy that we received such nice things."

"So who did he marry?"

"He married this lady name Susan. Susan is real nice. She had twins a year after they got married. We keep in touch."

When Jeff stopped talking, he and Alycia noticed the same thing -- they were talking. He was sharing his life with her, telling her intimate stories about his family. This was new for him and he liked having Alycia there stretching her eyes and latching onto his every word. He thought what a perfect rainy Saturday morning for sharing.

Tricked

"You know Selina, all this exercise stuff really makes me feel good. I feel so strong. If it wasn't pouring outside, I would go running. I can't believe it's been raining all morning."

"You think it's these exercises, but you're feeling strong because you don't have that mess in your system anymore. We should have locked her up."

"No Selina, don't mess with her. She's crazy. I get sick every time I think of how she was drugging me."

"That's why we need to do something about it."

"I know, but please, let's wait I'm not strong enough to deal with her yet."

"We'll wait."

"It hasn't been a week yet and I already love Snoop Doggy Dog. Even though he just totally dis women."

"What do you expect? He's a dog." They both laughed.

"I'll admit though, if I had my chance I'd do him." Selena confessed.

"For real, I wouldn't, I still cringe at the thought of men." Trudy frowned.

"Well, lately that's all I've been dealing with."

The two women got to the point where they knew that it was time to talk about them. Selina turned the music down and Trudy sat on the floor with her legs folded.

"So how are they? Have you converted?"

"Not really. To be truthful, I never got over you. Men were the only way that I could save myself for you all of these years. I've been waiting for you. I missed you so much. When I didn't hear anything from you, I considered only one other woman and she's not into the life. So there was no one else."

"I guess I knew that you were waiting. But as time passed, so did my thoughts about us. I'm sorry for allowing things to go the way that they did. I loved you so much, but I was greedy. It wasn't that I was ready to take on the world. It was just that I was ready to explore other possibility." Trudy paused, then took a deep breath to continue. "Trish had come up to me one night in the Village. She said that she wanted to give her boyfriend his fantasy wish for his birthday."

"Which was?"

"He wanted to watch her make love to a woman while he took pictures. At first I laughed but then when she said that she was serious and that he would pay me a thousand dollars if I did it, I agreed."

"While we were still together?"

"Well, yes and no. I agreed because I wanted the money. Aunt Moo started threatening me about paying her rent. She said that I owed her seven hundred dollars in back money and that she wanted me out, unless I paid. I didn't want to be on the streets with you, my room was our home. So I figured that I would get the money, leave Aunt Moo, and get an apartment for us. But that's when you said that you weren't ready to take on such a big move. I got mad, broke up with you and did what Trish had asked me to do."

"Did they pay you?"

"Yeah, that's probably what kept me until this day."

"Trish's boyfriend said that he would give me two thousand dollars if I would spend the night. He said that he had to go some where and that Trish didn't like being alone. So I agreed. The next morning when I got up Trish was already dressed reading the paper. She said that her boyfriend left me twenty-five hundred dollars and then she started crying. It was all an act at the time but I was so happy to see all that money, I thought her tears was real."

"Why was she crying?"

"You're not going to believe this, but she said that after I fell asleep, he came back and they had a fight, she said that he accused her of being dirty and stupid. He said that he didn't want a woman that was stupid enough to do anything he said and then he collected his things and said that he was never coming back."

"What?" Selina said amazed at the lengths Trish had taken.

"But the real truth was that Trish paid him to pretend to be her boyfriend so that she could get me in the sack. That was her money he paid me with. She cooked up the whole thing and probably gave me something to knock me out that first night."

"That sort of reminds me of how we met."

"Yeah, I know, I guess it doesn't feel so good when you're on the other end."

"So how do you know she did this?"

"After I held her and tried to calm her down. She held me back and kissed me. She begged me to stay. She said that she loved him very much and that she wasn't ready to be alone. I didn't want to stay because she wasn't a good lover, but her place was so clean and nice. There were beautiful things all around and it just made me feel special. I told her that I had to check on my aunt and that I would be back in an hour. Afraid to let me out of her sight, she insisted on driving me. On the way to Aunt Moo's house she told me to grab some clothes. She said that she would pay me for a weeks worth of companionship and then she began begging me some more."

"So then what happened?"

"When I got to Aunt Moo's I gave her the money she said I owed her, and then I stuck the rest under the floor board in my room. It should still be there."

"So that's how people get caught up into things like that huh -- Money."

"Yep. Money it was. Everyday she would do something really special for me. I liked it. I liked it for about a good year. Then she started smothering me. I couldn't go to the store across the street without her peeking out the window at me. She wanted to know my every move. When I confronted her and told her that I thought she was being insecure and that she should look into doing more with her life, she exploded. She told me that I had nerve to talk. She said that I was stupid and greedy. When I questioned her facts, she laughed at how she tricked me into being her lover. She laughed that it was years ago and that I was still there with her."

"So why didn't you leave then?"

"That was the night of my first strong dose. Two days after that argument I was still drowsy and needed her to help me around the place. She apologized for saying the things she said to me. She said that, it was out of anger and that the only reason why she took such drastic measures was because she found me very stimulating and attractive. She said that it was love at first sight and that she'd do almost anything to have and keep me. I was so sick I just forgave her. The next day after that, it all seemed like a dream, but it wasn't."

"Stop, don't tell me anymore. This story is making me sick to my stomach."

"I know, and I keep asking myself why. Aunt Moo kept us so poor and unattractive that I just jumped at the first chance of what seemed like paradise. I never was attracted to Trish. She's so dead looking, and has a horrible smell, even when she's clean. I just don't know why I stayed so long."

"Forget it. I don't want to talk about it anymore."

Selina got up from the floor and put on some music.

We're going to be late

Gary unzipped the suit bag and hung his suit over the bedroom door. Tonight was the big Children's Benefit where he was going to be honored.

"Gary, I don't know why you're complaining, you stay with me most of the time. If Dice is like your brother then what's the problem? *Hand me my brush.* Everyone has situations that sometimes are out of their control. I'm sure Queetha will keep the place nice enough that you won't know that they're there."

"Queetha? *I should have worn my blue suit.* I didn't tell you that fool left Queetha."

Maya's eyes widened and her mouth flew open.

"What?! I know he didn't leave her. Isn't she close to nine months pregnant? *That suit looks just fine.*"

"Yeah, she's close to nine months pregnant and so is Sharice. *Help me with my tie.*"

"Sharice? Who's that?"

"Sharice is Dice's new fiancé. He claims that when he was with Queetha she treated him like a dog. He said that she hated him. *You're choking me.* That she never loved him and that she just used him for what she needed him for and nothing else. *I hate this tie.*"

"I could believe it, I didn't find Queetha friendly at all. She kept her arms folded and barely said a word. *Here zip me up.* I tried to bring up different topics to catch her interest but she just looked at me. Don't tell me Dice got the other girl pregnant too?"

"Yup. *Do I have any dress socks here?* I don't know why Queetha gets such a bad rap. I never had any problems with her. I think she's sweet."

"So are you going to talk to her, you two seemed so close, maybe you should find out whether Dice is telling the truth? *Your dress socks are in my stocking drawer.*"

"I called Queetha late last night, from what she's told me, she doesn't want Dice back at all. She said that he did what he could do for her and now Sharice can have whatever is left."

"And you still think she's sweet?"

"Yeah. Maya, you don't know, Dice has a lot of shit with him."

Maya just shook her head from side to side and wondered *how come men are so blind.*

"I find it amazing how this girl Sharice could be so careless to get pregnant by a married man. *I like your haircut.*

"I don't think it was being careless. They needed this baby. Both of them were in a bad relationship and were too insecure to get out. *That dress is going to have all the guys talking tomorrow.* This baby is their bond. They needed something strong enough for them to take a stand. Besides, their in love, every time I see Dice he's dancing around with those high hips of his."

Maya laughed. "So let's invite them over for dinner."

"Maya please, I have to live with these people I don't want to see them if I don't have to. *Where's my wallet?*"

"Oh Gary, c'mon, I'm curious to see this Sharice. Two women pregnant at the same time? That Dice is some busy man. *I haven't seen your wallet.*"

"Too busy if you ask me. And don't think I don't know what you're up to."

"What?"

"You just want to look Sharice over. I know how you women do."

"I'll admit to that, but what I really want to do is check out her head. I can't believe a woman in this day and age would be so crazy as to have a married man's child. *There's your wallet, on the floor.*"

"Believe it. Now can we get off of this subject?"

"No, I'm not finished do you think that he loves her enough to stay away from his first family?"

"Yeah, he used to stay at my house all the time anyway. Queetha didn't allow him to play his music."

"No wonder he left, I couldn't live with a person like her, she sounds bossy. *Like my new lipstick?*"

"*It's alright.*"

"*Alright? Gary it matches perfectly with my dress. I shopped all day for this shade.*"

"*Let me taste it.*"

"*That's alright.*"

"I am really surprised at you. You never talk about people, just to think I was hesitant about telling you the situation because I thought you was going to go off about him leaving Queetha with the pregnancy and all."

"Gary, I respect all of your friends and I like Dice because he has manners and he always makes me laugh."

"You mean cause he's always flirting with you. Enough with the mirror, you look like a sexy fashion model."

"Anyway, I never said anything about his wife because she's a part of him and he's a part of you. But now that this has happened I'm kind of happy for Dice."

"Happy for him? *C'mon we're late.*"

"Yeah, remember that time we went over to their house for dinner, and Dice's brother came over to borrow Dice's suit for his big interview?"

"Oh yeah, Queetha wouldn't let his brother wear the suit."

"I thought that was so embarrassing, then right in front of him, she jumped in Dice's face and said, "I bought that suit for you, not your brother. *Lock the door.*""

"That was kind of cold."

"Kind of? That was petty, selfish, unloving and ignorant. If she bought it for him then it's his, and if he doesn't mind that his brother wears it, why should she?"

"*Watch your step.* That was the same night that he met Sharice."

"It was fate."

"Just like with you and I."

Maya leaned over and kissed Gary on the cheek.
"Keep your eyes on the road."

Friends & Lovers

"He may have beaten me in court, but I still owe him for what he did to me at Booties."

"Let it go Dane, they did what they felt they had to do. I've known Tyrone and Wes for years, they're not the violent type. Just like Sarah, you bring the violence out of people."

"You wasn't saying that a minute ago when you was begging me not to stop."

"Come on Dane, I'm not talking about sex. I'm talking about life. I know you're upset but, I have to admit, I didn't think that you really loved Wes."

"I don't."

"Yes you do, you called me by his name twice. You wasn't making love to him, it was me. It's alright to still be in love, but why would you want to hurt them?"

"Because they hurt me!" Dane could no longer hide his pain. "Over a silly little picture, my life with Wes is over! I don't deserve that! Yes, I do still love him and I'm going to fix that little Tyrone once and for all."

"Listen to you -- you sound crazy, do you really believe that Wes will take you back?"

"He took me the first time."

"I know, but I know Wes, he only had you because you are good in bed. It was like a mid-life crisis, he needed something different. He loves Tyrone. I don't think anyone can come between them."

"I did." Dane bragged.

"Yeah, but that only made their love stronger. I hear that they're even getting married."

"Married? No! Please don't tell me their getting married!" Dane said holding his heart.

"Next month. They're having a big celebration and everything."

"Oh No!" Dane cried. "I'll die if he marries Tyrone. I hate Tyrone."

"Why? Tyrone hasn't done anything to you. As a matter of fact, I remember when you use to like Tyrone."

"I never liked that cheap imitation of Wesley. He's so phony, always wearing expensive clothes like he's a movie star. I hate him, I hate him!"

"Calm down Dane, it's not the end of the world."

"Oh shut up and listen, I want you to ask Carl to snoop around and find out all the details about this so called wedding."

"For what? They're not going to invite you."

"Just do what I say. I have a plan."

"Look Dane, if you're planning on crashing the wedding, I won't help you get this information."

"Yes you will, because you enjoy being with me." Dane said licking Jay's fat stomach."

"Come on Dane, don't torture me, you know you got it going on, don't ask me to hurt Wes, he's an old friend."

"And I'm a new lover." Dane said waving his tongue in and out of his mouth.

My favorite men

"Allen was brilliant in court."

"You paid him enough." Tyrone said hanging up his Armani wool jacket.

"As hard as I tried not to laugh, I had to, did you see Dane's outfit?"

"That was funny. I can't believe she finally cut off that tacky blond hair."

"And that suit, I didn't recognize him at first you know he usually wears loud colors. I can't believe he had on a descent brown suit. He must have thought that he was going to win."

"The haircut is what I couldn't believe, he looks much better as a man than a wanna-be woman."

"Yeah he must be planning on going back home to his momma. Got a real man's haircut and wearing men's clothes." Wesley shook his head. "Too bad he couldn't fool the jury. Can you believe he tried to blame me for the burn on his face?"

"That and the virus is where he hung himself. He didn't even have it, but as usual he went too far and would say anything to get some money and back at me. I'm glad Allen got Sarah to testify. I felt so sorry for her, she really loves him."

"It's true, I hated seeing her up there crying like that. I'm glad that you wrote her a check for her damages, she really seemed like she appreciated it."

"Putting up with that mess, she deserved every dime of it."

"I'm just glad that it's over, now we can plan our wedding."

"Our wedding . . . I like the way that sounds." Wesley leaned over and caressed Tyrone's thigh.

"I'm looking forward to the bachelor party, its going to be a night to remember."

"Who you telling? Charles and Eddie have already been buzzing around asking when and where."

"Those two are so nosey. I can't see how they lived together without waking each other up to find out what the other one is dreaming about."

"That's too funny."

"Oh yeah, I forgot to tell you, Carl came up to me yesterday and said that he heard that we were tying the knot."

"So?"

"It was just the way he said it. He wanted to know was he invited and when were we going to do it."

"So, everybody has been asking that."

"Yeah, but Carl was acting like he needed the information for something else."

"Like what? What did you tell him?"

"I told him that he was not invited and if I wanted him to know our business I would be telling him instead of him asking me."

"I hope you didn't get nasty."

"Just nasty enough to let him know that I knew what he was up to."

"And what's that."

"I not sure but I know that he used to go out with one of Dane's close friends. What's the guy's name with the freckles?

"Jay?"

"Yeah Jay, Carl and Jay use to be kissing in Washington Square Park all the time."

"So what's the worst they can do, crash the shower?"

"I don't know but I just didn't like the way he was asking me, I could tell that he was being phony and didn't really care what our plans were. He was asking for someone else."

"Well, I wouldn't worry about it, the shower will be right here in our home and I'm sure no one outside of our guest list will get past Mr. D. You know how serious he takes his job."

"Good. Speaking of lists I was working on one last night."

"I hope you didn't invite everyone we know. I want to keep it under thirty guys. You know how homosexual's bachelor parties can get."

"I left you eight people to add, I did twenty-two. Now I don't want to give it away but two of the people are a surprise."

"Knowing you, I can only imagine." Wesley said smiling, relieved that he was done with Dane and court and everything was finally going well for them. "Read the list tell me who is on it."

"OK, I got Brian, Steve, Gene, Kelly, Jerry, Alexander, Charles, Louis, Tony, David, Phil, Sanford, Jose, Mario, Ward, Thomas, Seth, Eric, Mike, Amos, Hodge and Paul."

"You did well, those are my favorite men." Wesley laughed.

"I knew you would have approved."

"Who's Eric?"

"Oh, Eric is a new friend of mine, he lives in Jersey."

"Where did you meet him?"

"I don't even remember, but he's a model and I promised that I would invite him to the next party we have. He's good people."

"Great. So are you ready to set the date?"

"Yeah, I think we should do it in October."

"Next October or next month October?"

"Next month October. So our party will be in two weeks."

"Fine, you make all the arrangements I'll design something scandalous for us to wear."

"We're going to need something scandalous, because I bet before the party is over there will be a scandal." Wesley joked.

Oh God please

The drops of blood that colored the water beneath her were unreal. Roz sat still, closed her eyes and prayed that what she thought was happening wasn't. She eased up and wiped herself clean. Then she flushed the blood stained tissue and walked slowly out of the bathroom. When she reached her bed she kneeled down beside it and prayed again.

Oh God, I know that you have the power to give and take, so

Please let me keep my baby

I don't know how or why this is happening to me, but

Please let me keep my baby

If I've done anything wrong or said the wrong thing,

forgive me and please let me keep my baby

I know that you make choices that we don't understand, but

Please let me keep my baby.

Before Roz could say another word she felt a sharp cramp from within then a heavy warm gush sliding down between her thighs. She jumped up and rushed to take off her clothes only to see the deep color of blood that stained them. She cried, *Oh God, please let me keep my baby. Please let me keep my baby.*

Before wheeling Roz into her room, Lance dried his eyes trying to cover the emotions he felt. After receiving her D&C, Roz was still asleep, but Lance could see that her eyes were swollen like she had cried all night. When Roz's mother and Maya came into the room, Roz woke up and the tears started falling again.

After coming home from the hospital with nothing to do or look forward to, Roz went into a state of depression. Even though Lance consoled her and told her that they could try again whenever she was ready, she felt like she had let him down. She was ashamed and couldn't grip the situation, because she didn't have an explanation for it.

She held up the rattle that she received in the mail two days before she lost her baby and shook it until it made her cry some more.

"My baby was supposed to play with this. My baby was supposed to shake this rattle. Oh God. Why did you have to take my baby?"

Roz persuaded Lance to leave her alone and give her some time to be by herself, she said that she needed a couple of days to clear her head. Needing the same thing he obliged. Days had passed and Roz didn't know it, she didn't open her blinds, pick up her phone, or answer her door bell. She would just walk around with the rattle in her hands asking God why. After days of going through his own state of depression, Lance came to see her. He wanted to tell her that chapter in their lives was over. It was time to look to the future, to stop dwelling over the past. He said that God knew best and he did what he had to do. At first, Roz didn't want to here it, she ran in the bedroom and locked the door behind her, then she picked up a folded towel and wrapped the baby's blanket around it and held it tight. She rocked it from side to side and whispered sweet nothings to it. Lance pounded and pounded on the door, begging her to open it. He wanted desperately to know what she was doing inside. When Roz wouldn't open the door, Lance grabbed the rattle and told her to listen close. He destroyed the rattle, breaking it into tiny little pieces. He told her that it was over, to please let go. When Roz heard the rattle shatter into pieces, she dropped the make believe baby and ran to open the door.

"That's my baby's rattle." She looked at him with thick tears.

"Roz, it's over."

"My baby's rattle." She mumbled on her knees, picking up the small pieces.

"C'mon honey, get up."

"Why did you break my baby's rattled?!" she screamed like a crazed woman.

Lance was forced to let his tears roll. He loved Roz so much and hated seeing her like this. He cried as she pounded his chest with her fist.

"I hate you! I hate you!" she rambled now punching him with less strength.

Lance patiently waited for Roz to calm down then he hugged her and asked her to pray with him, to put their baby to rest. Roz dried her tears and began to pray.

Doubled-Crossed

The noise from the sirens didn't disturb the lovers nor did the pounding on the door. Jeff and Alycia were into one of their deep sessions and tuned everything but what was going on between the sheets out. Alycia heard the pounding but thought it was Jeff's heart beating. Jeff didn't hear a thing he was too busy handling his business. When the pounding continued Alycia tried to get Jeff to slow down so that she could at least ask who was there. But without a word, Jeff convinced her that whoever it was, had bad timing, wanted something stupid and wasn't important enough for them to stop or slow down. Alycia agreed with the moaning that came out of him and continued on with their afternoon marathon. That worked for a short while but then the heavy pounding resulted in the kitchen door crashing down onto the kitchen floor, they both jumped up.

"What the fuck!" Jeff reacted like he was real tough.

"Oh no, it's the police!" Alycia announced as if Jeff hadn't noticed.

"Cover your nipples!" Jeff said reaching for his shorts.

Pleased at the sight of Alycia's breast the round officer smiled and said. "I have a warrant for one Jeffrey M. Turner."

"Yeah, that's me." Jeff volunteered boldly unaffected by the police presence.

"You have the right to remain silent ..."

"Hold up! Wait a fucking minute." Jeff said. "Let me get dressed."

It wasn't until they handcuffed him that he noticed that he had on Alycia's gold blouse with pearl buttons instead of his gold shirt with black buttons.

"Wait! I can't go with this on!"

"Anything and everything you say will be held against you . . ."

"Jeff what should I do?" Alycia whined.

"Call Cheryl."

"*Cheryl?*"

"Yeah, her number is programmed on the last button of your phone."

Without hesitating Alycia called Cheryl.

"Hi Cheryl, this is Alycia, Jeff asked me to call you."

"Let me guess, he got arrested?"

"Yeah, how did you know?"

Cheryl's laugh was uncontrollable when she stopped she covered the mouth piece of the phone and repeated Alycia's words to everyone in the room around her.

"Tell her that you've been through it fifty times." Alycia heard someone say."

"No, no ask her how does it feel to be his latest victim." another one added.

"Who's that? What are they saying?" Alycia asked.

"Don't worry about it. How much money did he leave?"

"None, the police took it all."

"Did they take all the money that was in the silver box?"

"Yeah."

"Well look in your pink house coat all the way in the back of your closet."

Not knowing what to do, Alycia immediately dropped the phone and ran to the closet.

"There's about forty thousand dollars here. How did you know money was there?"

"Wild guess." Cheryl replied sarcastically. "Get dressed and meet me at the World Trade Center, I'll be standing by the entrance of building two."

"Wait, let me get a pen."

"You don't need a pen just meet me in front of Two World Trade Center."

Needing to be near him, Alycia slipped into Jeff's shirt. She danced into her tight black jeans and wore the new Timberland boots he had given her. *Where should I put the money?* She thought out loud. But she couldn't find a good answer because Cheryl's voice and laughter stayed on her mind. *How did she know that I needed to get dressed?* Alycia tied her right boot and separated the money into two parts. She slipped the bulky envelopes in the inside pockets of her jacket.

Cheryl was already there waiting when Alycia arrived.

"What took you so long?" she barked.

Stunned by Cheryl's pretty face, Alycia found herself explaining that she couldn't get a cab.

"Just give me the money." Cheryl said snatching the envelopes out of Alycia's hand and walking away.

"When will he be home?"

"Home?" Cheryl turned around with one hand on her hip. "You mean my house?" She stretched her eyes and pointed to her chest.

"Well no, I was talking about mine. Jeff said that he's staying with me now."

"And you believed him?"

"Yes." Alycia said as sincere as she knew how. "Cheryl, I don't know if he's told you yet, but we're in love. Jeff loves me."

"Loves you? Girl, just look at you when are you going to open your eyes? Jeff don't love you, he don't even love himself."

Cheryl's confidence made Alycia feel insecure about her relationship with Jeff. *Was he that good?* Looking at her reflection through the glass doors she realized that she was so involved in helping Jeff that she forgot to comb her hair, put on make-up, earrings or perfume.

"Look, I'm not going to stand here and argue with you about who he loves. You need to get over him and find someone else to fill your needs." Now ashamed of her appearance, Alycia attempted to walk away.

"Fill my needs?" Cheryl stopped her by grabbing her shoulder. "I know you didn't say fill my needs. Girl, I was going to save this for later but since you asked for it." Cheryl said waving her head and finger in Alycia's face. "How do you think I knew that the money was in your pink robe?"

"He must have told you that he put it there, for emergency reasons." Alycia act like it was no big deal.

"Wrong! Last week while you were at work, after we got finished working it out in your bed, he gave me the robe to wrap up in while I fixed his lunch. He practically screwed me while I had it on. Just as I was about to leave, he told me to put the money in the robe pocket, and place it in the back of the closet on the floor. Didn't you find the robe folded on the floor?"

"You're a damn liar." Alycia said slapping Cheryl across her face as hard as she could.

"Bitch, are you crazy?" Cheryl responded with a punch to the stomach.

The two women fought it out for about a minute before Cheryl threatened to cut her.

"Don't make me slice you I was just letting you know what the brother is about. Now let go of my hair!"

When the Port Authority Police came running towards them Cheryl hid the razor.

"Everything is alright officer, my sister and I just had a little disagreement."

Then Cheryl placed her arm around Alycia and hugged her.

"I swear I have nothing against you, we just happen to love the same man. Believe me I know the truth about him hurts. The only reason why I came into you're home, is because he left me and now I'm hurting. Jeff don't love us, he's using us against each other. He don't deserve either one of us."

Relieved to hear those words, Alycia held on tight to Cheryl's body and they both cried.

"Look, I got an idea," Cheryl said stepping away from Alycia a little embarrassed that they were embracing. "If you want, I could tell Jeff that we had a fight and that the police took the money from us. We could leave him where he belongs. We can split the money, you can have twenty and I could have twenty."

Alycia smiled and accepted the offer. The two walked to a nearby restaurant and talked over their feelings about how women should stick together and leave men like Jeff alone.

Twice as Dice

"Gary, Gary wake up! Sharice had a boy! Sharice had a boy! And she named him after me. My first son! Gary wake up, did you hear me?"

"Man, get out of my bed. I heard you. I heard you. Congratulations, now goodnight."

"C'mon Gary, we have to celebrate, she had a boy, Lynwood Stanley Johnson, Jr.! Don't that sound rich?"

"Yeah, yeah it sounds rich. But Dice man, you have to get out of my bed. I just got in about an hour ago and I'm tired. Do me a favor and close the door behind you."

"Man, you ain't no fun."

"Yeah, that's right leave, little Lynwood is going to want to see you first thing in the morning."

Dice closed the door and danced around the apartment. He went to the refrigerator and made himself a big fruit salad, but just picked out the grapes. Then he sat on the couch and smiled dreaming about playing ball with his little man. Then he fantasized about the sweet revenge it would be when Queetha found out that he had a son, something he always wanted.

After about two hours of sleep, the phone rang. It was Queetha's mother she screamed that he should meet them at the hospital right away, that Queetha was having the baby. Dice jumped up, grabbed his coat and went straight to the hospital.

Queetha had a boy, too. When he came into the room to talk with her, she told him that she knew she pushed him to do the things he did. She said that she still loved him and to prove it, she was naming their son after him, Lynwood Stanley Johnson, Jr.

She's sexy and smart

Their conversation was intense. Each woman told elaborate fantasy stories and compared notes on the way Jeff made love to them. Cheryl testified that, because she was light skinned, Jeff poured hot chocolate syrup all over her body and didn't stop eating it until it was all gone. Alycia had to top that, with her story about the time when Jeff burst into her home. While she was in the tub, she said that he was so out of breath, running up all those stairs that when he came into the bathroom he drank two cups of her bath water before he got in. Both women pretended to be excited for the other.

Two minutes after waving goodbye to Cheryl, Alycia hopped a cab and went straight to the courthouse to bail Jeff out. Regardless of anything that Cheryl had said, Alycia couldn't wait to see her sweet, loving Jeff. She had to warn him about Cheryl, tell him what kind of vindictive person he was dealing with and tell him about the plan Cheryl made for the money.

****

After receiving the disappointing news that Jeff would have to stay in jail until he got a court date, Alycia went home to twenty-eight sleepless nights. That's how many nights it took before Jeff's release. Alycia counted them by marking hearts on each day of her calendar and placing a prayer in her bible for his return.

The minute the clerk handed Alycia her receipt and Jeff's release papers, Alycia threw her arms around him and in detail told him what Cheryl had planned.

"Damn baby and you didn't want to do that? I think you're the dumb one." Jeff said hailing a cab.

"Huh?"

"I gotta hand it to Cheryl, she's smart, she did what I would have done. She was going to take the money and run, smart. Smart girl. She knows that I would have gotten out sooner or later."

"But, Jeff. I was the one that got you out, doesn't that count for something?"

"Hey, I didn't say it didn't. I'm just tripping about Cheryl. She was finally going to pay me back." *And she would if it wasn't for your dumb ass!* Jeff thought to himself. "She would have had me too." Jeff was just a little pissed at Alycia for being such a sucker. He didn't like suckers. (Well he did but, not that kind). Jeff looked out the backseat window, blushing, thinking about how sexy and smart Cheryl was and how he missed her cleverness. The more he thought about her, the more he knew that Cheryl had set Alycia up. Cheryl knew that Alycia was pitiful and would get him out as soon as she could. She was just setting the stage for his return. Cheryl knew that Jeff would come home excited, angry and hot for her.

"Why are you smiling? What are you smiling about? Jeff I hope you're not thinking about her?"

"About who? You're the only woman on my mind." he lied, then leaned over and gave her a smooth kiss to shut her up, so that he could daydream about the good time he was going to have with Cheryl. He knew that he wasn't getting the money back, so she would have to compensate some other way, his way.

"Jeff, let's just go back home and pretend that this never happened. I know you want to eat something. I'll cook us a special dinner and we could . . ."

"Yo! My man, let me out right here! Look baby, I'll meet you back at the house, I'm going to get the rest of my stuff and let Cheryl know that it's all about me and you."

"But, Jeff?"

Jeff slammed the cab door ignoring Alycia's last call. His mind was on Cheryl right now and Alycia couldn't touch it.

After paying the cab Alycia went upstairs again without Jeff. She had been waiting for twenty-eight days and there wasn't a thing left for her to do. The refrigerator was filled with so much food she could hardly close it. The house was spotless. With nothing else to do, she grabbed the Absolut vodka out of the bar, poured two shots into a glass, added some cranberry juice and squeezed a slice of lemon into the mix. After her third drink of this, she beeped him, ten minutes and no return call. Alycia got up went into the bathroom, stared in the mirror and cried. She got so upset, she threw up. That was Monday, on Friday she was still throwing up and Jeff still hadn't returned. Finally it dawned on her that she hadn't seen her period. She tried counting the days but last month was filled with worrying about Jeff and she couldn't think straight. After talking to herself, she decided that maybe she did have it, she just couldn't remember, just like going to work last week, she knew she went but couldn't remember anything that happened or who she spoke with. Everything was about Jeff and now Jeff was gone.

Her last smile

Trudy reached under the floor board to get the money to bury her Aunt Moody. She passed out at the morgue when identifying her Aunt's body. The cause of death was an overdose of pills. The police said that they had found her lying on the sofa with ten one hundred dollar bills in her lap and a smile on her face. Right then Trudy knew just who was behind her aunt's death and she began fearing for her own life.

****

It seemed like the whole neighborhood turned out for Moody's funeral. Everyone knew her as the friendly fat lady with the nasty mouth that sat half naked on the front porch. Moody had her ways but for the most part she was popular and well respected. Trish even attended the funeral, not to pay her respects but to gloat about how she did Moody in.

"I knew I would have find you here." She approached Selina like she had a knife under her shirt. "You could have at least told me that you were leaving."

Disgusted to be in her presence Trudy avoided Trish's eyes and whispered, "Did you do it? Did you kill my aunt?"

Surprised and impressed that Trudy was smart enough to figure it out, Trish's responded "What do you think? She didn't deserve to live, she was a fat slob -- you said so yourself. When I asked her to tell me where you were staying, she stuck out her hand and begged me for a thousand dollars. I gave it to her and then she kicked at me and spit in my hair. She said that she wouldn't tell me where you were if her life depended upon it. But I knew your aunt, she's just like you, greedy, so I told her that I would give her another thousand if she told me the truth. I told her that I wanted to just let you know that I found someone new. So she changed her tune and offered me a drink, when she got up to get it, I slipped her something good, something that would make her sleep forever. I wish you could have been there, it was beautiful. She gagged then did this dance like she was going out of her mind and then she collapsed. She tried to reach out to me, her eyes begging me for help but I just looked at her and grinned. Then she mustered up enough strength to reach her hand out to me for help and that's when I got back at her and spitted in her face. She got the message then that I was not there to help but to harm. She struggled about a minute more and then took her last breath and died. I stared at her ugly face for a long while and it just didn't look happy so I added a smile. It was easy. I just put my finger between her dry chapped lips and made her smile. Then I left her there with the money. I knew that you could use it for the burial. What a waste. It would have been way cheaper to cremate her fat rusty body."

Trudy flipped and grabbed Trish by the throat.

"You sick monster!" she shouted stomping all over her. "How could you be so cold? That was my aunt, my blood." Trudy cried kicking Trish as hard as she could.

When Aunt Moo's children realized their cousin was in a fight, without knowing why, they joined in and help Trudy beat Trish into a bloody a mess.

****

The first night after finding her aunt's body, Trudy went crazy. She wanted to go to Mexico or anywhere to hide from Trish. "I know she did it Selina, I know she did it."

Before Aunt Moody's death, Selina told two guys on her job about the accusations that Trudy made against Trish. She was afraid and thought that Trish should go to jail before she did any more harm. One of the guys remembered Trish's name from a news article, with a similar incident, that left her lover dead. The news article said that Trish was being held, but had to be released because they didn't have enough evidence. The girl's family was quoted as saying that they believed she was being poisoned by Trish. Trish retaliated by saying that the girl had a bad drug problem and overdosed. Selina asked him did he remember how long ago he had read the story, and what paper was it in. After two days of looking, she tracked down the story and called the detective that was in charge of the investigation. The detective advised Trudy to wear a tape recorder if she ever planned on being around Trish. The advice was good, but who knew that they would have to use it so soon?

Minutes after the fight broke out the detectives came running in and pulled the crowd off of Trish. They heard everything and placed handcuffs on her promising her a very long vacation as they carried her out of the funeral home.

The big payback

Thumping music escaped the walls of Wesley's apartment. The place was in full effect. Lavishly decorated in hot pinks and purples and judging from afar you would think there were celebrities in attendance. Ru Paul, Donna Summers, and Diana Ross impersonators were all there. Along with life size cardboard cutouts of Arsenio, Montel and Cher and if that wasn't enough, Wesley had paid management an additional twenty percent to hire a staff of all male waiters who would work the party dressed in only two pieces: a hot pink bowtie and a purple g-string bikini.

The couple's custom made *Happy Chair* was a gift from Utopia Classics a fashion designing company that is trying to pull Wesley from Bakari. The chair was loaded with all kinds of ticklers and gadgets to make the boys happy when they sat on it. Long curly lavender ribbons hung from the mixture of pink and lavender helium balloons that made the room appear magical. Like hanging beads the strings had to be parted every time you moved to go to the other side.

The Ru Paul impersonator was the bartender and appeared to be the big hit of the night. Most of the guys crowded around him flirting and making dates. Although pretty much of a waste, everything was elegantly arranged. Wesley left no room for disappointment. Platters of lobster tails, shrimp, fruit, cheese, sauces and dips where offered by the flirtatious group of servers. The food looked delicious, but instead of eating there was a lot of laughing, kissing, hugging, picture taking and touching going on.

At about 3:00 am, Tyrone announced that it was time for the entertainment. The double doors swung open wide as the huge pink cake with two miniature groomsmen on top, rolled into the room.

"There better not be a woman inside." Paul joked.

The hired staff was excellent in setting up the presentation for the show. Without noticed every candle was suddenly lit and all the lights were turned down. The music was eerie as the lid of the cake slowly flipped open. A long black leather arm stuck out, five fingers spread open and waved around the room. Slowly moving upwards like it was on an escalator, the leather covered head began to show. The boys applauded.

"Oh my goodness, it looks like cat woman." Paul joked again.

"Where are you going?" Wesley whispered to Tyrone.

"I need to adjust the spotlight, it's not high enough. Here sit." Tyrone patted the seat. "It's your turn to be happy."

Paul was right the person did have on a cat woman costume. When the body rose it revealed that there were two men. One man sitting on another man's shoulder -- face to groin the men pretended to be having oral sex. The audience went wild, whistled and applauded.

"Save some for me." Gene yelled.

Now facing the crowd, the mask man slowly pulled off his mask and pulled out his gun. It was Dane. Dane fired shots directly to the Happy Chair hoping to kill Tyrone dead. But Wesley was in the chair, and it was Wesley that was shot four times.

Before Dane could run out the door, Tyrone reached in his potted plant and pulled out his gun and caught Dane in the head, back, leg and shoulder. Not knowing what to do, Ru Paul screamed and ran frantically in every direction.

"I don't understand what's going on?" She said throwing her head back, allowing her lovely blond wig to get caught in the flame of a candle.

"Oh my Stars! Someone help me!" she screamed taking the attention from the shooting scene.

"Take it off!" someone yelled.

"I can't its glued!" she screamed running straight to the bathroom.

Minutes later, Tyrone was arrested, Wesley was rushed to the hospital under critical condition, and Dane was dead.

Ashes to ashes, dust to dust

Dane's death knocked the whole gay community for a loop. Men where falling out crying all over the streets about how much they were going to miss Dane.

It took Sarah for a loop, too. It was just a few months ago that they had shared so much love, laughter and friendship. It didn't matter that weeks before his death she wrote him off, vowing to never trust him in her presence again, regardless of what people said about him, he was still her child, her gift, her son. Sitting in the back seat of the funeral car, not ready to say good bye Sarah cried a big cry. This was the 2nd son she had lost.

Sarah's real son Tony was her all and all. She loved that boy with everything she had. Some accused her of loving him too much. They said that she was raising him soft, treating him like a baby all the time. Always pampering him and doing everything for him. Never letting him stand on his own, or do for his self. So when it came out that Tony was slipping around with boys instead of girls, they all blamed Sarah for treating him that way. Sarah paid the gossip no mind, they were all just jealous because her son was pretty enough to be a girl and their sons were ugly. But little did Sarah know that it would be her boyfriend that would break her heart and take the one person that she loved most away from her. Sarah's boyfriend Silas hated Tony; he hated the fact that Sarah gave her son more attention than she gave him. He would start arguments with her over petty things that she would do for Tony, anything to take her time away from her son. So when Silas found out that Tony had an interest in boys, he threatened to kill Tony if he ever caught him shaking his ass or flirting with boys.

Silas claimed to be a real man and no sissy was going to be sleeping in the same house were he slept. Neither Sarah nor Tony took Silas's threat serious. Sarah was in denial about Tony lifestyle and Tony thought that Silas was just a pathetic asshole.

Therefore, the two of them went on about their lives paying Silas little attention. So when Silas came home from work one day, which really meant home from the bar and found Tony and his friend in Tony's room playing music and lying across his bed flipping through GQ magazines he got mad. He burst through the room door hoping to catch a better act. Then he ordered them out of the house. Tony's friend wasted no time leaving but Tony didn't move to quickly, he was pissed that this man was telling him to get out of the home that his mother provided for him. If anyone should leave it should be Silas. So he took his time getting on his jacket and when he got to the door he told Silas "I hate you" and then turned to leave. Silas grinned and said "Good" and then with all he had he lifted his foot to kick Tony to help him down the stairs, but because of the few too many drinks that Silas had he lost his balance and the two of them came crashing down the long flight of stairs. Silas's 310 lbs landing on top of Tony's thin 120 lbs frame. Silas was all broken up from the fall and was rushed to the hospital, but Tony wasn't that fortunate, he was dead from the impact of the hard ceramic tile floor and Silas's weight crushing down on him. Before being arrested in the hospital, Silas cried that it was an accident. He said that he slipped and that he wasn't trying to hurt Tony, but Tony's friend was at the bottom of the stairs and he said that he heard the exchange of words and saw Silas kick Tony and fall behind him. He said that it was an accident that Silas fell, because he only meant for Tony to be hurt by kicking him down the long flight of stairs.

"C'mon Miss, we gotta do another funeral at 3 o'clock, you gotta get out of this car, go inside and cry." The driver said as sympathetic as he possibly could.

By this point all of Dane's friends were standing around the car as if someone famous was about to come out of it. They mobbed her as she step out of the car and they all wanted to have their turn holding her, kissing her and telling her how much Dane loved her. There was a lot of love in the air but it was messy, very messy.

After Sarah took her seat on the front row, she closed her eyes and thought about her Dane, she smile at the thought of his smile the time he got his first big tip from Miss Price. Miss Price loved the way she looked when Dane got through with her hair and make up, she told him that she had never looked that good in her life and handed him an extra $20 bill. She remembered how it changed him, giving him so much confidence in his craft. He was so proud of that $20 bill that he placed it along side Sarah's faded, first $5 dollar tip that was taped on the wall above the cash register. Then as Bobby got up to sing "How Can I Say Goodbye to Yesterday" Sarah blushed at the thought of the night Dane came home to tell her how special his new friend Bobby had treated him on their first date. He was a good boy she told herself a million times since his death. He didn't want to harm anyone he just wanted to be loved, that's all. She poured out a big cry and fell sideways in her seat listening to Bobby's beautiful voice. Dane's friends rush to her aid fanning her and holding her up. After a few cards were read someone got up and read this poem entitled Forever In My Heart.

Dane, you are forever in my heart.

Even though you're not here,

We will never be apart

I will see you again

There will never be an end

To the love we had

Farewell my dear friend

It was Remy, another one of Dane's many encounters that brought the ceremony closer to its end. There was a lot of sobbing going on. All the guys took it bad. Crying and talking to Dane through tears asking "Why?" telling him that he was "the best that they ever had" just carrying on profusely. Finally the procession started and it was time to get the last view of Dane's body. From the back row the ushers started leading people to the front. That's when all the guys up front started fixing themselves up for the final fashion show in Dane's honor.

The first person from the back row walked slowly up the aisle. Carrying two dozens of white roses and wearing dark shades, he took his time allowing everyone one to gasp and get a good look at him. Mid-way up the aisle he was identified. "That's Him!"

someone whispered loudly. "Oh no he didn't!" Another said. "That's him, that's Wesley" one man was telling another. "That's the guy who Dane got killed over."

Pleased at the site of Wesley the man replied.

"Ooh Chile, he is to die for."

When Wesley reached the casket he removed his shades, revealing his tear stained eyes. He placed the roses across Dane's chest and bent down to give him a farewell kiss and that's when the coma broke. Dane woke up and found himself in the hospital bed sweating and crying. It was all a dream. After five days in a comma Dane was still alive and had dreamt that he was dead. He saw his life pass him by and was now in the hospital bed crying and praising God for another chance.

To God be the glory

After the big scandal, Dane's friends couldn't wait to get to the hospital to gossip about everyone's take on the unfortunate yet, juicy event. They wanted to know what Dane plans were to get revenge on Tyrone and Wesley, plus they wanted to offer their support. Little did they know, they were in for an even greater shock than what already had occurred.

Thankful to see his friends face again Dane hugged Remy and Bobby with everything he had. Then he tearfully thanked them for the beautiful flowers and well wishes. He apologized for still being in his pajamas and not straightening up his room. But the guys could care less about all of that they just wanted to get started on the plans for revenge. So once the niceties were out of the way, Bobby started.

"I know you can't wait to get out of here to get back at them fools."

"Yeah, you know we're 100% behind you and this time Tyrone will be getting his." The two chuckled and hi-five.

"Just let us know how you want to do this and it's done, you don't even have to get involved we'll take care of those two for you."

Dane was quiet, strange and distant. He looked at his friends and said. "Why would I seek revenge on them? They saved my life."

Remy and Bobby laughed. "OK Dane, stop with the jokes." "We know you got shot four times but come on -- I know you want to get back at them fools."

Dane started slowly.

"The old Dane might have, but I don't feel that way. They are my brothers and I don't want to see any harm come to them or to anyone else for that matter."

"You can't be serious. I know you're not gonna let them get off like that. Man you looking at doing time and everything. You think they gonna forgive you for attempted murder? C'mon now Dane, what's up with that?"

"Guys you don't' understand. I had a revelation. There is something you guys need to know about me." Dane then paused and said. "I'm through."

"Through? With what?" Bobby laughed knowing that Wesley wasn't even an option.

"With all the mess in my life, I've decided to live the rest of my life serving God."

Bobby and Remy fell over laughing so hard that they knocked over a vase of flowers. Then Remy noticed a child like expression on Dane's face and said.

"So what are you saying?"

"I'm saying no more homosexuality for me. No more men, no more other peoples husbands, no more drugs, no more lies, no more stealing and scheming, no more picking fights, no more cursing and most of all no more Dane. My name is Daniel Strong and that's all I ever want to be referred as."

"Daniel Strong?!" They both said looking at one another.

"That's right Daniel Strong. Look guys the last thing I want to do is judge you and the others for the way you choose to live. And I know I've always said that life was: to each his own and that we all have to live and die for ourselves but . . .,"

"Save it." Bobby interrupted and stood up straight. "You can't be serious about giving up all of this." he said grabbing himself below.

Dane quickly turned away and closed his eyes. "Don't ever do that in my presence again."

"Turning down meat? Oh yeah, he's definitely on medication." Remy added. "He don't realize what he's sayin'."

"I know exactly what I'm sayin'. If you would just let me finish." The men were now arguing.

"No, there's no need to finish, you're through, remember and since life is to each his own you should keep your sermon to yourself. I like the way I'm living and I know you still like it. Right now, you're just trippin'. But let me get you straight on one thing, sick or not, don't you dare judge me." Bobby was now heated and pointing in Dane's face. "C'mon Remy" The two headed towards the door.

"I'm not trying to judge you and nobody else. I'm just trying to get you to understand that what I used to be a part of . . . will never be again. I used to feel the same way you do and throw to each his own, in everyone's face. That was my way of hiding behind silly words and clichés. I figured my life was my own and I could live as I pleased, but that is not the case. I am here for a purpose – God's purpose. I know this all seem to be a bit much for you right now but know that although he allows us to make decisions on our own, he still has power and dominion over us. He is our creator and we should be so thankful for what he's done. We should always give him the honor and the praise. I wasn't honoring him when I was behaving less than the man he called me to be. I can't say what's wrong or what's right for you. But as for me," Dane paused and lifted his head towards heaven with both hands stretched out. "I'm going to serve the Lord." Then he broke into tears. "I was dead, hear what I'm saying. Dead! And he pulled me out. God found something in me that was special enough to save. Can you believe that, something in me? Me, who has done all to shame him. Me, who have never took the time to thank him. Me, who did any and everything to pave a way for hell in my life? Knowing that he saved me, I won't ever turn my back on him again. Oh how I love him. And I know that he spared my life for a reason. He saved me so that I could help others like you. I was chosen to deliver a very valuable message about his Glory. Listen guys, it's not too late, free yourself of your sins, and hold on to his unchanging hands."

Knowing Dane was on medication Bobby felt sorry for getting upset and said.

"Look man, get some rest, we'll check you out in the morning. You're tired. Get some rest. You've been through a lot and you're not thinking clearly."

"Yeah Dane, I mean Daniel. You're tired, listen we're sorry you got shot up and don't worry we got your back. Get some sleep we'll talk more about this in the morning."

"Please guys don't feel that way, don't feel sorry for me, because I'm happy, real happy. Listen, getting shot was the best thing that could have happened to me. I would still be lost had I not got shot. Don't you see? This is God's way of opening my eyes, his way of getting my attention and hopefully yours too. He's offering me another chance, a new opportunity to surrender to his will. See before this happened, I thought I had all the answers. I thought I didn't need God. I thought I could take care of myself and live as I please. Deep down, I knew better, I knew I wasn't living right. My days were filled with activities I know wasn't pleasing in God's sight. And what a lot of people don't know is that I grew up loving God. My daddy was a preacher and even though he taught me right from wrong I still got lost. You'd be surprised, but there are things in my life that I never told anyone about. And it was these things that encouraged me to be weak and seek pleasures outside of God's will. So I turned my back on God and I ignored what I knew was right. I know God loves me. He always has and yet instead of being patient and waiting on him, I wanted a quicker fix so I turned to worldly solutions and continued to do things that would give me instant gratification. Drugs, men, stealing, cheating, lying you name it. I did it all to ease my pain. Each day adding another element that pushed me further away from his Glory. Right or wrong I did things my way. I was my own God and what ever pleased me is what I did. All the time knowing that I was going against everything that mattered. I was so busy trying to erase the pain on my own that I pushed the thought of God out and didn't hear his voice when Wesley beat me and left me for dead or when I forced Sarah to burn me. Neither incident moved me to repent. But getting shot was my last chance to get it right. You guys don't realize how close to dead I was. I was there passing through the tunnel, I saw the light it was guiding me closer and closer and my spirit was fading fast knocking on death's door and even after I let go, Christ held on to me and whispered life back into my spirit, into my soul. That's how much he loves me, enough to save me. He didn't have to do it, but he did it anyway. Because he loves me, he woke me up and started me on my way. It's his unconditional love that forgave me and offered me a new life. And I know now that he didn't do this so I could continue living sinfully. He saved me so that I could help someone else and I'm so ever grateful for the night I got shot." Dane was now very emotional and raising his voice.

"For me it's not To Each His Own, its To Each God's Own. We are his own! His own children, his own creation, his own! Can't you understand that? Don't ever think you are doing something by yourself, because without him, nothing is possible. Nothing! So please don't feel bad for me. Rejoice in knowing that I'm healed. I'm healed!

The two men were partially convinced but too stunned to absorb it all.

"So it's over, your not mad and Tyrone and Wesley?"

"No, not at all, I want to thank them and ask them for forgiveness. I want to tell them all about God's Glory. I want to talk with them and explain my whole situation and prayerfully they might join me in reconsidering their lifestyle before it's too late."

By this point, Dane wasn't looking at either guy. He gleamed forward and smiled as if he could see Christ and was talking directly to him.

"Man, you're starting to freak me out with all this talk. You can't be feeling well. We'll talk to you tomorrow."

"Don't wait until tomorrow." Dane cautioned. "It's not promised to you."

Remy and Bobby looked at each other in amazement. They could not believe that Dane out of all people was declaring that he was no longer in the "family" and didn't want to seek revenge. It was his signature to get back at anyone who dared to cross him. They listened to Dane for as long as they could and then they both gradually headed out the door.

Dane was so caught up in the spirit moving about him that he hadn't noticed that the guys were gone.

"Hear what I'm saying. Grab on to him now. Repent. Change your ways. I pray that you take heed. God has given me a second chance and he'll do the same for you. I didn't deserve it, but he had mercy on me and has forgiven me for all the wrongs I've done. Give him a chance to move in your life." Dane begged. And then with the little strength he had Dane attempted to get on his knees to pray but his condition was too severe, so he turned to the side and lifted one knee a little, closed his eyes and started to pray.

"Dear Lord, I'm so ever grateful for your mercy. Thank you for sparing me. Thank you for speaking life back into my soul. Thank you for this new day and opportunity to speak your name. Oh Lord Thank you. I know that I have sin, but Lord, I thank you for looking beyond my faults and into my heart. Lord, you know the pain I've been through -- you are the only one that knows my past. Lord you've forgiven me when I wouldn't forgive myself. And Lord I just want to say thank you. Thank you for showing me the light. Thank you for speaking to me in a place where I could hear your call. Lord, I promise not to ever turn back. I'm so happy to be free. Free from all the ugliness and pain. Free to lean on you. Just Free! Lord, I promise to do right by you. I promise to do your will. Lord, I will not let a day go by without sharing the good news about your unconditional love. Oh Lord, thank you. I will forever praise your name and live according to your word for the rest of my life. In Jesus precious name, Lord this is my prayer. Thank you Jesus! Hallelujah! Thank you Jesus!"

The Gift of Love

One year later and still a few months before the wedding, Tyrone started worrying about the perfect gift for Maya. He knew that it should be something for the two of them, yet he was still more concerned about Maya. Tyrone wanted his gift to be special after all that she had been through. He thought long and hard about what would make her coo inside. Not jewelry, not a new car and certainly not a mink coat. Then he remembered the woman, the woman that kept Maya up thinking for many nights. The woman Maya gave money to everyday, the woman that she never stopped talking about.

After telling Wesley his far fetched plan to find the homeless woman and get her all cleaned up to bring to the wedding, they decided that nothing else could top a gift like that. So after a couple of visits and showing the homeless woman Maya's picture, they convinced her to trust them. Wesley made arrangements for the woman to live in the apartment that they once lived in and then handled all the arrangements of hiring her live-in help. After a few days of just 'Bless you son', from the woman, the woman started melting and telling them a little about herself. Without blinking or looking at them, she stared out the window and slowly told her story.

"I'm not that old, about fifty-one, fifty-two. I use to live with my sister, I gave birth to a set of twins a boy and a girl. When my kids turned three months, my sister found out that they were also her husband's kids, so they kicked me out. My sister couldn't have children and that's why he lied and said that we was doing it for her. I was supposed to have my children for her, but that wasn't it at all. We was in love. I still love him. He wasn't meant for my sister, he was meant for me. You see me and my sister are also twins, he just married the wrong one. They say my sister was the smart one, and I was the pretty one, but we both were pretty, she just didn't know it. She was always jealous of my beauty so she called me dummy. Day in and day out, I was considered dummy instead of my name. So when I tried to pack up my kids, she threatened to take me to court, said that I wasn't fit to be a mother, said I was too dumb. She said that sneaking around with a married man was against the law and that they would put me away. I wasn't that dumb, I didn't believe her but he told me not to fight her, to leave everything up to him, so I did. He loved me, I know he did. A couple of days after they throwed me out, he found me and took me to a hotel and made love to me like he wanted me to remember it forever. It was just like the first time, beautiful." the woman paused and allowed tears to fall from her eyes. "I'd would of done anything for that man, anything he said. After all the love making was over, he told me to meet him at the 33rd Street Station on Saturday at 3:00. He said that he and the kids would be there and that we all would move to Brooklyn. So I did, for thirty some odd years I've been waiting, but they never came. Only my daughter, she came, but she don't even know me. She don't even know that I'm her momma."

Tyrone and Wesley stared at each other confused, about the daughter? Wesley hugged the woman and told her that it was alright, that if she wanted them to help her locate her children that they would.

After they got home that night they talked about the story the woman told them. They blamed the man and her sister for her condition, using her and adding to her already low self-esteem. But they still were puzzled about the daughter. The daughter she said that came. What daughter is she talking about? And why would her daughter come and leave her there? Then it hit them that she may be talking about Maya.

"Oh God Wes, I don't know if this is such a hot idea now. What if she's Maya's mother?"

"Don't be silly, that lady ain't Maya's mother, though they do favor. Remember she said that she had a set of twins, Maya's not a twin is she?"

"You know Maya always shuts down whenever I bring up her brother. I'm pretty sure they are twins, but you'd never know it because they're not close. I maybe wrong, but I think he's older than she is. I don't know, I've never even met her brother Gregg, but I did see his picture, they could pass for twins. You know what?" Tyrone sat down with his hand covering his mouth. "What if she's Maya's mother? Wes, you don't know what I'm feeling I think we stumbled upon something big. Oh no, I don't know what to do. Will Maya be happy? Or will she be . . . Wes! I can't take this. I'm getting goose pimples all over. Oh Wes, she's Maya's mother. I bet you she's her mother."

"I bet you she's not."

"Are you kidding? I could have dropped when she walked out of that spa. She was so filthy when we picked her up that I just knew she was dark skinned."

"Me too, but even with the ground in dirt, I could tell that she had beautiful eyes."

"I know, but when she walked out of the spa, her skin glistened just like Maya's and did you check out the way she walks. You can't tell me that they are not family."

"Yeah, that freaked me out the way her lips and eyes were so in sync when she talked. She is a spitting image of Maya. You mean Maya is a spitting image of her."

"What's Maya's number, I'm going to call her right now."

"Yeah, you call I have to figure something out." Tyrone said thinking back to the time when Maya left town to see her aunt in the hospital. He remembered her saying that her aunt raised them.

Wesley shook his head laughing he could not believe that Tyrone had gone so far as to make this woman out to be Maya's mother. He went over to the phone and called. But Maya wasn't there so it was Gary that said "Yeah, Maya's a twin." Now Tyrone and Wesley sat there holding their hearts, afraid of what they found.

"Look, the wedding is just weeks away, why don't we wait until after everything has settled down to find out the truth."

"Yeah, this is too much for Maya right now she's already going crazy with details about the wedding." Tyrone swallowed hard. "She's Maya's mother."

After a restless night, Tyrone couldn't wait to confront Gary about his discovery.

"Look Tyrone, I know you mean well, but Maya is finally at a point were she is happy about everything. She just got off of the roller coaster with you and that scandal. Look man, I appreciate where you're going with this but I don't want to blow this thing out of context, and right now you're pushing your luck with me. I'm trying real hard not to . . ."

Gary hesitated he wanted to tell Tyrone to get the hell out of his and Maya's life. He wanted him to know about the strain he placed on their relationship, he wanted to tell him about the many nights that Maya couldn't sleep, how she cried and worried about him being jail. He wanted to tell him how she lost weight, how she missed work. He wanted to tell him how he missed his woman, how he missed making love to her and seeing her laugh and smile. He wanted to tell him that if he didn't get out of his face he was going to kick his ass. But Gary was no fool, he knew how Maya felt about Tyrone and since they were friends before he met her, he could never go there and expect her to understand.

"Gary I hear you, but just hear me out. I'm ninety percent sure that this woman is Maya's mother. I wanted to surprise her with the news, but then I thought that it would be best to check with you. I just want you to meet her then tell me what you think. I promise if you disagree, I won't bring it up ever again, this I promise.

Gary took a long sigh he didn't want to have anything to do with Tyrone, especially since he just got out of jail for attempted murder. It was still too fresh, enough time hadn't passed and he wasn't in the mood for buddying up with him or Wesley. He had enough of their mess and was tired of the constant drama. Now Tyrone was trying to convince him about a homeless woman being Maya's mother. A woman who lived on the streets for thirty years that could possibly have AIDs or something but, that wasn't the only thing that turned him off, the main thing was that Tyrone was involved and that meant that whatever it was it would be exhausting. All he wanted to do was just love Maya, grab her by the hand and run off with her. Yeah, Maya had mentioned this woman more than a million times but that was because she felt sorry for the lady. Tyrone was over doing it as usual, trying to hard to please Maya and make up for all the trouble he caused. It seemed like he was always trying to win her over. Reluctantly Gary gave in promising himself that this was it, after this he would never be bothered with Tyrone again.

"Ok, I'll meet this woman, but I'm telling you," Gary surprised himself and pointed his finger in Tyrone's face. "This had better not be a waste of my time, if this lady doesn't' look like Maya to me, I'm out and you better keep your word and not mention it again. Deal?"

"Deal, let's go." Tyrone agreed knowing that he was right and when Gary meets this woman he's going to pass out.

"Go? Go where?" Gary asked already regretting his decision.

"Wesley took her over to Louise Beauty and Spa salon on Kearny Avenue this morning, he's been with her all day and I promise that I would meet them there between 4 and 6 for dinner. It's just a little after 4. C'mon it won't take long I'll call Wes and tell him that we will be joining them for dinner."

"Dinner, man just tell him that we will meet them outside of the salon, I'm not trying to have dinner with y'all, I got things to do." Gary said praying that someone from the hospital would beep him so he would have to leave.

"Fine, whatever." Tyrone said with some irritation, he was losing patience with Gary and his standoffish attitude. "I'll drive." He volunteered still proud of his fancy red Jaguar.

"You'll drive you. I'll drive my own car." Gary replied.

Tyrone hopped in his car and slammed the door, he couldn't believe Gary was acting like this, he had never seen this side of him before and he didn't like it. But then he knew that Gary had a right to feel this way, he knew that Maya was putting him through the ringer the last few months because of everything that happened with he and Wesley. He felt bad for losing his patience and decided to let it go. Plus he couldn't wait to say "I told you so."

Once alone in the car, Gary too, had regrets he was sorry that he was so hard on Tyrone. From what Maya said none of this was Tyrone's fault, he was a victim in it all and did what he had to do. And now here he was trying to not only make Maya's life better, but also this woman's. Gary didn't think for a minute that this woman could belong to Maya but he knew that stranger things have happened so when Tyrone pulled into the parking lot, he pulled right beside him and smile.

"Okay I just dialed Wes and told him that we were in the parking lot, c'mon let's go around the front. As they were turning the corner to the front side of the salon Gary saw Samaya.

"Oh Wow!" Was the best that Gary could do surprised by the striking resemblance. "I can't believe my eyes."

"Told you." Tyrone said smiling now even more convinced that he stumbled onto something big.

"Wow, hi I'm Gary, how are you?"

Samaya took her time to speak her first thought was that Gary was so handsome and deserving of her daughter. "I'm fine" she mustered with a soft but genuine smile.

"You are so beautiful." Gary quickly admitted.

Samaya dropped her head and nodded a thank you.

"I'm sorry, I didn't mean to embarrass you" Gary said now touching her fingers and lifting her hand so that she would lift up those beautiful eyes to him.

"Hey Tyrone, where did you say we were eating?" Gary asked now hungry to find out more about this woman that looked like his sweet baby.

"But I thought you said that you had things to do." Tyrone joked, seeing that Gary wasn't going anywhere.

"Naw man, I said that I didn't have anything to do."

"Well she mentioned that she wanted some soup." Wesley offered. He had already gotten to know a great deal about Samaya and was fascinated with her gentleness and her peace, he wanted so much to be in Maya's shoes, he knew who his mother was, but his father was the mystery. And after this experience he decided to seek him.

"Then soup it is, my treat, let's go to *Spoons*." Gary suggested not waiting for a reply "Miss um, um, would you like to ride with me?"

"Forgive me." Wesley offered. "Gary, this is Ms. Samaya."

"Sa Maya?"

"Yup, Samaya." Tyrone said like I told you.

The four went to *Spoons* and had a very pleasant yet straining conversation. Samaya wept and she told Gary the whole story of how she had wound up at the train station for so many years. She told him about the first time she saw Maya going to work and how she knew that Maya was her baby girl. She told them all how embarrassed she now was for Maya, and how afraid she was that Maya may reject her.

She asked them for help, she wanted them to give her some time to pull herself together. She wasn't ready to meet Maya. Everyone agreed except Gary, he wanted to let Maya know that night. But Samaya tears made him promise not to tell. Then Tyrone had a brainstorm.

"Why don't we call one of those talk shows?"

Wesley gasped, "That's perfect, and I have just the show. You know I have good friends at Harpo, I designed the gown Oprah wore to the NAACP awards Sunday night. All I have to do is let them know that this is important to me and within a couple of weeks we'll be on the show.

"We?" Tyrone asked with surprise.

"Well, yeah, I was thinking about searching for my father too."

"Oh I didn't know." Gary offered apologetically.

"That's all right I don't want to go into it right now, this is about Maya." Tyrone grabbed Wesley hand and squeezed it under the table and then Samaya began to speak.

"Will she know that I'm the same lady? Please let's take that part out. I don't want her to think that her mother is a total nut, because I'm not. See you people don't realize but when you love a person the way I loved Rufus, . . . well your heart is capable of splitting in two, I loved him so much that I couldn't do anything but wait for him. I may have been there for years, but in my mind it wasn't even a week. It was just long enough to realize that he wasn't coming. I know that I'm not making much sense to you, but it felt good to want so bad. Waiting in that station gave me something to hold on to. I couldn't hold on to him, once I got up and left, it would have been all over then. I wasn't ready for it to be over, he was still mine and as long as I had on the clothes that I left out to meet him in, I could hold him. As long as I had on that raincoat and kerchief I put on to see him – he was still with me. So those items and everything that was on me was for him. I can't explain it no better than that, and you may think that you don't ever want to love someone that much, but I'll tell you this, outside of God, there's no greater love than that. Rufus was a gift, a true and pure pleasure he was. I felt so much love for him, in my heart, not my mind and not in a physical place, but it was full and rich, in my heart. The love was so intense that no matter what I saw, read or felt, everything appeared beautiful, everything was blessed around me, there was no bad, no ugly, no rude or coldness, just sweet heaven sent love. And I'm going tell you a little secret. Very few get to experience that kind of love. I imagine it being in line with those who will enter the gates of Heaven. It's such a glorious experience, such a pleasure to be chosen to feel love like that. Have you ever felt that way before?"

The three guys just nodded, first yes, then no. They were all mesmerized by what they had just heard and believed every word of it. They believed that love could be that real and each of them knew what they were feeling about their relationships didn't measure to what she had just described. Her words were so strong that they had forgotten that just a few days ago, she was a muddy, cruddy looking bag lady asking for 'spare change.' They felt close to her now and forgave her just like they knew Maya would.

Showtime

When Maya got her invitation to go on the Oprah Winfrey show, she screamed and jumped up and down.

"I love Oprah. Thank you so much Tyrone. What is this show about? Is it the one where she's going to be giving out all kind of goodies? Or is it a make over show?" Then she threw her hands on her hips and said. "I know you don't think I need a make over. Could it be she wants to cover my wedding? Oh my goodness it is, isn't it?"

"No, no and no." Tyrone said not offering any hints. I already told you I don't know what it's about all I know is that she wants you to appear. Now let's figure out what you're going to wear."

"Hmmm, how come I don't believe you? You're up to something I can tell. And judging from the way that Gary's been acting, I think he's in on it too. What is it? Oh c'mon tell me.

"Tell you what? I don't know anything. I think you should wear something casual. Some fancy wide leg pants, maybe blue and a crisp white top. Yeah, add your silver jewelry and wear your hair out. I think that's a classic look for television."

****

Maya and Gary flew out to Chicago for the show. Coming down the escalator they could see the chauffer holding a sign with their names on it. They got into the limousine and rushed off to the studio. In minutes the Harpo staff snatched Maya up and took her back stage. Feeling a little nervous without Gary by her side, she started to question everyone about why she was there.

"You'll soon find out, just relax." The make-up artist told her.

Gary sat in the front row along side Tyrone and Wesley. Samaya was in the dressing room across from Maya's getting her make up done as well.

The show began and Maya was called to the stage. After introducing Maya to her audience and the folks at home. Oprah revealed that there was someone special in the studio that wanted to meet her. Then she asked Maya if there was anyone special that she wanted to meet. To everyone's surprise Maya said that she longed for her mother. She said that she was raised by her aunt and never felt the mother love that she knew existed somewhere for her. When Oprah asked her did she know what happened to her mother Maya said no and then told a tearful story about how she only remember the negative stories her aunt told her about her mother. Stories that she never believed were true. By the time Maya finished telling her story about her strange and lonely childhood, everyone in the audience was feeling sad and in tears. Then Oprah announced that she had a huge surprise for her.

"It's your mother!" Oprah announced as the audience applauded.

Maya jumped to her feet and cried. Right away she recognized that it was the homeless woman.

"Oh my God! I can't believe this. I actually prayed and day dreamed about this happening a thousand times. How did you get here?" Maya burst into tears and ran to her mommy like she was four years old all over again.

Finally being able to hold her baby girl, Samaya just broke all the way down and cried. After getting most of the tears out, Oprah asked Samaya if she would share her story of love and homelessness. It was hard for Samaya to speak so she motioned for Wesley to take the stage with her and while holding his hand, she repeated the story she told the guys and all of America saw homelessness in a different view. Maya was overjoyed by the big surprise and couldn't thank Oprah, Tyrone, Wesley and Gary enough. She held on tight to her mother and the show ended on a very happy and tearful note.

Ribbon in the sky

A week before the wedding, Wesley brought over the gown he designed for Samaya to wear. It was a beautiful soft pink gown with clean, elegant lines. It was perfect for the mother of the bride to wear.

Seeing her at the church brought tears to his eyes. He walked over to her, kissed her and complimented her on her stunning beauty. He pinned on her flowers and told her how happy he was to be a part of this beautiful story.

Coming down the center aisle of the Okras restaurant, Maya saw all her family and friends. She held Gary's arm tight and thanked God for allowing everyone to be there, especially her mother. Every since their first date, Maya had always wanted to have their wedding reception at Okras. She loved the beautiful decor and embraced the warmth inside the restaurant. The band played Stevie Wonder's *Ribbon In The Sky,* while Toy, with her happy self, introduced for the first time, Mr. & Mrs. Gary Steven Cooper.

As they entered the dining area, everyone but Alycia, stood up clapping to receive the newlyweds. Alycia was too busy feeding Jhazzi, her and Jeffrey's three month old son.

Selina had forgotten where she was and whistled at the handsome couple as they smiled for pictures. Trudy elbowed her so that she wouldn't whistle again.

While Queetha sat faithfully trying to get little Lynwood Stanley to stop crying, Dice made the best man's toast. He wished them much happiness and a house full of healthy children.

Roz with her big eight month belly grabbed Lance's hand and waddled over to the handsome bride and groom and gave them a big hug and kiss. Handing Jeff the baby, Alycia got her turn to kiss the bride and hug the groom. She was so proud of Maya and excited about the wedding she would soon have.

Tyrone was second in line to dance with the bride. He and Wesley were the ushers for the dazzling couple.

The newlyweds were swollen with gratitude from the love they had for each other and the love they received from their family and friends.

It was a beautiful, cold, clear and sunny winter day. Most brides would prefer their wedding in June, but you know what they say...

Your feedback on this book is welcomed!

Email your comments to
info@valeriechandlersmith.com

If you've enjoyed reading

To Each His Own

Visit
www.valeriechandlersmith.com

for details on upcoming projects and events